# CLEAN AIR

ALSO BY SARAH BLAKE

FICTION
*Naamah*

POETRY
*Let's Not Live on Earth*
*Mr. West*

# CLEAN AIR

*a novel*

# SARAH BLAKE

ALGONQUIN BOOKS
OF CHAPEL HILL   2022

Published by
ALGONQUIN BOOKS OF CHAPEL HILL
Post Office Box 2225
Chapel Hill, North Carolina 27515-2225

a division of
WORKMAN PUBLISHING
225 Varick Street
New York, New York 10014

This is a work of fiction. While, as in all fiction, the literary perceptions and insights are based on experience, all names, characters, places, and incidents either are products of the author's imagination or are used fictitiously.

Excerpt on pp. 27–28 from "DEP Issues Code Orange Air Quality Forecast for Philadelphia Area" (PA: Pennsylvania Department of Environmental Protection, 2017). Reprinted with permission from the Pennsylvania Department of Environmental Protection.

Excerpts on pp. 51 and 129–30 from "Triple Your Impact for Clean Air" and "Take a Stand Against a #ToxicNeighbor" (Harrisburg, PA: PennFuture, 2017). Reprinted with permission from PennFuture.

Excerpt on pp. 93–94 from Katie Shepherd, "Ash Falls Like Snow Across Portland as Wildfire Tears Through the Columbia River Gorge" (Portland, OR: Willamette Week, 4 Sept. 2017). Reprinted with permission from the publisher.

Excerpt on pp. 105–7 from Jamie Sams and David Carson, Medicine Cards (New York, NY: St. Martin's Press, 1988), pp. 89–92. Reprinted with permission from the publisher.

Excerpt on pp. 171–72 from "What Are the Spare the Air Days?" (San Francisco, CA: Bay Area Air Quality Management District, 2017). Reprinted with permission from the Bay Area Air Quality Management District.

LIBRARY OF CONGRESS CATALOGING-IN-PUBLICATION DATA
Names: Blake, Sarah (Poet), author.
Title: Clean air : a novel / Sarah Blake.
Description: First Edition. | Chapel Hill, North Carolina : Algonquin Books of Chapel Hill, 2022. | Summary: "In a near-future world where tree pollen has made outdoor air unbreathable, a woman's safe but tedious life is thrown into turmoil when she witnesses a murder and her young daughter starts sleep-talking about the killer"— Provided by publisher.
Identifiers: LCCN 2021038451 | ISBN 9781643751061 (hardcover) | ISBN 9781643752228 (ebook)
Subjects: GSAFD: Mystery fiction.
Classification: LCC PS3602.L3485 C54 2022 | DDC 813/.6—dc23
LC record available at https://lccn.loc.gov/2021038451

10 9 8 7 6 5 4 3 2 1
First Edition

*For my son, Aaron, and my mother, Barbara,*
*whose generations I am torn between*

# CLEAN AIR

Dear Cami,

We couldn't breathe the air. To some people it seemed quick, sudden even. To some it seemed gradual. In hindsight, everyone said the signs were there. It was in the trees, the pollen. It happened in spring. And while spring doesn't happen at the same time everywhere—we saw it happen one place first, and then another, and another— how could we have stopped it? What I'm trying to say is, some people, most people's response to catastrophe, as it approaches, is muted. That was ten years ago: the Turning. It killed more than half of the world's population. And the resulting world, the world we built from scratch, it's not how I was taught a postapocalyptic world would be. It presents itself like a gift.

## CHAPTER ONE

Izabel moved through her morning routine. She poured Cami's juice into a sippy cup. It was "spill-proof," but that didn't mean it didn't leak. Izabel wedged it beside containers of snacks in Cami's lunchbox. She zipped it up and put it in Cami's backpack, which had flaps of fabric on the side to look like elephant ears. The trunk was embroidered on the front. Black plastic eyes had been sewn in until they were flush.

Then the shower turned off. The water stopped running through the pipes in the concrete slab beneath her. She knew Kaito was patting himself down with a towel, but she couldn't hear that. Instead she heard the cars outside. One of her neighbors was playing music. Sometimes she felt as if she could hear every neighbor through their plastic walls.

Kaito would be stepping out of the bedroom soon. If she timed it right, the three of them would be in the kitchen together as they got ready for the day. Not that she didn't want to be alone with Cami, only that she preferred not to be.

She broke off an oversized banana, cut it in half, and left it where Cami sat at the island. Then she poured soy milk into a bottle and took it with her into Cami's room.

"Good morning, honey," Izabel said.

Cami didn't move.

"Wake up, wake up, wake up." This time she put her hand on Cami's leg.

Cami's brow furrowed.

"I have your milk. Do you want your milk?"

Cami's eyes popped open and then closed again, and then she rolled them open—with great effort it seemed—and the whites of her eyes were slightly pink.

"Good morning, mi amorcito."

"Hi, Mommy."

Izabel handed her the bottle of milk. She was four, but she insisted on bottles still. And Izabel couldn't bring herself to care.

Cami sat up and drank, eyes closed again.

When Izabel tried to leave, Cami pulled at her. So Izabel turned her body to face the same direction as Cami, and she let Cami lean back into her. It was a lovely, peaceful moment. One she got to have every morning. She chided herself for spending it, mostly, thinking of what she had to do next.

She pulled herself away. "We don't want to be late." She went to the bins of Cami's clothes and picked out an outfit for the day.

Cami held out the empty bottle.

"Are you done with it?"

Cami nodded, awake now, alert, a little animal.

"Then you know what to do with it. You know where it goes."

Cami ran out of the room and put the bottle by the kitchen sink.

"What's next?" Izabel asked, following her.

"Teeth brushing!"

"Good morning," Kaito said, stepping into the kitchen.

"Daddy!" Cami ran into his arms, and he scooped her up and kissed her twice on the cheek.

"Better go brush your teeth," he said.

In the bathroom, Izabel put toothpaste on both of their toothbrushes as Cami peed in the toilet.

"Can you wipe yourself? Do you know what to do next?"

"I know!"

Izabel brushed her teeth while she watched Cami. She wiped herself with a nearly normal amount of toilet paper. She flushed the toilet. She washed her hands. She took the toothbrush from the cup.

"Did you wet this?"

"Uh-huh," Izabel said, toothbrush in her mouth.

And then Cami brushed her teeth and spat. For a minute, you could be convinced that she could take care of herself, that she wouldn't start crying when she couldn't get the Velcro on her shoes to line up exactly.

Back in the kitchen, Cami picked up her banana and held it over her head and said it was the moon both ways.

"What do you mean?" Kaito asked.

"Full moon," she said, turning the sliced face of it at him, perfectly round and dimpled with color like any good asteroid-blemished surface. "And . . ." She turned it so the arc of it was above her. "And . . ."

"Crescent," he said.

"Crescent moon!" she said.

"Very good," Izabel said, taking the banana from her, pulling down the peel, and handing it back. "Now you better eat."

Cami and Kaito looked at each other and Izabel knew it was some sort of acknowledgment that Izabel was the serious one in the house. But she didn't know if that were true. Yes, she was serious now, with them, but she didn't know if she would have been, if she wanted to be, if she'd started this way.

When Cami was done with her banana, Izabel took her to get dressed. Cami wanted to pick out her own outfit and Izabel reminded her that every night she asked her if she wanted to put out clothes for the next day.

"But I don't know what I want to wear *then*. That's a different day."

"I know—so this is how it works. For now."

"This doesn't match with my mask."

"Everything matches with your mask. That's how masks work."

"It's not denim, Mom!"

Izabel let out a single giant laugh and then started laughing so hard she could feel tears in her eyes. "Where did you learn *that*?"

"It was on one of your shows."

"It was?"

Cami nodded.

Kaito came in the room. "Are you two okay?"

Izabel couldn't stop laughing. Her sides were hurting now.

"Mommy thinks I told a joke."

"But you didn't?"

Cami shook her head.

Kaito kneeled at Cami's feet and started to dress her.

"I told her this outfit doesn't match my mask."

"You're right—that doesn't sound very funny."

Izabel was getting her breath back. "I said her mask matches everything!"

"That's true," Kaito said.

"And then Cami said, 'It's not denim!'"

Kaito smiled at Izabel.

"See. Daddy knows it's not funny."

"It's a little funny," Kaito said.

"Maybe you had to be there." Izabel felt herself getting annoyed.

"He was here," Cami said.

"Not in the room," Izabel said. "It's an expression."

Kaito nodded.

Cami looked satisfied with that. She always looked to him for the final say on a matter.

"Shoes next!" Cami yelled, and she ran out of the room.

Izabel wanted to scold Kaito for not backing her up better, for not laughing, for not telling Cami to trust what her mother says. But then he stood up and kissed Izabel on the forehead. He was sweet. He was kind. She didn't want to have a fight over a feeling she couldn't quite articulate.

At the front doors, Cami had put her shoes on the wrong feet. Izabel switched them. Next her coat went on. Then her backpack. Then her mask, down around her neck for now.

"Are we early?"

"A little," Izabel said. "Is it joke time?"

Cami nodded.

Izabel brought out her tablet and opened a kids' app that had a daily joke on its main page. "What color do cats like?"

"What?"

"*Purrrrr*ple."

Cami laughed. "I get it."

"Yeah, you do."

The doorbell went off. Izabel put Cami's mask up, around her ears, under her eyes, pinched it over the bridge of her nose. She checked it, following its black border over her cheekbones. The emerald green covered her cheeks and continued down below her jaw. A small black circle of plastic sat to the left side of her mouth. From her eyes, she could tell Cami was smiling. Izabel hugged her.

"Have a great day at school," Izabel said. And Kaito waved from the kitchen, where he was making coffee.

Izabel pressed a button on the wall and the first set of double doors opened. Cami went through them. As soon as they closed behind her, the second set of double doors opened, and she went out those and ran to the car. There was a burst of air in the small room, a quick blast to clean it out, a small safeguard, keeping one batch of air from another. It obscured Cami for a second, but Izabel was used to that. She watched her every morning like this. As tired as she was of nearly every moment of her life, some parts still filled her with fear. Cami getting to a car was one of them.

Cami pressed a button on the car and the door opened for her. She got in, the door closed, and off the car went. Izabel would get an alert on her tablet when the school checked her in.

At this point, she would usually eat breakfast with Kaito before his workday started, but she didn't want to talk to him right now. She knew she'd start a fight. Neither of them needed that.

She went to the bathroom and sat on the toilet and peed and looked around on her tablet. She opened her favorite app. It ran news articles and newsletters and email blasts that went out years before the Turning. She could lose herself for hours in the news of the past. When humans thrived—too well. When we were drinking all the clean water. When we traveled so often we ripped holes in the ozone. When we couldn't see another way. When we melted the ice caps and debated the commodification of natural resources and thought we would need seed stores.

She usually didn't remember which year was which. Little memories across her childhood of local and global traumas that she couldn't sort chronologically. Today, legs hard against the toilet seat, she tapped on *2020*. The summary popped up. A bad year. A global pandemic. Everyone wearing masks then, too. She was eight years old. Her mother was alive. They were happy.

She tapped on *Most Popular*. An article came up about the garden eels in an aquarium in Tokyo. It was becoming hard to monitor their health. They hid from their keepers. They had grown fearful of humans as the aquariums sat empty during quarantine.

In an attempt to make them more comfortable, to make them betray their instincts, they were arranging a festival. For three days people could call in and video-chat with the eels. They were going to set up five screens in front of their tank. There were rules. You couldn't be loud or obnoxious. They wanted smiles and waves and soft conversation.

Izabel's tablet dinged that Cami was checked in at school. She sighed. She felt something in her chest drop, like a ball, a short but satisfying distance. She put the tablet on the floor, wiped herself, pulled up her pants, washed her hands, and picked up the tablet again. It wasn't even 9 a.m. Kaito would still be in the kitchen.

She decided that she'd rush out, kiss him on the cheek, and go to the mall. She didn't know what she would do there, but it was better than staying home. The days dragged on until Cami came back. And when Kaito came out of his office for lunch or for a break, she felt like he was critical of how she used her time, even though he didn't say it, even though he insisted he didn't think about her like that.

But she was critical of herself in that way. Even if she cleaned everything, got all the laundry done, responded to emails, ordered the groceries, scheduled dentist appointments. Even then, she wondered what she was doing inside her perfect life, where she was perfectly comfortable, and she'd survived the Turning, and she'd fallen in love, and the world had been taken back, some of it, and they'd had a child, and their child flourished, and they wanted for nothing, and no one was homeless, and no one was hungry, and what they had learned was that anything could be accomplished, if it were for few enough people.

She got dressed and went into the kitchen. Kissing Kaito's cheek felt better than she wanted to admit. His skin was smooth and smelled good, from an aftershave he liked, something he picked out himself. It made her feel special that he used it, that he shaved, because he never had to see anyone but her.

She could feel her unhappiness with him wane. And it would come back, too. She knew that.

She pressed the button on the wall that called for a car. She looked back at him over her shoulder, and they smiled at each other as if they would have sex if she were staying. It was an easy enough smile to give when they both knew they didn't have to deliver.

She looked back at the panel on the wall that called the cars and opened the doors. It also had the display for the air filtration system. She looked at this snapshot so often she hardly saw the specifics of it anymore, only that everything was green and well. All the filters were functioning properly. There were no errors in the system. But today she saw that the air quality was at 98 percent.

"Kaito," she said. "The air quality is at ninety-eight percent."

"Hmm."

"Isn't it usually at ninety-nine percent? Or one hundred percent?"

"There are no errors?"

"No."

"Then I guess ninety-eight percent is fine."

"I guess so," she said.

## CHAPTER TWO

That night, the alarm went off all through the plastic dome. The lights went on. Something had failed. Probably something small, but when Izabel woke, the back of her throat already hurt.

She heard Kaito moving through the house, having woken before her, quicker to gain his bearings. He came back into their room with her mask. His was on.

As soon as she'd taken the mask from his fingers, he was off to Cami's room with her small mask, and Izabel followed.

Cami was still asleep.

Kaito put the mask over Cami's face, moving her black hair to put the straps around her ears. Izabel looked out the sheer plastic window of Cami's room. No other houses were lit up like theirs.

Izabel coughed, which made Kaito move faster. He picked up Cami in his arms and they rushed to the front of the house. Izabel pressed a button on the wall and a thick plastic sheet dropped down, ruffled and bent. She pulled it to the floor, straightening it, making sure it reached. And then, carefully, she began to seal it around the edges. She had to push some of Cami's toys out of the way.

While she did this, Kaito turned on the small air filtration unit that was strong enough for the new, small room they'd created. He also tried to wake Cami. The unit turned green to show that the air was safe.

A voice came through the intercom system. "A mobile unit is two minutes away for repairs. An ambulance is on the way as a precaution. Have you all reached the safe room?"

"Yes," Izabel said. She watched Kaito trying gently to wake Cami.

"I can cancel the ambulance if it's not necessary. Is it necessary?"

"I don't know."

"Excuse me. Can you speak up?"

"I don't know!" Izabel took off her mask and put her face close to Cami's. She was warm and her skin was its normal color and her chest was moving up and down with her breath, though Izabel couldn't feel it through her mask. Cami looked like a sleeping princess with her black hair against her emerald green mask, a princess from a strange new kingdom.

"We need the ambulance," Kaito said.

"Of course," said the voice.

Izabel put her mask back on. They waited for the sound of the sirens to come and replace the sound of the alarm.

"Are you okay?" she asked Kaito.

He nodded. "My throat hurts."

"Mine, too."

Kaito reached down and ran his hand over Cami's head.

"Do you think she could be sleeping through this?" Izabel asked, knowing it was a stupid question.

They could hear the sirens now.

"We should clean up this space," Kaito said.

And it was true. They'd gotten too comfortable. What was supposed to be their safe room was filled with toys, shoeboxes of knick-knacks, old diaper boxes filled with art supplies.

The doorbell went off when the ambulance pulled into the spot outside their house, and then they heard the EMTs come inside.

"Masks on!" they shouted. "Confirm."

"Masks are on!" Izabel yelled back.

The EMTs unsealed the room, put Cami on a spine board, and connected her mask to an oxygen tank. Izabel and Kaito followed them out of the house, through the double set of doors, passing the small robot that was already repairing the air filtration system.

The ambulance was so covered in pollen it was yellow. It was early April and peak pollination for cedar, elm, and willow.

"Bad night?" Kaito asked once they were inside.

"The count is high," one of the EMTs said. His nametag read BEN. He touched a screen inside the ambulance and told it to return to the hospital.

The other EMT's nametag read UZAIR. He set to work putting sensors all over Cami. Screens began to show her pulse and her oxygen level.

A green light went on in the ambulance that meant it was safe to take off their masks, but before they could raise their hands to their faces, Uzair said, "We'd ask you leave those on given the level of exposure you've already had tonight."

Izabel and Kaito nodded.

Finally Ben said something about Cami. "We see this a lot in children. They're the most affected."

"But they're usually fine," Uzair added. "We'll know more at the hospital."

And they weren't far. Izabel could make it out faintly through the yellowed windshield. There was a button to clean the windows, but it was behind the EMTs.

Kaito took Cami's hand, which made Izabel want to touch her. She put her hand on Cami's foot and watched Cami's eyes. They were still. She wasn't dreaming. Izabel remembered how, as an infant, Cami laughed more often in her sleep than at any silly thing Izabel did. And Izabel wondered if Cami's body was only practicing this new behavior or if Cami had figured out something truly funny in the dream. Like Izabel slipping and falling. Like Izabel choking on a piece of corn.

Izabel didn't like going to the hospital, because of all the time she'd spent there with her mother. She'd spent even more time there during the Turning, but that's when everyone lived at the hospital—everyone who survived—and it didn't feel like a hospital then, but an elaborate fallout shelter, with taped-over windows and doors and the constant buzzing of filters and generators.

Visiting the hospital now was much more like when she'd been there with her mother. When her mother was dying. The halls were clean and carts of medicine and equipment lingered by doorways, and nurses and doctors popped in and out of rooms, and all the lights were on.

At the hospital they wheeled Cami's bed into a room and told Izabel and Kaito that a nurse would be with them shortly. Izabel couldn't believe they would leave them alone with an unresponsive child. She thought a doctor would be waiting at the door to rush in with them, like in old episodes of *ER* and *Grey's Anatomy* when an accident had been called in ahead of the ambulance. But then, maybe, if they weren't worried, she shouldn't be either.

Kaito got up and began to examine her. Before the Turning he'd been a doctor, a surgeon, with the da Vinci Surgical System. He still got called in, on rare occasions, to remove a prostate or uterus. But now they needed someone with his skills for the robots.

He got an otoscope off the wall and checked her pupils. There was such an ease in his wrist as he flicked the light into each eye.

WHEN IZABEL'S MOTHER was dying, Izabel didn't spend every moment at her bedside. Her mother slept often, and Izabel roamed the halls and sat with people in the ER, seeing how the injuries were calculated and weighed against each other. The wheezing child got taken first, then the boy holding a cut on his eyebrow, then the man with his head between his knees.

Izabel was nineteen and studying to be a nurse at college. She had taken the semester off to be with her mother, even though she didn't know what that meant at the time. She thought it meant saving her. But she knew now: it meant creating months of memories that she could look back on with guilt.

A NURSE CAME in. Clipped to his shirt was his hospital ID, with his picture and his name, LUIS. He made a funny face at Kaito, and Kaito put the otoscope back on the wall. "I used to work here," Kaito said, staying next to Cami.

"Oh, okay," Luis said. "I'll be your nurse tonight. The doctor's coming in to check on your daughter soon, and I'm going to take some blood and then check you two out."

Luis took Cami's hand gently and extended her arm. He tied a band of rubber high around it. Izabel thought she saw a change in her veins, her soft skin. Luis tapped a finger on the crease of Cami's elbow and then wiped it with alcohol. Izabel wanted to stop him but she couldn't say why.

He put the needle in and the little tube that ran to the vial turned red and then the vial filled. He popped the vial out and popped in a second vial. Izabel imagined the hell Cami would've been giving them all if she was awake.

As Luis stuck stickers on the vials, he gestured at Izabel. "Is this correct?" he asked.

Each sticker read KALLOE, CAMILA 11-02-2038.

Izabel nodded.

Luis put the vials into a plastic bag. "I'll check you out first," he said to Izabel, and as he reached around Kaito for the otoscope, Izabel watched his arm brush against Kaito's back. But Kaito didn't move from Cami's side. Luis put a pulse ox on Izabel's finger and then looked in her ears and nose and mouth. "Anything bothering you?"

"My throat hurts," she said.

He got her a lozenge out of a giant jar by the sink. "It's a minor irritation. Otherwise you look good." He put the cuff on her arm for the machine to take her blood pressure. The lozenge tasted like cherry medicine, like the recipe hadn't been changed in a hundred years. The cuff tightened around her arm and then released. Luis put the numbers into a tablet.

Next was Kaito's turn. He finally left Cami's side to have a seat. Luis said he looked fine as well. He added Katio's numbers to the tablet, put the tablet on the wall, and left the room.

That meant there'd never been too much pollen in the air in the house. That meant Cami should be okay. That meant Cami should wake up. Why wasn't she waking up?

As IZABEL'S MOTHER got sicker, she slept more and more of the day. So Izabel explored more and more of the hospital. It didn't take her long to discover the morgue. Malik was the medical examiner and he seemed to take to Izabel right away, though she didn't know why. She wondered if he was warm toward everyone.

He let her watch autopsies. He even let her put on gloves and hold the organs. He had her place them on the scale, one by one, as he recorded their weights in pounds and ounces and muttered about the superiority of the metric system.

After her mother died that fall, Izabel tried going back to school. But she started failing all of her courses. *At least I have a whole semester to fail out*, she thought.

She didn't know what she wanted to do with her life anymore. She didn't know who she wanted to be. She didn't know what she thought about the words *profession* or *occupation*. She didn't like anything. Except spending time with Malik, who seemed to value her and the skills she was picking up in the quiet of the morgue.

It was there that she heard the first emergency warning.

"Where's the doctor?" Izabel said.

"They're waiting for the bloodwork," Kaito said.

"Couldn't they check on her before that?"

"Let's watch something on TV," Kaito said.

Izabel turned on the television and the local news was on, covering the opening of the first contemporary art gallery. The arts were booming, the news anchor said. The arts were having a rebirth. They, the people, were in a renaissance.

The emergency warnings were and weren't a surprise. When the trees had turned, two weeks before, to the south of them, it was clear people were going to die. A lot of people. When the spring had burst, crawling across the Earth, shift by shift, across hemispheres and regions, the world had been thrust into crisis, calamity, again and again. The only reason the emergency warnings were a surprise at all was because of human nature. The idiocy of human nature.

THE DOCTOR FINALLY came. Dr. Inaway, with a young man shadowing him. Izabel remembered hearing Dr. Inaway's name going out across the intercom system while sitting with her dying mother. *Paging Dr. Inaway. Paging Dr. Inaway.* Her mother would say, "Well, are you a doctor?!" Then she'd shrug and say, "In a way." And they would laugh. And her mother would cough. But Izabel and her mother had never actually met him.

As soon as he came into the room, Kaito's face softened. They must have worked together before. They shook hands and held each other's shoulders, how men do. It looked nice. And then Dr. Inaway shook Izabel's hand plainly.

"This is Gregory," he said, introducing his shadow.

Izabel and Kaito and Gregory all nodded their heads at each other while Dr. Inaway picked up the otoscope and examined Cami. Then he stood up and asked Gregory to repeat the exam. Dr. Inaway paid attention to him but also took the tablet off the wall, scrolled through something, and said, "Her bloodwork is clean."

Gregory finished and the doctor nodded at him.

"There's nothing wrong with her," Dr. Inaway said.

"There's *something* wrong with her," Izabel said.

"That's not to say something's not happening, only that, physically, she's in perfect health."

"What do we do?" Kaito asked.

"Best thing to do is wait. We'll roll in chairs that recline into beds for both of you."

"That's it?" Izabel said.

"We'll see what happens in the morning. And obviously we're

monitoring her closely. If anything changes, I'll be right back in here. I'm on shift until nine a.m."

Before Izabel could say anything else, he left the room, with Gregory behind him. Izabel realized Gregory had never said a word. She'd let him touch her daughter and look in her ears and nose and she had no idea what his voice sounded like.

Kaito turned the television back on—a rerun of *America's Got Talent*.

WHEN THE EMERGENCY warnings began, everyone in the hospital gathered in the cafeteria. They rolled all the air scrubbers there. All the med carts. All the beds they could fit. The oxygen tanks. They handed out surgical masks. They taped up vents and holes around pipes, everything as best they could. There were hundreds of people—patients and staff and a few stragglers like Izabel.

That was the day Izabel and Kaito met, assessing how much food there was, calculating rations. Malik chose both of them to work with him to figure out that particular problem. Izabel didn't say, *This is pointless—we'll all be dead soon*, but she thought it. She also thought Kaito was the most beautiful man she'd ever seen.

That night they stayed up watching news coverage of the dead. People on their porches, in their cars, whole families on their sofas. Someone wearing a gas mask took the footage and sent it to the local station. They showed his twitter handle on the bottom of the screen as the video played, @survivalsnotahoax. Izabel took Kaito's hand.

## CHAPTER THREE

Izabel and Kaito left the reruns on. Every hour Luis checked on them, and every hour he found them still awake in the reclining chairs next to Cami's bed. Eventually he offered them something to help them sleep, but they refused. He pointed at the button on the wall that would reach him. As if they didn't know.

Someone on the television was singing for the judges. Someone who was probably dead now. But no one complained about the reruns. Izabel wondered if everyone was like her, if they wanted to bury themselves in the past, like her app offered, like the Turning hadn't happened. But, no, probably not. They probably liked that the show was funny sometimes, and that other times it made them cry, when mothers in the audience cried, when children were darling. It was feel-good television.

ON THE SECOND day of the emergency warnings, the second day quarantined in the hospital cafeteria, the local news featured clips that were sent in from all over the Northeast. In every clip, the survivors were wearing masks of all different kinds, kinds Izabel didn't know the names for then, but would come to learn: half mask, full-face, canister type, continuous flow, self-contained, particulate, cartridge. Usually a family or organization had seen the warning signs across the world, and they had prepared. Some were still sheltering in their unsealed houses, their furniture and floors beginning to turn yellow.

"Kuchi-sake-onna," Kaito said under his breath as the footage poured in.

Izabel prodded him.

"An old yōkai story my brother used to tell me, to scare me."

"Tell me," Izabel said.

"Just a woman who would go around in a mask asking people if she were pretty and then take off the mask to reveal that the corners of her mouth had been slit to her ears."

"That's horrible. What did you call her?"

"Kuchi-sake-onna. 'Slit-mouthed-woman.'"

"It's like the Heath Ledger Joker," Izabel said.

"I thought of her as soon as I saw the trailer!"

"But in a surgical suite, everyone's in a mask. Does it scare you then?"

"A little," Kaito said. "But that's one room. This is the whole world now. A whole world of kuchi-sake-onna."

IZABEL CLIMBED INTO bed with Cami. She kissed the side of her head, on her temple. She kissed her cheek. She kissed her on the lips like Cami was the sleeping princess she so resembled in Izabel's mind. But Cami didn't wake up. Izabel watched her chest move up and down.

She remembered the dreams that she used to have in quarantine. Sometimes she was a tree. Sometimes she was the pollen. She ran the back of her finger down Cami's arm.

More times than she wanted to remember, Izabel was the kuchisake-onna in her dreams. But she went around saying, *Why so serious?* like she was the Joker, too. She was as confused about who she should be in her dreams as she was in her life.

She reached up and touched the corner of her own mouth. And Cami's chest kept going, so steady and quick. And Izabel finally fell asleep.


ON THE THIRD day of the quarantine, the local news stopped. The studio must have been decently airtight, but without the air scrubbers and the oxygen tanks and masks of their own, they didn't last all that long.

After the signal dropped and the television played static, Izabel and Kaito kissed for the first time. Izabel felt like Ariel— like if she hadn't kissed him by the time the sun set on the third day, she would've been turned back into one of the humans that died.

When the news came back on, it was from D.C. They had taken more precautions there. Many of the government buildings had filters, oxygen, masks, plastic sheeting, tape, food. They were taking in survivors. The halls were filled with sleeping bags, and every outlet had a power strip with a dozen smartphones plugged into it.

Over the next week, the officials who hadn't died were holding meetings. They were a smaller version of the government everyone was familiar with. They talked about the budget. They had scientists video-conference in with updates.

And it became absurd. When they started discussing defense contracts. When they started talking about whether pollution was to blame, if China was to blame, and if actions should be made against them, a show of strength. Or if not strength, then remaining viability.

When one tech company stepped forward with a plan, the government tried to debate it, restructure it, get bipartisan agreement for it. They approved parts of it and not others. They suggested ways to cut corners. They tried not to broadcast any of that, but reports got leaked. And the next thing everyone was hearing was that, with the help of the civilians in the capital, there had been a sort of coup.

THE TECH COMPANY moved forward with their plan. The roads that would be maintained were chosen. And then the robots appeared, moving through the deserted streets. Izabel watched as they demolished buildings and cleared debris past a perimeter they'd marked. The work was loud and methodical and went on for months.

During those months the new government set up a network for survivors to find the most successful strongholds and get themselves there. The hospital was one of them.

Izabel and Kaito set to work with Malik to create a safe entryway to the morgue, where people could be hosed down. And then they created a safe passageway from the morgue to the cafeteria. They wore hazmat suits as they worked.

Another team worked to expand the safe area past the cafeteria, to include a large waiting room that they filled with more beds. Another team washed linens, vacuumed mattresses, and wiped down every metal and plastic leg, handle, frame, and wheel.

The robots delivered food supplies, and better respirators, too.

Izabel watched the robots build frames of rebar in the earth. She watched them put in pipes for plumbing that kept spiking up for future hookups. They laid wiring in bright colored tubing. They put in coils for heating. The earth was the most complex she'd ever seen it.

Next they poured the cement. All around the hospital was a clear, flat foundation with hundreds of perfectly placed plumbing and electrical hookups. It looked like something simple was beneath it. It looked simple itself. It looked like nothing had been there before that. Certainly not a whole town.

Poof. History wiped clean.

And then the new town went up. They used kits. It was easy, fast, practically noiseless. It looked like colonies that Izabel had seen pictures of, set up in the desert, to simulate life on Mars. Perfect and barren. Their plastic domes.

KAITO WOKE IZABEL up by shaking her shoulder.

"Is she up?" Izabel said.

"No," he said. "Look."

On the television was a breaking news story. In the middle of the night, someone had taken a weapon to the side of a home, slashing the sheeting, and a family of four was dead inside.

"Police are reporting that the family was having financial trouble and they believe this was a targeted, singular event. We will continue to update you as this story develops."

"Holy shit," Izabel said.

"What is going on?" Kaito said, straining his voice to keep it quiet. "We haven't had a murder since before the Turning."

"I know," Izabel said. "They'll get him."

"A few hours ago they report that we're living in a renaissance, and now this."

As IMPRESSIVE AS it was—the tearing down and rebuilding of an entire town—it still took too long. Malik died before they were relocated into the domes. Izabel slept for days and Kaito called it grief.

When she went back to her work of shepherding people into the hospital, people were coming in carrying their dead. Izabel held more than one person's dead child while Kaito hosed the pollen off of both of them near the morgue's drain. Izabel was grateful the suit's facemask kept her from looking down.

IZABEL HAD THOUGHT no one would kill another person again. Not after what they'd all been through. Kaito paced the room.

The next news update had the names of each of the family members, and photos of them alive and smiling. Karen and Peter Coughlan and their two children, ages two and three, Tammy and Tavi. Izabel felt sick.

Izabel shook Cami. "You have to wake up, mi amor." She shook her hard.

Kaito wrapped his arms around Izabel's arms, and her chest, pulling her away, pulling her into his chest. "You can't shake her awake," he whispered into her ear.

THE TURNING WAS ten years ago. 2032. That's how people talked about it. Though it took more than that year for the world to experience the full effect of it, and less than a month for any city or town to all but die off. But it was easier to call it, vaguely, the Turning. To not recall which month took which town. To let it slip out of time. To let it become the generic past tragedy of the world.

The nation hadn't even set a day of remembrance. No day off from work, no vigils, no annual way to keep saying goodbye. And Izabel appreciated that.

Izabel's mother died enough months before the Turning that Izabel held on to the date of it—October 21, 2031. Her mother in the at-risk population. Her mother, early-susceptible. Her mother, sometimes called one of the Canaries.

IZABEL TRIED TO calm down in the reclining chair, but she kept her eyes on Cami. *It's been too long.* That was all she could think.

"Distract yourself, Izzie," Kaito said. "We have to wait."

She knew he was right. She opened her favorite app again. She tapped on *2017*. She would have been five years old. Even if her mother had shown some sign of sickness, she would've been too young to realize what that meant, would mean, for the both of them. She tapped on *Today's News.*

This came up:

### The DEP Issues a Code Orange Air Quality Action Day Forecast for the Philadelphia Area

. . . On air quality action days, young children, the elderly, and those with respiratory problems, such as asthma, emphysema and bronchitis, are especially vulnerable to the effects of air pollution and should limit outdoor activities.

The U.S. Environmental Protection Agency's standardized air quality index uses colors to report daily air quality. Green signifies good; yellow means moderate; orange represents

unhealthy pollution levels for sensitive people; and red warns
of unhealthy pollution levels for all.

To help keep the air healthy, residents and business are
encouraged to voluntarily restrict certain pollution-producing
activities by:
- Refueling cars and trucks after dusk
- Setting air conditioner thermostats to a higher
  temperature
- Carpooling or using public transportation; and
- Combining errands to reduce trips.

For more information, visit www.dep.pa.gov.

Izabel recalled the maps they made that tracked how the
Turning had moved, as if they only needed to understand it. Just
as her mother might have gotten this email and then refueled
her car that night in the dark. An action that saved nothing and
no one.

Izabel closed her eyes and tried to trigger goose bumps over
her body in waves, like she experienced when she got acupuncture,
which the acupuncturist said was her chi. And she could trigger it
slightly. And she hoped it was her chi. She hoped something was
moving inside her that she didn't understand.

She stood up suddenly and went to the med cart.

"Put in your code," she said to Kaito.

"It might not work."

"Put it in."

He did, and the cart unlocked. Izabel took out a syringe. Kaito
didn't have to say anything because she knew he was thinking,

*What are you doing?* And he knew she was thinking, *You know I'd never hurt her.* And so she continued.

She took Cami's foot in her hand and held the syringe next to the side of her smallest toe. This was the point that hurt Izabel the most in acupuncture. She took a big breath in and as she let it out, she pierced Cami's skin.

Cami whined.

## CHAPTER FOUR

"Can you open your eyes?" Izabel said.

"Ow," Cami said.

"Cami. Can you open your eyes?" Izabel said more firmly.

"I don't want to."

She softened her voice. "Come on. Yes, you do. I'm here. Daddy's here. Open them up."

Cami opened her eyes and whined again.

"Good job," Kaito said. "You're doing so good."

She closed her eyes into wrinkles to make a point of it.

"Did you see where you are?" Izabel said.

Cami squinted to peek out. "Where are we?"

"We're at the hospital," Kaito said.

"Why?"

"You wouldn't wake up," Izabel said.

"Was it morning?"

"No," Izabel said.

"Then why would I wake up?"

Izabel let out a small laugh.

"It was noisy," Kaito said. "We woke up."

"I wake up when it's morning. I stay in my bed. Unless something's wrong."

"That's right," Izabel said, and she kept laughing lightly, like a bird was caught in her throat.

THE SPRING AFTER the Turning was gentler, in that the air did not become increasingly *more* toxic. It held the levels. Kaito and Izabel settled into a dome together. They were madly in love, which Izabel remembered mostly by how often they were touching—holding hands as they walked, being under his arm on the couch, sleeping with limbs across each other in their new bed, and standing close enough that she would often turn and kiss his shoulder.

Kaito proposed after they'd been living together for two years. And Izabel said she couldn't marry him because the world was too new.

Thousands of kits had become a town in those two years, a real, functioning town. But it was hard to believe. Could they really survive like this indefinitely? Could there be a meaningful future for them, for any of them?

But about a year later it felt real to Izabel, despite herself, the possibility of their future taking shape, and then she said yes.

Though some things about the town would never feel right. How almost everyone over sixty had died and Izabel rarely saw an old person. And almost every child under ten had died. So Izabel saw infants, yes, but then teenagers, and nothing in between.

When Izabel was pregnant with Cami, so were a large group of women in the town, and it made Izabel feel like she hadn't chosen to get pregnant at all. Like she hadn't had countless conversations with Kaito, weighing the pros and cons, considering what was hope and what was foolishness. It felt instead like it was an imperative of her species at work.

DR. INAWAY CAME in, happy to see that Cami had woken up, and he said that he wanted to discharge her. Gregory and Luis were with him, and Luis went about undoing every cord he'd attached. Lines went flat, numbers dropped to zero.

They had to go home, and Izabel hadn't thought of that consequence of waking Cami. She hadn't thought about having to leave the safety of the hospital when a murder had just happened, when the domes were vivid in all of their vulnerabilities. And they still didn't know what had happened to Cami. It seemed to Izabel that Cami could lose consciousness again at any time. What was stopping her?

"You don't need to observe her overnight?" Izabel said.

"No," Dr. Inaway said, smiling. And Gregory smiled behind him. Like they were delivering nothing but good news.

AFTER THE DOCTORS left, Izabel said to Kaito, "That's it? We never know what happened?"

"You know that we don't know enough about the environment and its effects."

"Doesn't it bother you?"

"Of course it bothers me," Kaito said.

"Can't you talk to them?"

"It wouldn't change anything."

Cami said, "I want to go home."

"You don't even want to try?" Izabel said.

"Mom! I want to go home!"

Izabel snapped at her—"Is that how you want to say it?!" And she was surprised she would talk to Cami like that, so soon after fearing she'd never see her awake again.

"No, Mommy," Cami said.

"Okay, okay," Izabel said, collecting herself, righting herself. "Let's go home."

It was so early in the morning that the car that came for them was clean of pollen. It must have come straight from the porting station. When the green light came on inside, they pushed their masks down around their necks. Izabel looked out the window at their small town and the dense forest behind it, the old city mixed into the trees, buildings overrun with vines and blooming wildly in the sunlight.

Cami was starting to seem like herself again. She asked if she would be going to school that day.

"No," Izabel said, "not today. We'll play at home today."

"Yay!" Cami said.

Izabel smiled at her.

"Can Dad play with us?"

"He can if he wants to."

"I'll play with you a little bit, but I have to work today."

"Yay!" Cami said again. "I want to play a three-person game. One-two-three." She touched each of them with her finger. Then she twisted her head around to look out of the back of the car and began waving.

"What are you waving at?" Izabel said.

"That tree!" she said.

Izabel saw all the trees near the north edge of town and didn't bother asking which one.

Cami sat back down in her seat, pleased with herself, and as the car pulled up to their house, Izabel watched Cami pull her mask up, over her mouth, without any prompting. Child of this world, she knew what to do.

It only took a few hours for Izabel to regret not taking Cami to school. Izabel put together five snacks—graham crackers in one small bowl, cheese crackers in another, blueberries, a cut-up banana, chocolate chips—and put them all in front of Cami so Izabel could stop getting up and down, up and down, at Cami's every whim.

Cami watched a show on the television, and Izabel watched an old show on her tablet. An episode of *Property Brothers*. The brothers walked a family out into a backyard with a pool and a covered patio with a grill. *Wow*, the family said. *This is amazing. This is better than the inside.* They showed another few shots of the backyard from different angles.

"Obake blueberry!" Cami yelled out, holding a giant blueberry in front of Izabel's face.

"Not so close, Cami."

Cami took her arm back, still waiting for Izabel's response.

"Yeah, that's really big!" Izabel said.

Cami popped it into her mouth and went back to her show.

All of the blueberries looked giant to Izabel. Cami had never seen a regular-sized blueberry. After the Turning, produce grew larger, larger than anyone thought it could grow, and it grew more resilient, too. It was the first thing the country learned how to profit from. They encouraged fields of growth and built gargantuan robots specifically to traverse those fields and harvest the produce. It was one of those robots that Kaito commanded from his home office.

Cami began to ask Izabel questions about nothing. "Why are

trees green?" Chlorophyll. "Why are days twenty-four hours?" That's how long it takes for the Earth to spin once around its axis. "What *is* twenty-four hours?"

Izabel always answered and Cami knew she always would. Izabel was the kind of woman who knew answers and liked that she knew them. She liked that she knew words like *chlorophyll*. She liked that she could teach them to her daughter. But it was not satisfying, like a conversation. And it was not her television show of past people, imagining them lounging in patches of grass.

Izabel turned to Cami. "Maybe there's a class we could do at the community center this afternoon—what do you think?"

"Yeah!" Cami yelled.

"Do you think that's a good idea?" Kaito said, leaning out from the back room.

Izabel shrugged. Cami was dancing around the room.

"Do you want to rest, Cami?" Izabel asked.

She didn't answer. She just danced.

"Cami," Izabel said. "Cami, stop for a second and answer."

Cami stopped. "I don't want to rest."

"Thank you."

Cami went back to dancing.

Kaito laughed. "I guess it's fine." He went back to work. Izabel could hear him adjusting himself into the backless chair, his knees on the kneepads, his hands disappearing into the machine, his head mostly obscured, enough to create the world around him with a sense of the periphery. He would be there for hours.

Izabel pulled up the schedule at the community center and found an arts and crafts class starting soon.

"An art class?" Izabel said.

"Yes!" Cami jumped, and she ran to get her mask.

THE CAR THAT came to them now was a little yellow with pollen, normal. They passed a few streets of perfect homes, domed and gray, under their own layers of pollen, left to sit. Cami pushed the button that rinsed the car's windows.

They ended up behind a car with a young man in it. He was sitting to the left side of the car, and his right arm was outstretched. He made his hand into the shape of a gun, pointed his finger at a house, bent his thumb and bent his arm like he was experiencing a recoil, and then he straightened his arm and did it again. He pretended to shoot every house they went by. Izabel was transfixed.

"What's he doing?" Cami said.

"He's pretending to shoot the houses."

"Shoot them how?"

"With a gun."

"What's a gun?"

"An old thing," Izabel said. Every time he shot, she could hear, in her head, the sound effects that children used to make for gunshots, that she used to make as a child.

The man's car turned a different direction. Izabel and Cami both moved around in the car to better watch where he was headed.

"Is he a bad guy?" Cami said.

"I don't know," Izabel said. But she felt like he was. If his car hadn't been so covered in pollen maybe she would have been able to make him out. Describe him to the police. She felt her hands shaking. Was he last night's killer?

They reached the main street of the town. They passed the school, the spiritual center, the entrance to the mall and its network of long domes. The community center came next. Izabel remembered what used to make a main street: a market, a post office, ice cream shops with lines out the doors.

THEY MADE IT to the classroom as the arts and crafts class was starting. Another child ran over to hug Cami, a friend from school. Her mother was standing by the wall. She was a tall, Black woman, and the letters of the alphabet were taped up behind her. The letters had *Sesame Street* characters beside each of them. Elmo was holding acorns in front of the *A*. And for *T*, Cookie Monster was holding a tree's trunk, standing beneath its full branches.

"You pretend to be something," Cami's friend yelled out.

Cami began to act like a robot.

Izabel decided to introduce herself to the mother. "I'm Izabel."

"Andy," the other mother said.

"What's that short for?"

"Andromeda."

"Really?" Izabel said.

"Yes. My parents liked the Greek myths."

"Even the ones about stringing up women." Izabel was trying to be funny but it came out wrong.

Andy tried to laugh anyway. "My mother thought the world would end from the rising waters."

Izabel imagined every woman in the world as a metaphoric woman, chained to the rocks for the sea monster, which turned out just to be the sea itself. She said, "Sorry. I didn't mean—"

"It's okay. I like my name."

"I like it, too," Izabel said. And she meant it.

The women went back to watching the children. Izabel felt she'd failed again at small talk, how she always did, but she was so tired from the night at the hospital that she didn't care. Instead she kept thinking about the myth of Andromeda and about the rising sea levels that everyone was so obsessed with thirty years ago.

Before the Turning, Izabel knew that the flooding of the world was one possible future apocalyptic event. But Izabel had always thought of the waters as passive, like an enormous bloating woman. Humans had melted the ice caps and done this to her. Humans had raised the temperatures, and she took in the land that came with her new size.

Now she was imagining the waters flooding the world intentionally. That was an animosity that Izabel hadn't considered. And she liked the agency of it even if it scared her.

Izabel overheard the children talking again, the robot game over now.

"Who is older—your mom or your dad?" the other girl asked Cami.

Cami looked at Izabel.

"Your dad," Izabel said.

"My dad," Cami said to the girl.

"That means your dad will die first and you will die last."

"I don't think I will die at all," Cami said.

"We don't have to talk about that," Andy said.

"It's okay," Izabel said, and though she knew she shouldn't, she leaned down to the girl who was not her own and said, "You know, death isn't that predictable."

"Why don't you two play robots again?" Andy said, pushing her daughter away.

Izabel stood up. Andy was looking right at her.

"What do you do, Izabel?"

"Just a mother," she admitted. "You?"

"I do some legal work for the factory, and other places."

"From home?"

Andy nodded.

Cami came up to them. "Mommy, my foot hurts."

"I know, honey. I told you we had to give you a little prick."

"I don't like shots though."

"I know you don't, but you don't even remember."

"But now it hurts," Cami said.

"Did it bleed?" asked the other girl.

Cami looked at Izabel—shock on her face, probably shocked she hadn't thought to ask her mother this herself.

"No, it didn't bleed," Izabel said.

"I like when I bleed," the girl said. She leaned toward Izabel like Izabel had leaned toward her. "And I like to rub it on things."

*Touché*, Izabel thought.

"That's enough of that," Andy said, and she shoved the girls away again by their shoulders.

"I would make my whole dress blood," the girl said, walking away.

"Enough," Andy said sternly after her.

Izabel heard Cami say, "I'd love your blood dress."

"Kids are weird," Izabel said.

Andy pushed out a laugh again, trying not to be embarrassed. Izabel knew that laugh. And maybe Izabel couldn't comfort her completely because she *was* considering how strange their daughters were. She was thinking, *If these girls were older, bigger, stronger, might they be the type of people who could slash through the wall of a family's home?*

She watched the girl hug Cami again, and Cami stood stiffly in her arms.

She thought, about each of them, *Is this how a killer would behave?*

## CHAPTER FIVE

That night, after Izabel put Cami to bed, Kaito got called back to work in his machine. Izabel lay in bed alone and watched another old show about real estate. This family, like all the families, said their yard was a priority. They evaluated it based on the shade it provided. The fence. They asked if their dog would be happy there.

Izabel remembered asking her mother for a dog almost every day for a year, until one day her mother yelled at her, "It isn't going to happen!" And Izabel wasn't sure why that had done it over everything else, but she never asked for a dog again. Maybe she knew what the truth sounded like.

Cami didn't ask for a pet like Izabel had. She saw pictures of dogs and cats, saw them in books on her tablet. At the mall, there was a small indoor "zoo," which was more like a business, trying to breed animals and bring them back as pets. They saw a litter of rabbits once.

"Wow," Cami said, and then she walked away.

"That's it?" Izabel asked. "You don't want to really look at them."

"I looked at them," Cami said indignantly.

"You're right," Izabel said. "You did."

THE REAL ESTATE show finished, and Kaito was still working. She heard nothing from his office—the machine doing its work quietly behind the door. Izabel switched to an episode of *The Millionaire Matchmaker*, one she'd already started at some point. She was at the part of the episode where Patti was screening women for her millionaire, three at a time. Patti was looking for career women, for women who wanted children, for women who were okay with dating a Black man. Patti was telling a woman to "step it up" for the mixer.

And then Izabel heard Cami thrashing around in her bed.

Izabel put the tablet down and rushed into Cami's room.

"You're okay. It's okay," Izabel said, placing a hand on Cami's chest.

Cami started to cry.

"What is it, honey? What is it?"

Cami opened her eyes. "I asked why I can't touch any of them."

"What?"

"They showed me why."

"Why what?"

"Mommy!" Cami stood up and hugged Izabel around her neck.

"It's okay. Lie back down. I'll lie down with you. Would that be good?"

Cami nodded.

"It's okay." She kissed Cami on the forehead.

After Cami was back to sleep, Izabel couldn't go back to watching, to seeing if Patti had made a match. She decided to take a shower.

For Izabel's birthday, Kaito had their shower floor tiled. And she did delight in it, the tiny squares alternating in texture and color. A shining green showed through slick glass. A textured opaque olive green that sparkled silver in places.

It wasn't enough of a change to the room that she forgot where she was, and that was smart of Kaito. Izabel would have hated it, as if they were pretending, or forgetting the time before the Turning. He knew how she felt about that. She let it slip out. That worry. That little anger she kept and polished like a silver spoon.

An industry had formed in the town to disguise the rooms of the plastic domes to look as if they were not of plastic. Inset walls, tile work over the concrete floors, custom kitchens, built-in bookshelves and entertainment units. Anything was fair game as long as the access to the electrical, the plumbing, and the HVAC was clear.

It took a few years of stability before businesses like this began to crop up. Then it took only months for them to succeed. The companies had names like ArtInside, Personal Design, Classic Interiors. Izabel wondered if they were part of the renaissance, too.

Her mother would have called her tiled floor a *flight*. Everyone deserved those, her mother used to say.

As Izabel showered she imagined everyone, as a society, finding a way back to McMansions. And other spoils. Displays of wealth. She imagined the television producers chomping at the bit, already prepared for the new version of *MTV Cribs*.

Izabel rubbed her toes into the tiles and grout. She considered less pleasant things. She wondered if somehow she had caused the break in their air filtration system. If she'd cooked something she wasn't supposed to and clogged a filter. If she hadn't operated the doors correctly. Something rote that somehow became *un*rote by mistake, by her unpredictable body.

She thought she heard Cami crying and she turned the water off. The house was silent. Her hair was filled with suds. She turned the water back on and rinsed out her hair. It sounded like Cami was crying again, but this time she didn't turn the water off to check. She needed to take deep breaths as she finished conditioning her hair, to hear what sounded like crying and not respond.

When she finished and turned off the water, the house was still silent. She was right to not stop, to take her time, but she had to tell herself that over and over.

She dragged her foot over the tile to help the water down into the drain. She wanted to keep mold from growing in the grout for as long as she could. She inspected the plumbing coming up through the concrete slab.

No cracks. All sealed and caulked and perfect. And it was only another week before an inspector would come around for their quarterly check.

BACK IN HER bedroom, Izabel touched her tablet. Alerts ran down the screen. Another family had been killed.

Izabel tapped through and the News app opened. Under the story of the newest murder were stories about the school talent show, the newest fruit in the market.

She tapped through on the top story and a video of the police chief came up. "We no longer think these attacks are personal in nature," he said. "If you have any information on the attacker or the attacks, please get in touch with us immediately."

She went into Kaito's office.

"What's going on?" he said.

"Another family."

"Jesus."

"I think they think it's a serial killer now," Izabel told him.

"I'm going to apply to move."

"To where?"

"The capital. You know how they've asked me to move there, to their training center, to teach people remote piloting." He paused. "What do you think?"

"Sure," she said, but she didn't know what she thought about any of it yet.

"Did I hear Cami crying before?"

Izabel had almost forgotten. "A bad dream," she said. "What are you working on?"

"A robot got stuck and I'm cutting him out."

"Does that happen a lot?"

"Out harvesting, yeah. But this was right outside of a town's perimeter."

"Which town?"

"One in California."

"Can I see?" she asked. She didn't know why she hadn't ever asked before. She didn't know why he'd never offered.

"Yeah," he said.

He got out of the machine and she got in. She thought she'd see the whole picture of it: the massive robot, the horizon, the ocean, a sunset maybe. But instead she saw one part, of only one of the robot's joints, tangled in a mess of green. The scene of it curved around her eyes until it hit blackness, and the blackness of the machine swallowed her such that she forgot the rest of her body was in her house. She had to focus on the sensation of the chair under her thighs to remember.

"So zoomed in," she said, sitting up, letting the well-lit office take her body back from the machine in one swift, dizzying pull.

Kaito said, "That's what it's always like."

"I hadn't thought about it that way."

"All this time?"

She nodded and stood up, giving him back his seat. "I'm proud of you," she said.

"I love you," he said. "I'm going to go submit an application."

"Right now?"

"I won't be able to sleep until I do," he said.

She nodded. She wanted to think of an action she could take that would make her feel more settled. But when she couldn't think of one, she crawled into bed with Cami.

When Kaito and Izabel first got together—even though it felt like the world was ending, even though one version of the world *did* end—she slept the best she'd ever slept. Cramped in a hospital bed. In a room filled with hospital beds. It felt impossible.

She wasn't sure when that feeling stopped, but maybe it was in the domes.

Izabel wrapped her arms around Cami and pulled her in. She didn't worry if it would wake her, the way she did when Cami was younger. She listened to her breathe. She listened to her intently, carefully. Not for comfort. She listened as if Cami's breathing would give something away. She wanted to know whether tomorrow Cami would wake up how she had every morning of her life, or if she wouldn't, again.

But maybe she'd been breathing just the same at the hospital. Already Izabel couldn't remember.

Izabel woke up the next morning to Kaito screaming. She propped herself up on her elbows and saw him on his knees at the door to Cami's room. He wasn't crying but maybe only because his eyes hadn't had a chance to make the tears yet. His face was red and his mouth was wide like a doll's.

Half-asleep, she said, "You're going to wake her."

Kaito started to regain his composure. "You're covered in blood," he said.

"What?" She looked down and she was, and so was Cami. She started grabbing at all of Cami's limbs. She was warm. Izabel couldn't find a cut anywhere. Cami's chest was still rising and falling.

"It's all over your face," Kaito said.

She touched her chin. "Shit," she said. She jumped out of bed and ran to the bathroom. She'd had a nosebleed. Seeing her mouth covered in blood she instinctively licked her lips and tasted it, salty and metallic. She pulled her shirt off over her head and started to run the hot water.

Kaito followed her in. "What can I do?"

"Nothing. I'll do it."

"Do you want me to strip the bed?"

"No, I said I'll do it."

"Are you mad at me?" Kaito said.

"No, I'm not mad at you." She was mad at her nose and her allergies and the air.

"Don't you think Cami might be scared if she wakes up surrounded by blood?"

She hadn't thought about it like that. "Okay," she said. "Do whatever you can in there, and keep bringing it to me. The blood'll stain."

He disappeared again and she ran the hot water over her shirt, got a little hand soap, ran it over the blood, grabbed the cloth up in each hand and rubbed it together. Kaito came back with the sheets and her clothes and little Cami behind his legs, covered in blood.

"You woke up, honey?" Izabel asked.

She nodded.

"Want to jump in the shower with me real fast before school?"

"Will you come with me?" Cami said.

"To school?"

Cami nodded.

"Sure, honey."

"I can keep doing this," Kaito said, pointing his nose toward the sink.

"Okay," Izabel said. "Keep the water hot."

In the shower, Cami held a washcloth over her face so that water didn't get in her eyes, like she always did.

"Look up," Izabel said. "It won't go in your eyes if you look up."

When the washcloth got too soaked, she handed it back to Izabel with her face crinkled up. Izabel wrung it out and handed it back to her.

When Cami was clean, she slapped the wall with her washcloth and laughed when it splashed back at her.

Izabel went over her own body and got rid of every mark of blood.

BY THE TIME they were dressed again, their teeth brushed, breakfast eaten, Kaito had finished with the sheets and clothes and gotten them into the washing machine. He kissed them at the door.

When the car arrived, Izabel and Cami put on their masks, went out the first set of doors, and waited for them to close behind them before going out the next. Outside, Izabel heard the burst of air in the small room. They walked quickly to the car.

On this ride, the car in front of them had a child in it, also going to school. How Cami must look sometimes, when she rode to school by herself. The light turned green in their car and Izabel and Cami lowered their masks.

The little boy was playing a game with his hands. Cami was looking out at the trees again, but Izabel watched the boy. It looked like one of his hands was attacking the other. And the other was taking it.

At the school, Izabel and Cami's car stopped behind the child's, but their car stayed locked. It would only unlock at the designated spot, the one in line with the door, the shortest distance to the dome of the school.

The boy got out of his car and started to run in. Halfway there he tripped and fell forward, catching himself with his hands. Then he looked at his hands and panicked at the blood. He tried to wipe it away on his pants. *He's taking too long,* Izabel thought.

Izabel tried to open the car door with the button, but it didn't work. She banged on the window and tried the door's manual handle, but it wouldn't unlock. The boy looked back at her. Finally, their car slid into the designated spot and on one of her attempts, the door flew open.

"Mom!" Cami screamed.

Izabel looked back and Cami's mask was off. That's when Izabel realized hers was off, too. She slammed the door closed again and reached for Cami's mask.

"I'll do it," Cami said, getting her hands in the way of Izabel's. "Do yours."

Izabel looked back at the boy. A teacher had come out and was moving him into the building. Izabel put on her own mask. She tried to calm down. Cars had built up behind them.

Cami took Izabel's hand and opened the car door with the button on the panel. They walked in like nothing had happened.

MR. LIND GREETED them inside the school. The boy was nowhere to be seen, but Izabel guessed that he was in the bathroom washing up. Maybe someone was changing his clothes.

Cami ran off to play with the children.

"We missed Cami yesterday," Mr. Lind said.

"That's why I wanted to come in," Izabel said. "We had a problem with our air filtration system and Cami responded oddly, slept through the alarm and the ambulance ride, and we were in the hospital for a few hours."

"I'm so sorry," he said.

"She's been okay since we got home, and the doctors said she's perfectly healthy."

"That's good news."

"But I wanted you to know. And please let me know if there's anything you notice today."

"I will," he said, and then one of the children began to cry. "I better get back to it."

"Thank you," Izabel said. She pressed a button to call a car and waited awkwardly by the door, trying not to be a distraction. Cami looked at her a few times, and they waved at each other, but Cami always went back to what she was doing. Then the boy appeared. He had at least five Band-Aids on his hands. He was happy. He was fine.

## CHAPTER SIX

Back in the car, she decided to go to the mall instead of going home. She typed in her destination, and as the domes ticked by, she began to think that maybe she shouldn't have let Cami go to school, because of the murders. She thought back to the classroom. Weren't there fewer children there than usual? Were those parents right? Smarter? Prepared?

The car pulled up to the mall and she went inside. She reasoned with herself that the bloody nose, washing the sheets and clothes, tending to their bodies in the shower, it had all distracted her. She hadn't considered Cami *not* going to school. If she had, she would have kept her home. Like a good mother. But now it was too late. Cami was already there.

Izabel walked to the salon to get a pedicure. She sat in a row of women high in massage chairs, across from another row of women low at their feet. Usually the salon had the news on, but today they had found a collection of old music videos to put on. *Smart*, Izabel thought. But then, Childish Gambino's "This Is America" came on. He shot the choir and went back to dancing. Everything reminded Izabel of her proximity to death.

She reminded herself that Kaito let Cami go to school, too. She imagined what he would say. *Home isn't any safer than school.* That was right. And Cami loved school. Izabel tried to stop worrying. She opened her app, tapped on *2017* again. Five-year-old Izabel. Kindergarten Izabel. She remembered a picture her mother kept from Izabel's first day of school—she was standing on a tree stump at the bus stop.

She tapped on *About the Air*:

Code orange. Code red. What goes through your mind when you hear those words? Are we talking about a fire, a federal emergency, or a medical evacuation?

No, no and NO.

For the young, the elderly and those who have difficulty breathing, or for those who have heart conditions, these words mean bad news when it comes to the air we breathe. When a code orange day is announced, it means that the air quality exceeds U.S. Environmental Protection Agency pollution limits. The air is unhealthy to breathe for sensitive groups of people.

A code red day means that the air is unhealthy for everyone.

How many coded color alerts do we need? The answer is simple: NONE.

We can't afford to let pollution standards slip because we will get more code red air quality days that impact everyone's right to breathe clean air. Our state and federal legislators need a wake-up call. . . .

Izabel knew the pollution would have done them in if the trees hadn't. Another possible future. God, how surprised all the environmentalists must have been. Someone must have laughed about it.

The nail technician grabbed Izabel's shoes and walked her over to where she could dry her nails. "Thank you," Izabel said, sitting down.

She unwrapped a candy from a dish of candies and imagined her mother getting that email, not knowing what was coming. Izabel hadn't signed up for any local emails when she got to college, when she was supposed to be crafting her adult life. She ignored everything she could.

She knew her mother would tell her it was okay. "You gotta watch out for yourself in the way that works for you. I do that."

"I'm a selfish person," she said to her mother, countless times.

"That's survival. That's in your genes," her mother always said back.

And then Izabel did survive when her mother didn't. So she started fighting herself and those simple instincts. Now she was stuck, not selfish, and not good at surviving either.

SHE WENT TO the privacy pods in the mall next. They were windowless and soundproof. Sometimes the people who worked at the mall used them for naps. But Izabel used them to scream and yell and curse and dance and be alone, as an adult, totally alone.

She signed up for an hour with the man managing the pods. His nametag read SASHA. Then she sat down to wait for one to open up. There was one other person in the waiting room with her. He had a briefcase by his feet.

"Getting work done?" Izabel said.

"Yes," he said. "You?"

"Oh, no. Just . . . need some time."

"Everything okay?"

Izabel tried to hide it, but she looked him over. She couldn't tell if he was being genuine. He had nice shoes. He was showered. His clothes fit him. This put her at ease for some reason.

"Sorry," he said. "I think that was, umm, sort of knee-jerk. Not taking into consideration that we don't know each other." He laughed a little.

"It's okay," she said. "I'm Izabel."

"Patrick," he said. They shook hands.

"Patrick," Sasha said.

Patrick got up, grabbing his briefcase. "Nice to meet you," he said.

"You, too," she said.

Shuffling by them all, leaving a pod, went a man who had been crying.

In the privacy pod, Izabel was finally ready to read today's actual news. The family that had been murdered last night had been identified. The news had photos, again, of each person smiling. This time a married couple, Talia and Miriam Berenson, and their son, Rey, and Talia's mother, Floss. Three generations.

Izabel was sure she recognized Floss from her days in quarantine at the hospital. *Was the family really so lucky*, she thought, *to have survived in different places and be reunited? Had they been so lucky, only to be killed, ten years later, at random like this?*

She put the tablet back down. At a small desk, there were pens and paper. And a shredder to shred the paper, too. It was part of the delivery on privacy—something you could write and the cloud would not store.

She sat down and started writing.

Dear Killer,

I want to put you in a shiny electric car and program it to go to the Arctic. To charge itself when it needs to, but stay locked. I'll put food and water in there, and enough air filters for you to keep changing them. But not your mask. And maybe once you're in the Arctic, maybe you can breathe the air without anything on your face. You can let your cheeks and chin and lips get wind-chapped. You can beg for your mask. I can't have you here anymore. Near my house.

She shredded the paper.

Dear Killer,

Maybe you're not really killing families to kill them. Maybe you're sending a message. Like you're straight out of *The Sopranos*. Maybe there are a lot more people who owe you money, who need that message, who need to pay up. Who is it? Is there some underground gambling ring I don't know about? Somewhere, is there someone having fun?

She shredded the paper.

Dear Killer,

I've been trying to come up with ideas for my own underground gambling ring. I've heard stories about cockfighting and rat races. All sorts of things you can bet on. I've thought of pretty dark ones. Like betting on which animal would live longer when exposed to the air. Can you believe we still have animals, killer?

She shredded the paper. A light went on in the pod that meant her time was up.

Izabel went to the food court to get something to eat. A young man named Lucas took her order, a poké bowl with ponzu and cucumber. She wondered if life would be so different without name tags. If life would be so different if she never learned another man's name in her life.

As she ate, there was a breaking news story on her tablet. A federal agent had been sent in from the capital to help with the investigation—Inspector Paz. The article showed her picture. She was not smiling. Izabel thought she looked like a woman who could get things done.

She took her empty bowl and chopsticks to the window with the conveyor belt that went back to where they washed the dishes. Next to it, on the wall, was a poster someone had taped up. It was Baba Yaga's house on chicken legs with skulls all around it that were drawn a little too realistically. But it was kind of beautiful to feel another kind of fear for a second.

Back at home, Izabel and Kaito shouted quick hellos to each other.

"Everything good?" he asked, coming to the door of his office.

"Yeah," she said.

"And Cami was fine?"

"Totally," she said. "Any news on the application?"

"No," he said. "I'd tell you." And he disappeared into the dark room again.

She tried to think of something useful she could do. *I could finally go through Cami's winter clothes*, she thought.

So she put clothes that Cami had grown out of into a bag, after unfolding the shirts, holding them up, looking them over, checking each tag, and folding them up again. She stretched her arms and arched her back and then went through another drawer. It felt like accomplishing something. But then she was done.

There was less than an hour before Cami came home. She went to the couch with her tablet. She turned on an old show where people made cakes competitively.

IZABEL PAUSED THE show when Cami was about to be home. She went to wait between the two sets of doors with her mask on.

The doorbell went off when Cami's car pulled up, right on time. Cami ran into the small room and hugged her. Izabel lifted her off the ground. The air rushed over them and then the inner doors opened and they stepped into the house.

They took off their masks and Izabel leaned over to help Cami take off her shoes and then she kissed her toes. Cami giggled.

"How was your day?" Izabel asked.

"Great!" Cami said.

"What did you do?"

"Mmm, I don't remember."

"Nothing?"

"I sang a song to my friends! But that wasn't during school."

"Oh, I see."

"That was after school, waiting for the cars."

"Gotcha. And who are these friends?"

"They're nice."

"Do you know their names?"

"No," Cami said, smiling.

"No?"

"I want kisses, Mama."

"Where?"

"On my belly." Cami lifted her shirt.

Izabel kissed her, left and right, so she had to move her nose back and forth into her stomach until Cami squealed.

"I want to eat!" Cami said.

"Okay, let's get you set up."

Kaito came out of his back room and Cami ran to him. Izabel went to slice an enormous apple for Cami's snack.

"Hello!" Kaito said. "How was school?"

"Great!"

"Anything good happen?"

Cami shrugged. "Daddy?"

"Yeah?"

"I want you to tell me a scary story."

"I've got to get back to work."

"One story," Cami said.

"One *short* story?"

"Yeah. About the dragon."

"Okay. Once there was a dragon with eight heads and eight tails. His body was so huge that it covered eight valleys and eight mountains and trees grew all over him."

"And his stomach was covered in blood!"

"That's right," Kaito said. "And he would come to this family's house and eat one of their daughters, every year. So Susa-no-O came and built a big wall around their land with eight doors."

"For eight heads!"

"Yup. And just inside each door was wine, thick, thick wine, and when the dragon burst in, every head slurped up the wine and fell asleep. And Susa-no-O used a great sword to defeat the dragon in its sleep."

"But he lost it?"

"He lost the sword in the dragon and when he looked for it, instead he found Kusanagi."

"The legendary sword!"

"The legendary sword!" Kaito repeated.

Cami picked up a foam sword and ran to Izabel and slashed her across the back of her legs. "*Ksh, ksh, ksh*," Cami said.

Izabel ignored her and said, "Okay, your snack is ready."

Cami ran to the table and sat patiently while Izabel walked the apple and a cup of juice over to her. Cami ate and watched *The Backyardigans,* an old show of animated animals, playing pretend and singing elaborate expository songs about their every action.

Kaito kissed both of them before going back to work.

Izabel was sure she should never feel upset, not with a family as wonderful as hers. But as she fell back onto the couch, turning the cake show back on, about to find out who once took home a $10,000 prize, as she felt the ache in her back from bowing over a hundred little clothes like she'd said a hundred little prayers, as she arranged her head on a chintzy pillow that matched a vase and a throw and coordinated the room around a turquoise blue she once cared about, as she, Izabel, relaxed back into her life—she was upset.

## CHAPTER SEVEN

A week went by before there was another killing. Just as the news was calming down about it. Just as people were interested again in pictures of the new harvest of overgrown fruit, fist-sized strawberries, an artichoke the size of a basketball.

This time two people were killed, an older couple, Stacy and Kevin Hutchinson, in their sixties. Izabel could tell she felt less upset than when children had been killed, and she felt guilty about that. She caught herself thinking, *They lived long lives*, and, *They survived the worst of it. They got ten more good years.* But that was bullshit—she wanted more than thirty more years of her life.

From the morning news, she learned that the Hutchinsons had liked virtual golf and had volunteered at the community center. By the afternoon, the coverage was all about the next steps the town was going to take to prevent further killings.

A patrol would begin—electric cars would comb the grid of the town with newly installed cameras. And some would have police officers in them. Officers were already volunteering for night shifts.

Izabel imagined the predictable pattern the cars would take, predictable enough for a person to plan around.

Next they had two people on the news to argue the pros and cons of implementing a curfew. One woman shouted, "Wouldn't the killer be more noticeable if there were a curfew?"

The other woman said, "Families have a right to choose where they want to be at night to make themselves more comfortable."

"So what, we're going to have everyone sleep in the hospital again?"

"That's not what I'm saying."

Izabel thought about how they'd probably start the curfew soon regardless—and then the doorbell went off. She looked out one of the sheet-plastic windows near the front of the dome, and she saw a man walking up to their doors.

"Kaito!" she yelled.

She couldn't *not* let the man in. She knew that. She didn't want to *kill* him. But she felt a tightness in her throat knowing that she would let him into her house.

Kaito walked out of his office as the man walked through the doors.

"Good morning," he said. "I'm Marcus."

"I'm sorry, Marcus," Izabel blurted, too loudly. "I don't know—"

"Your quarterly inspection," he said.

"Ha!" she said, and her throat released itself.

"Are you okay?" he asked.

"Yes, I just forgot. And I'd been watching the news, and I guess I worked myself up a bit."

"It's awful," he said.

She turned to Kaito, who looked calm. "Didn't get you?"

"I had it on my calendar," he said, with what sounded like an apology in his voice, toward Marcus, for his wife's behavior.

"Do you mind if I get started?" Marcus said.

"Sure," Izabel said. "Thank you."

"Thank *you*," he said. "I'll let you know if I need anything."

Kaito went back to work and Izabel sat on the couch with her tablet. She needed something more distracting than usual. She put her earbuds in and turned on an old episode of *Bridezillas*. She watched a bride yell at someone over the phone as she walked down a sidewalk in the middle of the night. Bending over to yell harder, the bride took in giant breaths and turned herself pink. But she didn't cough. And the air was clear. And her face looked beautiful, bare under a streetlamp.

WHEN MARCUS WAS leaving, he said everything was in order. He said he didn't know why there was an air filtration system malfunction, but he could send the report over from the mobile unit, the one that was sent to do the repairs.

"Did you apply to move?" Izabel asked him.

He looked surprised, but he answered. "Yes."

She nodded.

"Did your family?" he asked.

"Yeah, we did."

"Good luck," he said.

"You, too."

He went back to his car, which had waited for him. It must have his equipment in it, things he might need, caulk and tape and quick-fixes that would hold until a specialist could come.

THERE WERE SO many applications to move to another town that they overwhelmed the committee. Usually the committee would respond on a rolling basis, but not this time. All individuals would be notified by email on May 1st at 5 p.m.

It was mid-April now and peak pollination for pine and poplar. Over the next two weeks, it would peak for beech, birch, maple, oak, and sycamore.

AFTER MARCUS LEFT, Izabel ordered more easy-seal plastic, and another filter—this one on wheels—so they could turn another part of their house into a safe room. The bathroom maybe. That seemed practical.

When Cami got home from school, Izabel took her to the mall, where Cami threw pebbles into the fountain.

"I wish—" she started.

But Izabel cut her off. "You're not supposed to tell anyone."

"Oh!" she said, and then quietly, "I wish everything was orange." Her favorite color.

Izabel smiled at her, and she thought about an orange couch on an orange floor with orange walls and an orange coffee table, all in Cami's hideous orange world.

Behind the fountain a section of the mall was closed off. A sign said WATER ATTRACTION COMING SOON. Izabel had read about it. A stream that ended in a long shallow lake. Kayaks and paddleboats. The ceiling would be extra low to help minimize the amount of air it would require. They would paint it like the sky.

Izabel had been excited about it. She missed the water, and running her fingers through a boat's wake, as it began, beside the boat. Her mother used to take her kayaking. The next day Izabel would always beg for them to go again, but her mother would press her fingers into her upper arms, into the backs of them, and complain that she was sore. "Another time," she would say.

Once, before the air turned, Izabel went by herself. She realized there was a way to move an oar through the water such that it looked right, but the boat hardly moved. And then there was the way that worked: her fisted hand perpendicular to the water, her arm bent to 90 degrees, and then the hard pull back, keeping the oar broad, with that drag, that resistance. She crossed a lake. She crossed back. The next day she was holding her arms like her mother had.

But the point, the point was that, with the murders, now the water attraction seemed frivolous.

CAMI KEPT THROWING pebbles and making absurd wishes. Izabel could hear a news report playing on someone's tablet nearby. People had started flooding a small security company in town with requests for cameras to be posted outside their homes. But there weren't enough cameras, or robots to post them, or workers to man the robots. The police had asked that the company not put up any of the cameras they did have, so there would not be a problem over who got them and who did not. The police asked that the people trust them to catch the killer.

IZABEL AND CAMI sat next to each other in the food court and shared a pile of French fries.

"I haven't woken up with blood again," Cami said.

"No, honey, of course not."

"I thought that once girls started to wake up with blood, it kept happening."

"You mean your period? That wasn't your period, honey. Didn't Daddy tell you? I had a nosebleed and it went all over us."

"I can't have a baby yet?"

"No, no. It was only a nosebleed. When you're older, you'll get your period. But it will just be blood between your legs, once a month. Not all over your head like it was the other day."

Cami's eyes filled with tears.

"Oh no." Izabel pulled her in. "What is it?"

"I wanted to have a baby."

"One day you'll have a baby. But not now. What would you do with a baby now?"

"I would read her books."

"Aww, people don't have babies when they're little. You can't even read yet."

"I can read a little!"

"That's true. That's true. You would be great. Really great."

Cami still looked upset.

"Do you want to go pick up a doll baby and you can practice having a baby?"

She nodded.

"Okay, wipe off those tears. Let's go pick out the best doll baby we can find."

But when they got to the toy store, Cami had already forgotten the ferocity of her own feelings. She opted for a stuffed emoji face—the cat head with heart eyes.

They went to the small indoor playground next. Andy was there with her daughter.

"Hey!" Izabel said. She was more excited to see a familiar face than she thought she'd be. She sat down next to her while Cami took off her shoes and put them in a cubby.

"Hi," Andy said. "Remind me of your name again."

"Izabel. And you're Andy."

Andy nodded.

"What are you two up to today?" Izabel asked.

"We went to the store with the racetracks, where they let you race the toy cars. Hestia loves that."

"'Goddess of the Hearth'?"

"Ugh, I know. We turn into our parents, right?"

"It's pretty."

"Thanks. She certainly lives up to the name."

Izabel wasn't sure what that meant, but she smiled at her. She liked a woman who would say something that made no sense.

"You guys?" Andy asked.

"We just bought that emoji pillow thing she's carrying around with her."

"Cute."

"No, it's not. You can say it."

Andy laughed. "I liked emojis when I was little, too."

"Yeah," Izabel admitted, "so did I."

"Did you have a favorite?"

Izabel thought. "That one that looks like it's gasping at something and turning blue and its eyes are all white."

"I remember that one! Do they still have it anymore?"

"I haven't seen it," Izabel said.

"Maybe because it looks like someone suffocating." As soon as Andy said it, she got embarrassed.

"It's okay," Izabel said. "I think about stuff like that."

Andy shook her head, pushed out a laugh, the way she had before when she was embarrassed.

Izabel wanted to ask Andy what she thought about the murders, but Cami ran up and said she was bored. She sat down and started putting her shoes back on.

"I guess we're leaving," Izabel said.

"See you," Andy said.

IZABEL WAS IN high school when her mother's asthma got really bad, and when she began trying everything to alleviate it. Izabel would be working on a paper and men would show up to clean out the ductwork.

"I heard it helps," her mother said.

Her mother had filters running in every room. She was trying new filters every month. She was burning through her retirement savings. At the time, it infuriated Izabel—her mother's shortsightedness—because Izabel expected her to live. She went around every day expecting it, like it wasn't much to ask.

When Izabel sat close to her mother, she saw the tiny chips at the bottom of her mother's top teeth. The forks were doing it, the spoons and the glasses and the mugs. They were the same ones she'd had for decades, but the nebulizer was weakening her teeth. The steroid inhaler was making them sensitive. Still Izabel caught herself thinking her mother was well, on the whole.

Izabel didn't know how she could have thought that.

At the mall's exit Izabel let Cami push the button that called a car. A light lit up over the spot marked 8.

"Eight!" Cami yelled.

Izabel nodded.

Above the panel was another taped-up poster, like the one of Baba Yaga in the food court. This one was of a kappa, the frog-like yōkai that waited at the edges of bodies of water for people that they could pull in and eat. At the bottom of the poster was a limb, an arm, bloody at the shoulder socket, where it had clearly been torn.

"Is that Walkappa?" Cami asked. Walkappa was a character from the show *Yo-kai Watch*, where the yōkai had been made playful, and mostly harmless.

"That's a kappa, honey. Who Walkappa is based on."

"Cool!" Cami yelled.

Izabel didn't know if she'd noticed the bloody arm, but knowing Cami, she probably had.

Izabel tried to imagine who was drawing these new posters. A new Banksy? Or just a teenager interested in old graffiti, or images of New York City's papered plywood walls? Or maybe they'd read some article about old propaganda, the fliers dropped from planes.

Another family came up and called a car. A woman by herself with three children. One on her hip, one at her hand, and one, about as old as Cami, allowed to wander a little farther. A child who will return to you when called. Izabel wondered if this woman was tricked somehow into having this many children this close together.

When a car pulled into spot 8, Izabel and Cami put their masks over their faces and walked through the mall's double set of doors.

KAITO FELL ASLEEP in Cami's room while putting Cami to bed. Izabel stayed up watching an episode of *Fixer Upper* where they were taking an old wooden house down to the studs. The air kept filling with dust.

Near the end of the episode, Kaito woke up and stumbled back to their room. "You okay?" he asked.

"Yeah," she said. "You want to go to bed?"

"Why? Want to talk about something?"

"A little," she said.

"I can do it. I'm awake enough."

"Did you apply for us to move anywhere or just the capital?"

"Just the capital. I didn't know it would be this competitive. I feel like I should have known."

Izabel didn't say anything. And then they both heard it—Cami talking in her sleep. They hurried to her room.

"I love orange. Do you have a favorite color?

*"No, I can't see colors.*

"Are you blind? I've seen a blind person but I haven't ever seen a blind child . . ."

It sounded strange, all in her little voice, this back and forth.

"What is she doing?" Izabel asked.

"I don't know," Kaito said.

"I know all of the colors. I know some of the colors in Spanish . . ."

"She sounds like she's awake," Kaito said.

Izabel nodded.

*"He killed another family,"* Cami said.

Kaito walked toward her.

Cami kept going. "He defeated them?

*"They're dead.*

"I don't like that word, say 'defeated' . . ."

When Kaito reached her, he shouted, "Wake up, Cami. Wake up."

Cami woke up and looked at them there in her room. "Are you *both* sleeping with me tonight?"

"No," Izabel said, "not tonight."

"Do you remember what you were dreaming about?" Kaito said.

"No. I don't think I have dreams."

"It was important. You're sure you don't remember?"

Cami shook her head.

"Okay, honey," Izabel said. "Close your eyes and go back to sleep."

"I sleep with my eyes open!"

"That's right. I forgot. I'm sorry. Back to sleep now."

Kaito stormed into the dining room. "What was that?"

"I don't know," Izabel said.

"Should we call someone?"

"And say what? Our daughter said another family's dead?"

That's when they saw the flashing lights of police cars and ambulances through the clear plastic windows. If they'd been a few houses closer, they would have heard the alarms of the sliced-open house.

## CHAPTER EIGHT

Izabel remembered lying in bed with her mother one night, and the windows began to light up red. She asked her mother what it was.

"The police," she said.

"Why are they here?"

"They're not here. They probably pulled someone over. Do you know what that means?"

Izabel shook her head.

"Someone was speeding, or went through a red light, and now they're getting a ticket."

The lights went white in the room and it was too bright to fall asleep. Izabel asked what that was, too.

"The police still. They can change their lights."

"If I were them, I would change them to green and blue for our favorite colors."

Izabel's mother kissed her on her forehead. "That's not a setting you can do."

"Can I look outside?"

"I'd rather you didn't," her mother said.

"Why?"

"Someone could have a gun."

"Will you look outside?"

Her mother looked out and then put her head back down on her pillow. "Yup, they pulled a car over."

"Did you see the police officer?"

"No. They must be back in their car, writing up the ticket."

"Can I look then?"

Her mother was growing more agitated. "No, you can't."

"I want to."

"Look, if they have a gun, if, for some reason, someone shoots, if you're looking through the window, a bullet can go through a window, but if you're down here, on your bed, the bullet can't go through the brick wall here, okay? Do you get it?"

Izabel was scared. She went stiff under the sheets.

"I'm sorry," her mother said. "It's not scary. Probably no one has a gun. Do you want to look through the window?"

Izabel shook her head.

"Let's go to sleep, okay? The lights will be gone in a minute."

Her mother put her arms around her.

Through her whole childhood Izabel worried about bullets tearing through walls and windows. Missed shots. The distances that bullets could travel. Which guns could fire through what. The size of rounds. Collateral damage. Accidents. Drunk people. Drunk people on Ambien. Every story she heard got layered into the scenarios she imagined. In almost all of them, her mother was tragically injured, while Izabel was left unhurt—the one who hears, watches, drops to the floor.

THE NEXT MORNING, the news showed a newly dead family's smiling faces. Six people this time: Carlos and María Calandria, and their four small children, each about two years apart, Imilce, Gabriel, Rubén, and the infant, Graciela. The news reported that they called the girls Imi and Gracie.

Izabel began to cry. Calandria was Izabel's maiden name. Her mother's last name. She didn't remember the Calandria family from the hospital, but maybe they'd moved from another town. Ten years was a long time. A lot of new people had come in. She pulled up the town directory to see if there were other Calandrias, but only Carlos and María came up.

Izabel thought she would cry forever. Not in a disruptive way, just with tears that fell down her face for the rest of her life.

TO DISTRACT HERSELF, Izabel began running through old gun scenarios in her head. A man enters a bank, a school, a synagogue, a Target, an ice-cream shop, a theater.

Her fear of bullets was a decades-old feeling that had been sparked by that man in the car. And now that she felt that fear again, it was easy to obsess over it, and its oldness.

In this new world, having a gun in a dome was like having a gun on a plane. If the dome is pierced, everyone dies. Only, not because of cabin pressure. No paper napkins being pulled into the sky first.

Not that there weren't tragedies here, without guns. A man died in a car once, when the first version of the filtration system jammed. And he wasn't found for hours. Not until the cars were called back to the porting station to be cleaned and charged for the next day. The person who oversaw the cars being run through the car wash—they saw the body as the yellow was rinsed away.

In all of Izabel's old imaginings of violent incidents, she was rushing to put pressure on a bullet wound on her mother's body. They weren't like the way she failed to save her mother in real life.

Lots of people told her that she hadn't failed her mother at all. That she rushed her to the hospital and they did everything they could do for her for days, and she died like almost everyone died.

But Izabel took the blame where she could.

ON THE NEWS, they showed a map of the killings, with four red dots over each destroyed house. They had guests on, commenting on possible patterns, possible distances that could be covered on foot, given certain suits. They kept trying to get Inspector Paz on the show, but she never came on. They would note it at the end of the show. "After many attempts to contact Inspector Paz, she declined to comment."

When Izabel was out, she overheard conversations about the killer sometimes. But more often people were talking about a book they read on their tablet, or how often they swept their kitchens, washed their sheets. Izabel felt uncomfortable at surprising times, like ordering lunch—having a full conversation over a counter with another adult and never mentioning the killings.

This wasn't a completely new feeling. She remembered it from when the town began. When she walked through the mall with a water ice and no one said, "How weird is this!" She wanted to yell it out, if no one else would, "Is this real!" or "I'm eating water ice!" But she didn't. It was as if everything in the world was saying, *Continue, continue. Hush, hush.*

IZABEL TOOK CAMI to the mall after her school day. She asked her, "You still don't remember what you dreamt about last night?"

Cami shook her head.

"Did you have a good day at school?"

"Yeah."

"Is there anything you want to talk to me about?"

"No."

"Okay then," Izabel said.

She put Cami into the free daycare and went to the privacy pods. She still felt sick at the death of six more Calandrias of the world, when there were hardly any Calandrias left. And she felt more sick when she thought about how Cami knew somehow, in her sleep, that they had died.

In the pod, Izabel began to write.

Dear Killer,

I want to tear it all down, too. But I don't want anyone to die. That's my predicament. With how things are, the tearing down and the killing of people are inextricably linked. The infrastructure. The infrastructure is both the infrastructure and the guarantor of life now. What you have done—is that the predicament coming to its head?

In one direction, the forced conclusion, to let it stand—that's where I am.

In the other direction, forced also, to tear it apart, one home at a time, huddled groups of deaths—that's where you are.

I wonder, if in the constant consideration of the predicament, one can be forced from one side to the other.

She shredded the letter.

Dear Killer,

When I'm ovulating I have more fantasies about sex. But fantasies is the wrong word for them this month. I'm imagining I'm having sex with you and I dislike it. Not that you're raping me. I'm liking the sex. And it's because I'm enjoying it, and you, that I dislike it. I'm feeling horrible about it at the same time as it's happening. Or sometimes I'm enjoying it but you're physically disgusting, for example you smell like fish, or your hair is unwashed. And I know, realistically, I couldn't enjoy sex with someone who smells like fish, but that's why it's just imagining something. And I hope, too, that I couldn't enjoy sex with someone who's killed people, but I know I probably could.

She shredded the letter. And then she wrote a letter to Cami instead.

Dear Cami,

I think there's a future where you grow up to be a serial killer. And me, too. But I don't wonder how I became disturbed. My mother's death. The Turning. I'm not the person I might have been. But you. If you become disturbed, you might wonder how that happened.

So let me tell you that your father has killed people—in a post-surgery-complication kind of way—and he's always moved on from that. All doctors have lost patients. And all families have made decisions about their aging parents. And people caused other people's deaths in car accidents, when they used to happen, when people drove cars.

I could go on, but it doesn't matter. What I'm trying to say is that we're all going to be held accountable for some amount of death at some point in our lives.

If you take some agency in that relationship with death that you will negotiate over the course of your life—if you do that— you won't be the first.

She shredded that letter, too.

Dear Cami,

Please know I would never kill someone. I hope that you don't need to hear that but maybe you do. Maybe I will have changed. Or I'll die before you know me well. The chance that I die before you grow up seems like a real possibility now.

I also want you to know that it wasn't hard to pretend for you that the world was well, normal, as it should be. My mother pretended with me. Police were killing Black men and women and children, trans men and women, unarmed, when their hands were up, or when they were running away, or sitting on a park bench. I was your age. My mother didn't tell me. I found out about it later, but when I was still a child. When I found out, I didn't understand why a thing like injustice existed. I didn't understand any unfairness, at its simplest form. I understood happenstance, how people died because a branch fell on their head. But not unfairness, dependent on *people*.

You will learn about World War II and how anti-Semitism traveled the world and you won't believe in a God I never told you about. You will learn about slave ships and slavery. You will learn about the mistreatment of women across every culture. Knowledge will pass in and out of you and change you until you are so lost. And then you'll go to work in the morning. Or you'll wake up to your own child and smile at them, despite yourself.

Izabel didn't shred this letter. She folded it up small and put it in her purse.

When they got home, Kaito pulled Izabel into their bedroom.

"We need to talk about this."

"About what?"

"Last night . . . Did Cami know—that that family had died?"

"How could she?" Izabel said, only saying it to sound like the rational one between them, maybe for the first time.

"I don't know," Kaito said, "but it happened."

"It sounded like it happened, but maybe that's not what happened."

"That sounded like gibberish, but I know what you mean."

"Thanks," Izabel said.

"I mean that's not—"

"It's fine."

"What do *you* think happened?" he said.

"The question that matters to me is, What can we do about it? Nothing, right? We can't tell anyone without sounding crazy and there's nothing really to tell. So what's the point in talking about it?"

"Because it was weird. It was weird, and I want to talk about it."

"Okay. Maybe another time then. I had a long day and I'm tired and I'm hungry right now."

"Fine," he said.

And they left the bedroom, annoyed with each other.

AROUND THE TABLE together, Cami asked for another story. Kaito told one about an old couple who lived a meager life and loved their dog very much.

"Shiro!" Cami said.

"That's right," Kaito said.

"She can't name anyone in her class but she remembers the dog's name," Izabel said, mostly to herself, as Kaito continued.

The story went that Shiro led the old man to a spot under a tree, and together they dug up a huge treasure. But their greedy neighbor saw and asked to borrow Shiro.

"The couple was too kind to refuse," Kaito said.

So they let their neighbor take Shiro. He led him all over, hoping Shiro would find more treasure. And when Shiro found nothing, the neighbor killed him.

Cami gasped even though she'd heard the story dozens of times.

The neighbor buried Shiro under a tree and did not tell the old couple what he had done. But when the couple asked him to return Shiro, he told them everything. The old couple asked to have the tree where Shiro was buried, and the neighbor consented. So they cut down the tree and made it into a mortar where they could crush rice for rice cakes. And when they used it, it made more rice than they could ever need and they never had to worry about being hungry again.

The neighbor saw this and asked to borrow the mortar.

"The couple was too kind to refuse," Kaito said.

But when the neighbor used the mortar a horrible smell came out of it, so the neighbor burnt it to ash. When the couple discovered what he had done, they said the neighbor should have only asked for rice cakes if he wanted them. Then they took the ashes home with them.

Back home the old couple scattered some of the ashes, and a tree, which had been dying, burst into bloom.

"But isn't it bad for trees to bloom?" Cami asked.

"It didn't used to be," Kaito said.

"But now?"

"Now it makes it hard for us to breathe," Kaito said.

"But the moral of the story," Izabel said, "is not to be *too* kind. You have to be able to say no."

"No!" Cami said.

"I think the moral of the story is to love fiercely and loyally," Kaito said.

"And what? You'll get rewarded?" Izabel said. "That's not why you should love someone."

"No, but you're rewarded in lots of ways for loving people."

"Sure. Of course. But that's not the most important moral."

"Say no!" Cami said.

"That's right," Izabel said. "Advocate for yourself."

"And your dog!" Cami added.

## CHAPTER NINE

A ndy found Izabel online and messaged her to see if she wanted to meet at the pool at the community center. Izabel said yes.

"Let's put everything we need into the big bag," Izabel said.

"I have your bathing suit," Cami said.

"Mine? Where'd you get my suit? Go get your suit."

"Okay!"

As Cami disappeared into her room, Izabel thought about how easy it was for Andy to find her online. Wasn't that true for everyone in town? With the directory, you could find out who lived in every house on the grid. This made the killer feel even closer.

Cami interrupted her thoughts. "This one, Mommy?"

"Perfect." Izabel smiled. "Into the bag!"

IN THE CAR, Cami waved at the trees on the north edge of town again.

"That's my tree friend!" she said.

"I know," Izabel said.

"What kind of tree is it?" Cami asked.

"Which one?"

"The tallest one!"

"Maybe an elm," Izabel said.

"An *emm*?" Cami said.

"An elm, E-L-M."

"*Ellllm*," Cami said.

"That's right," Izabel said.

And for the rest of the ride Cami said the word *elm* over and over, quiet, loud, fast, slow, with her voice high, and with it as deep as her child's voice could go.

THE POOL WAS filled with children wearing the community center's accepted flotation devices—all different colors but all the same shape around the children's arms and chests. Andy wore a bathing suit with a skirt around her waist and Izabel felt herself wading a little deeper into the water to hide her thighs.

"I love your suit," Andy said.

"Thanks," Izabel said, and after a beat, "Yours, too," in case Andy was looking for that.

"I don't know if I've told you, but Cami's adorable."

"Your Hestia, too."

"I like to think so." Andy smiled. "Are you married?"

"Mm," Izabel said. "Yeah, my husband's name is Kaito."

"What's he do?"

"He drives, controls, whatever, the harvesters. Do you know what I mean?"

"Doesn't everyone?"

"How about you?" Izabel asked.

"Oh, I'm taking basic income and doing a little legal work here and there."

"No, I mean, are you married?"

Andy looked down. "Widowed."

"I'm sorry." But then Izabel looked confused. She tried to hide it.

"Don't try to do out the math. It doesn't make sense, right? Hestia's too young for it to have been the Turning. He didn't die because of the air."

"I'm so sorry."

"It was three years ago," she said. "I've gotten used to how my life works without him."

The girls splashed at each other nearby.

"It was a heart attack," Andy said, even though she clearly didn't want to talk about it. She asked, "Do you take the basic income?"

"No, Kaito makes enough. Let someone else have it."

"I didn't realize how fake money was, before the Turning," Andy said.

"I think I did," Izabel said.

"Do you think about it a lot? The time before?"

"I think about my mother a lot," Izabel said, skirting her obsession with the past, all her time on the app.

"Did she die?" Andy asked.

"Yeah."

"Your dad, too?"

"I don't know. I didn't know my dad."

"My parents died together in their old car, one day when one of the trees went, in the middle of April that year. Sycamore maybe." She paused. "It's kind of sweet, right?"

Izabel tried to think of it as sweet. She really tried. She decided to change the subject. "You know what I've been thinking about?"

"The killings."

"I wasn't going to say that, but yeah, that, too."

"What were you going to say?" Andy said. She seemed glad to be surprised.

"I've been thinking about guns."

"Guns? I haven't thought about them in a long time."

"Exactly," Izabel said. "I started thinking about them and now I can't stop."

"You want to hear one of my stories about guns?"

"Yeah," Izabel said.

"When I was little, we lived in a super safe neighborhood, you know? Not like now, not like *so safe*, but for then. But we were near a city. When I got older I wondered how more crime didn't creep out over the edges of the city, but it didn't. Anyway, I'm little in this story, and my mom took me on walks every day in my stroller. And my dad tells my mom that a few days ago, a man in a sweat-shirt shot someone one road over from where we live, but further down. And she's shocked, you know. How you're supposed to be." Andy checks to make sure the girls aren't paying attention to them. "And then he tells my mother, a day or so after that, the same guy, he's walking around and looking odd, so a few people approach him and he just starts shooting them. But maybe nobody died that time—I don't remember. And you know, she's shocked again, *how terrible*, all the rest. And then about an hour later she's getting ready to go out on our walk and she's putting me in the stroller. My dad freaks out. 'What are you doing? What about the guy who's shoot-ing people?' And she's like, 'What am I going to do? Not walk?' He goes, 'Yes! Don't walk!'"

Izabel laughs.

"Would you go out and walk?" Andy asked.

"No!" Izabel said.

"See, I think I would."

"No, you wouldn't. With Hestia?"

"I mean, they win, if you don't keep living your life."

"But it's not a *them*. It's one shooter. You can't make a point against one shooter who's down the street."

"Right, but you're willing to put your life marginally at risk or you're not. You have a little fear or you don't. That's a choice you have to make."

"I don't know," Izabel said. Cami had come back over. She pulled on Izabel's fingers. "What is it, honey?"

"I'm a shark and she's a fish and I'm going to eat her."

"Hestia. Her name's Hestia. Can you say Hestia?"

"Hech-a."

"Pretty good," Izabel said.

The girls ran off again.

"What are you doing about the killer?" Izabel asked.

"What do you mean what am I doing?"

"Like we applied to move away. Everyone's been applying. It's all over the news."

"I saw that. You applied?"

"Yeah. I almost thought that all they'd have to do was look at who didn't apply and that'd be the killer." Izabel had raised her voice and people were looking at her.

"I didn't apply and I'm not the killer," Andy said.

"No, I'm not—I just—"

"I get it."

Izabel took a few short breaths until she calmed down. "Why'd you call me?"

Andy didn't understand.

"Do you like hanging out with me?" Izabel said.

"I do. I'm sorry if—"

"No, it's fine. I have trouble reading people sometimes."

"I like talking with you. I talk to Hestia all day, and she's great and all, but she's still four."

Izabel laughed.

When they got out of the pool, all of their toes were wrinkled. When they got into the changing rooms, Izabel felt the sharpness of the drier air returning to her lungs. She knew the others felt it, too, even if the children couldn't articulate that feeling yet.

LATE THAT NIGHT, Izabel told Kaito, "I'm not sure we made the right choice about the application."

"I think we did."

"I think we're acting out of fear."

"We *are* acting out of fear," he said.

"Like everyone else, like herd behavior."

"No," Kaito said. "It's rational behavior. We have Cami to think about."

Nearby Cami was saying, kind of singing, "A nice sleep . . . a nice sleep," over and over to her toys as she was putting them away on shelves.

"I know," Izabel said. "When I think of her, I think it's the right choice."

"Because it is the right choice."

"Look, don't minimize it. We hardly have anyone left that we care about to begin with. We'd be leaving them. And maybe leaving them to *die* here. And maybe we could stay and do something to help. Maybe there aren't enough towns left not to be fighting for one."

"I don't disagree, Izzie. I just hope there are enough people that we don't have to be the ones. Other people can fight. And we can take care of Cami."

"But maybe there *aren't* enough people left. What kind of probabilities do we need, to have enough people that want to, like genuinely want to, put up that kind of a fight?"

"I'm not a statistician."

"And I'm not asking you to literally solve the problem, Kaito!"

"What do you want me to say? It's black and white to me."

"So you can't empathize with me for two seconds?"

"No, I can't. Because I know you. I sympathize with you and you'll still be thinking about this tomorrow."

"I'll still be thinking about this tomorrow anyway!"

"When you do, you'll know that I'm pretty steadfast."

They'd both gotten angrier than they'd meant to. They looked over at Cami. She was still playing her game. Except now the game had changed. "A nice sleep," she sang, and then, in a low, monster-y voice, "*in the oven*!"

"Oh no, I'm in an oven!" she responded to herself. "This was supposed to be a good day!"

## CHAPTER TEN

The next day Izabel was still thinking about the possible move. And the day after that. She wasn't certain about whether they should do it. If she was honest with herself, she wasn't certain of anything. Sometimes the world felt false and fake in all its plastic. But many nights had gone by without killings and that felt good. *Maybe he won't kill again*, she thought, even though she knew that he would.

Cami woke up early and couldn't go back to sleep, so they all got up early. At the table, Cami wanted to play a drawing game. She brought over her tablet and stylus from her play area. "Please," she said.

"Which game do you want to play?" Kaito asked.

"The yōkai game," Cami said.

"Okay," Kaito said.

"You go first, Mommy," Cami said.

Izabel drew an avocado, split in half, a big circle for the pit in its middle. Then she held it up. "Now this is a regular avocado," she shouted. "Your normal, everyday, regular avocado!"

Cami giggled.

Then Izabel blocked her tablet from view with her left hand and drew a little face on the pit of her avocado and little wings coming out of the side and little feet out of the bottom. She pulled away her hand dramatically, as if she was making a big reveal.

Cami laughed more. "You have to name it now!"

Izabel wrote *AVOCONDOR*.

"Daddy's turn!" Cami said.

Kaito turned a salt shaker into a yōkai salt shaker and named him Saltierre.

"Like Happierre!" Cami said—another character from *Yo-kai Watch*.

"Your turn," Kaito said.

Cami drew a tree. "This is just a tree!" she said. And then she put the cutest smiling face on it. "Trenster!" she said. "Mommy, will you write it?"

Izabel wrote *TRENSTER* beneath Cami's tree.

"There's a name for a tree yōkai," Kaito said.

Cami stood up next to him. "What!"

"Kodama."

She danced in the spot she was standing. She held up her shirt. Then she threw her hands out like it was the end of a jazz routine. She said, "Kodama!"

ANDY AND IZABEL met up at the mall once the girls were at school. They sat in a coffee shop with high tables and stools.

"Do something you'd never do," Andy said. "To figure out if you should go."

It was the day before notifications would go out about the applications to move. Across from the coffee shop, men were setting up a stage. There were signs all over the mall that a ballet performance would take place that evening.

"Like what?" Izabel said.

"I don't know. Have your tea leaves read. Get a tarot reading."

"Do you do those things?"

"No," Andy said. "But I haven't ever been as torn as you look."

"I am torn," Izabel said.

"Have you ever been in the spiritual center?"

"We got married there."

"Oh yeah? By who?"

"It was a Quaker wedding, where everybody signs the certificate."

"Are either of you Quaker?"

"No." Izabel shook her head. "But it was on the list of wedding ceremonies they offered and we liked the sound of it."

"We had a Jewish wedding. My husband smashed the glass under the chuppah and everything."

"Was he Jewish?"

"Yeah."

"I'm a little Jewish," Izabel said.

"You?"

"Part of my family fled to Uruguay during World War II and a few generations later, you look like me."

Andy laughed.

"I don't know much about being Jewish," Izabel said, "or about being from Uruguay. I'm assimilated, as they say."

"Me, too," Andy said.

"Kaito still knows a lot about his Japanese heritage. He tells Cami all kinds of stories. I'm jealous."

"That's great for Cami, though."

"Yeah," Izabel said. She watched the men for a second. They

were setting up trusses for the lighting. She wondered if there'd be a spotlight to follow the woman as she's chased across the stage. "Ugh, he's so sure about what to do."

"I don't want to talk about it anymore. Leave. Stay. Maybe you won't get approved and the decision will be made for you."

"You're right."

Andy nodded and shrugged at once.

"Fine. I'll do a tarot reading."

Andy smiled. "Make the appointment now."

"Now?"

"Yeah, while we're sitting here."

"Okay," Izabel said. She brought out her tablet and booked a session with a reader named Maris. "Done."

"Good," Andy said, and she started talking about how much her parents used to like gardening together.

THAT NIGHT, IZABEL went into Cami's room and sat at the edge of her bed. She listened to Cami sleep-talk.

"I want to have the man who makes my sandwiches at the mall over for my next birthday party. He's my best friend.

*"What's his name?*

"I don't know.

*"Then I don't think you should have him in your house.*

"I like him.

*"But you don't know him.*

"I know him. I said I know him.

*"What color does he like?"*

Cami paused.

*"Who is in his family? What does he like to do?"*

She started to cry.

*"Don't be sad. I mean only that you should get to know him."*

Cami calmed again.

*At least her dreams are sensible,* Izabel thought. She also made a note to pay more attention to who was making Cami sandwiches at the mall.

As she went back to her bed, she found herself worrying over Cami's strange dreams, these cogent conversations. But then she thought, *What do dreams mean anyway?* She'd once dreamt she had sex with a man she found in a forest of bamboo.

WHEN THEY ALL woke up the next day, Cami had diarrhea. And then she threw up. Izabel wanted to put her in the bath but Cami refused. They lay on the couch and Izabel let Cami take a sip of diluted apple juice every few minutes.

"I feel better," Cami said.

"Your stomach might not."

"It does! I can drink more."

"You might make your stomach spasm if you overdo it. Do you want to throw up again?"

"No."

"Then we'll keep this up a little longer."

Izabel left her on the couch and walked over to Kaito's office.

"I need you to watch her today."

He pulled himself out of his machine and looked up at her. "Today? We hear about the application today."

"I know that," she said. She held back from saying something ruder, about reading a calendar and knowing what May 1st meant. Instead she said, "It's not for that long. I have this appointment."

"What appointment?"

Izabel bit her lip. "A tarot reading."

"Seriously?"

"Yeah."

"What for?" he asked.

"In case it might help me make a decision."

"About whether we should leave?"

Izabel nodded.

"And you think it might help?"

"I don't know."

"I'm all for it if it might help," he said, putting himself back into the machine.

"So you'll watch her?"

"Yeah. Tell me when you're leaving." His voice came out like he was so much farther away than he was, so much so that she reached out and put her hand on his back.

IZABEL GOT TO the spiritual center early. It was raining out, and the domes and cars were returning to their bare white bones.

The churches, the mosques, the synagogues—they never came back after the Turning. A few people tried to start the religious institutions again, once the town was established, but too many people found their beliefs broken. Izabel only heard, here and there, of people practicing more privately: Buddhist shrines set up in spare bedrooms, crosses with Christ's injured body above beds, mezuzahs between the sets of doors.

The spiritual center was first established for funeral services, because everyone needed those, regardless of how they felt about God.

And after that, people were getting married again. Big weddings. Not the rushed elopements that happened in the hospital, where couples proved to each other that love still existed, that it could buoy them in some singular joy. Not those. People were jumping over brooms again. They were tying their hands together and walking in circles. Chairs were being lifted over everyone's heads. And the brand-new toddlers of the world were carrying rings down the aisles.

Some of the practitioners at the spiritual center studied all the world's old religions. They were scholars more than anything. The people of the town thought of them as sacred, but they weren't often needed for anything in particular.

What rose up in place of religion was a revitalization of the spiritual and the unexplained. People wanted to believe there was an energy in the universe that connected everyone and everything, an energy that could articulate those connections, provide feedback, clarity, if one knew how to hold the conversation. And so there were rooms for reading tarot, tea leaves, the I Ching, numerology. One practitioner, Lucy, was well known throughout the town because she would hold séances.

It was all part of the renaissance they were in.

But Izabel didn't like being in the spiritual center; it reminded her of how her old world had transformed into this new one. Waiting in the lobby, she opened her app, tapped on *2017* again. The year felt just out of reach. She scrolled through the headlines until she saw one about a fire.

A wildfire that has been burning through the Columbia River Gorge since Saturday afternoon is now dumping ash on Portland as it tears through more than 3,200 acres of fir trees and brush in one of the area's most beloved natural areas.

Longtime residents of the city say this is the first time they could recall ash falling on Portland since the eruption of Mount St. Helens in 1980—a disturbing measure of the damage wrecked by record heat, parched forests and horseplay with fireworks . . .

... The fire started nearly two days ago when two teenage boys tossed fireworks from a cliff along Eagle Creek Trail. Dry brush at the bottom of the cliff ignited and the flames spread quickly, trapping more than 150 hikers on the trail. They were rescued Sunday morning.

On Monday afternoon, the winds in the gorge shifted— forcing further evacuations, shutting down the interstate and sending plumes of smoke into Portland.

Ash began falling across the city shortly before 5 pm.

The National Weather Service's Portland station says to expect ash to keep falling throughout the day Tuesday. "It's very light, so it doesn't impact the overall air quality much," the NWS writes on Twitter. "But the air is not great to start with, so staying inside is not a bad plan."

Portland Public Schools has announced it will end the Tuesday school day two hours early because of heat and smoke.

Izabel thought of the children breathing in the smoke. She leaned forward as she looked at old photos of Portland's fire. The ornately painted tiles of the spiritual center's floor became the backdrop to the photos on her tablet—entirely mismatched, entirely unjustified. The rain fell harder and harder on the plastic sheeting of the dome.

## CHAPTER ELEVEN

Once, Izabel and her mother got stuck at the beach in a thunderstorm. Izabel's mother thought they could wait it out at the aquarium. Izabel stood on a step stool at the touch tank, reached into the water, and touched a stingray that came up to her fingers.

A horseshoe crab was flipped over on its back in the tank, and Izabel's mother asked the girls who were working there, "Shouldn't we flip the crab right again?"

The girls smiled and said the crabs did that sometimes, to rest. The girls said the crabs liked it.

But it didn't look like it was resting, with its legs pumping and its book gills flapping.

Izabel waited for the stingray to come to her fingers again. She heard other women come up and ask the girls the same thing. *Shouldn't they help the horseshoe crab? Shouldn't someone?* The girls smiled again and repeated the same thing, as if they'd never answered that question before in their lives.

It was still pouring when Izabel and her mother left the aquarium hours later. They ducked into a candy shop and ate string licorice while they waited for the rest of the storm to pass. Lightning struck close and its thunder shook the building—the windows rattled in their frames like they were made of plastic. Izabel's mother touched one. "Glass," she said.

It seemed like the rain would never stop, like every street on that stretch of island would flood and they would be trapped there. So Izabel's mother said they would run to the car. Halfway there, they were already soaked. They stopped under a pagoda in the middle of a parking lot that was normally for valets.

Lightning struck again and Izabel heard her mother count the seconds between the flash and the thunder. When it boomed, her mother nodded, pleased with the number, and they continued. She grabbed Izabel up in her arms.

Her mother couldn't tell how flooded the street was, and when she stepped off the curb into the last street they had to cross, the water came up to her knee. She held Izabel tighter and Izabel remembered laughing. Or she didn't remember laughing but she remembered her mother saying, "It's not funny. This is dangerous."

When they were in the car, Izabel's knees shook when the lightning struck again. "It's not scary *now*," her mother said. "The car is grounded. The lightning can't hurt us here." But Izabel didn't understand what was dangerous and what wasn't, when she should be careful and when she shouldn't. Her mother took off her soaked shirt and rubbed her down with a towel. Then she draped the towel over Izabel's bare chest and buckled her over that.

On the drive home, her mother must have thought Izabel was asleep. She called a friend and Izabel heard her recount the storm, the water to her knees, the thought of being struck by lightning while that deep, with Izabel in her arms.

She talked about how, in moments like that, she could almost feel her death, the one that happened in a parallel universe, where the lightning did strike.

Her friend's voice came out loud from the phone. "Don't be silly."

And Izabel yelled, "She's not being silly!"

IZABEL WAS STILL focused on the sound of the rain on the roof of the spiritual center when a door flew open. Out of the room came a group of men and women in long white skirts, with small towels on the backs of their necks, all of their faces flushed. One man sat down across from Izabel in the lobby chairs, wiping sweat from his face and neck.

"What were you doing in there?" Izabel asked.

"Whirling," he said.

"Like dervishes?"

He nodded.

"I didn't know anyone still did that."

"Not too many of us."

"Are any of you actually Middle Eastern?"

"A few," he said.

"Why do you do it?"

"I like it."

"No, like, what's the purpose of the whirling?"

"Oh, to experience God. If you disrupt the physicality of the body, you can break from it and then you feel the energy that is always there."

"Like your soul?"

"If your soul is one with everything."

"So you don't believe in ghosts then?"

"I believe in everything," he said, obviously slightly annoyed at Izabel's voyeuristic questions.

"I'm getting a tarot card reading done," she said.

He nodded.

"I will speak to the energy, I guess."

He nodded again.

"Carl," another man said, behind him, holding two metal cups of water.

"Thanks," Carl said, reaching back and taking one of the cups. He downed the water, stood, and they walked off without a goodbye.

Izabel went to the bathroom and heard a woman dry-heaving into a toilet.

"Do you need help?" Izabel asked.

"No," the woman said.

Izabel peered under the door and saw that she was wearing one of the long skirts, and sitting on her knees in front of the toilet. She stood back up. "Can I get you some water?"

The woman hesitated. "Okay."

Izabel went back out to the table with the stack of metal cups and the jug of water with a little spout. Above the table was another poster. A woman standing in water and surrounded by dead children. La Llorona. Her mother used to tell her the story of La Llorona and Izabel had always hated it. She hated it more now, as a mother herself.

Izabel looked around, confirmed no one was paying attention to her, and ripped the poster off the wall, crumpling it into her fist. Then she took a cup of water back to the woman in the bathroom.

When the woman opened the stall door to take the water, she looked terrible.

"Is there anyone I can tell that you're in here?"

"No," she said, shaking her head. She took a sip.

"I think you should sit and put your head between your knees."

To Izabel's surprise, the girl did it, right then. The water sloshed in the cup.

"I'll hold it for you until you want it again," Izabel said.

"Thank you."

But then Izabel heard someone call her name in the lobby.

"That's me," Izabel said.

"Go," the girl said.

"Will you be okay?"

The girl nodded her head into the fabric of her skirt, which was sweeping across her bent knees in so many folds of white.

So Izabel left, and the woman who had been calling her name led her quickly to a room. She showed her where to sit.

"There's a girl sick in the bathroom," Izabel told her.

"Hmm, I'll tell someone," the woman said.

Izabel was left alone in the room for some time. It smelled of sandalwood. There were sticks in a pretty glass jar with oil in it. There was a dream catcher, stacks of tarot cards, books on tarot readings, but it wasn't what Izabel imagined—no purple tablecloth or shaded windows, no tabletops covered in knickknacks and crystal balls. No ambiance.

The woman came back and sat down across from her. "Thanks for waiting," she said.

It took Izabel a second to realize that this was Maris. "I'm sorry," she said. "I thought you just helped people get to their rooms."

Maris shook her head. "No. But that's okay. Good to help the girl." She looked right into Izabel's eyes when she spoke. "Are we ready to begin?"

Izabel nodded.

MARIS STARTED TO shuffle the cards. They were twice as big as playing cards. She loosely held half of the deck in each hand and let them fall over each other from the left and right until they were shuffled. She made it look easy.

"Do you have any ideas about what a tarot reading is?" she asked.

"Not really," Izabel said.

"Nothing?"

"That it tells you about the future."

"Yes, that's true."

"My friend thinks it will help me make a decision."

"Do you think it will help you?"

"I'm open to it."

"You don't have to tell me what decision you have to make. Just think about it." Maris handed Izabel the deck of cards. "Think about the decision, and when you're ready, hand the cards back to me."

Izabel took the deck of cards, thought to herself, *Should we leave?*, and handed them back.

"Okay, are we done with that now?" Maris said.

"With what?"

"With you not being invested?"

"I'm sorry, I—"

"Do you think you would believe in this more if I wore a head-scarf and had glitter all over this room? No, you'd have more reasons not to trust me. And normally I wouldn't care, but I think you need something from this, so let's do it."

"Okay."

"You're ready?"

"I'm ready," Izabel said. And she wasn't sure if it was guilt or shame or only how much she disliked disappointing someone, but she did feel ready.

Maris handed her the cards again. "Close your eyes. Take a deep breath. Think about the decision that's before you. Imagine you are on a path and it's splitting. To your left is one decision. To your right is the other. What does the left look like? What does the right look like? You are standing at the fork and you see both paths very clearly, but you don't know which to take. That is your question. Put that question into the cards. And when you're ready, hand them back to me."

Izabel did as she was told and took her time. She could feel herself filling the cards and they began to feel heavy and hot. She almost dropped them. It felt like she had to get them out of her hands.

"That's better," Maris said. She cut the deck, restacked it, and then spread it out in front of Izabel. Every few cards, one tilted up. "Take eleven cards, and take as long as you need."

Izabel started with every card that was tilted up. She was worried that Maris would stop her. That this wasn't really Izabel picking the cards, but the cards picking her. But Maris was quiet. When Izabel finished picking the tilted ones, she had seven, and a few new cards were up now, having been disturbed. So she picked those. She had ten. The last card she picked because she felt she should, and she wondered where that feeling came from.

Maris began to the lay the cards out, one to the left, one on its side on the top, two beneath it, which Izabel recognized: Death and the Five of Cups. Maris drew in her breath a little, but she continued. Beneath those cards were two more on their side. One was a heart with three knives through it. One was a knife dripping blood. Then there was one more to the right. And to the right of that one, the final four, were all on their sides, down the side of the reading.

"That looks bad," Izabel said.

"It is bad," Maris said, "but maybe not in the way you think. And there are good cards, too." She pointed to the card all the way on the right, the last card Izabel had picked. "The Empress. The Death card is not weighed more heavily than the Empress because it's scarier looking. Let's go through it.

"It looks as if two men are influencing you right now. To the left here, the King of Pentacles, above, the King of Swords. Is someone in your life a surgeon?"

"My husband used to be a surgeon."

"So this is him." She tapped on the King of Swords. "This card. It calls up precision. Does he have feelings about this decision of yours?"

"Yes."

"The cards say, listen to him."

"Who is the other man?"

"I don't know. The King of Pentacles. An earthly man maybe. Someone who works with his hands. You don't know who it could be?"

Izabel shook her head, even though somewhere in her she knew this was the killer. If there were any other man influencing her life right now, it was him. She wondered if he was showing up in every reading Maris did these last few weeks.

"What about the bad cards?" Izabel asked.

"I would say you are in danger. This is you here." She landed her index finger heavily on the card below the Death card. "The Queen of Wands. And this card below it"—she touched it with her thumb—"the Three of Swords, with this card to the right"—she placed her pinky on it—"the Emperor." She tapped the set of three cards together. *Thump thump thump.* "These are controlling cards. I would say the King of Pentacles knows who you are."

"No, he can't," Izabel said.

"I thought you didn't know who he was."

"I don't."

"Then how do you know that he doesn't know you?"

"I can't—"

"How are you getting home after this?" Maris interrupted her.

"I was going to take a car."

"Don't stop anywhere," she said. "Go straight home."

"I thought these cards might not be that bad."

"You're right. I'm getting ahead of myself. Let's look at the cards on the right. The Eight of Swords at the top. This means, the decision you feel you must make, if you feel trapped, that is of your own making. You must explore why you feel this way.

"Below it, the King of Rods, this is who you *could* become. Ambitious. Successful."

"If I follow my husband?"

"That I don't know. This is only a future-you that is in you already."

"And the last cards?"

"The Empress and the Ten of Pentacles. These show great stability in the home. Wealth. Security. Love. You are a mother?"

"Yes."

"You are a good mother."

Izabel nodded, unsure whether thanking her would be like thanking a card.

"That's what's important, isn't it?" Maris asked.

"Yes," Izabel said.

"Then follow your husband. That's what the cards say."

"And go home straightaway?" Izabel said.

"Hmm, that might be me saying that," Maris said. She smiled, but like she was hiding a sharp pain.

## CHAPTER TWELVE

For some reason Izabel didn't move to get up like she should have. She felt sick. She felt the presence of danger. And she felt concern, too, because instead of fear, she was feeling a kind of power. Izabel wondered if she would ever understand herself.

"Look, let's do something else," Maris said. "We have time. Do you want to pick a totem?"

"What?"

"Like an animal guide."

"Okay," Izabel said.

"It works the same, but we'll use this deck." Maris led her on another mini guided meditation as Izabel held the deck. She was glad that this time the cards didn't feel like before, like they were going to burn her.

Maris fanned the cards out again. "Just one this time."

Izabel picked one—the coyote. Maris got out a book, *Medicine Cards*, and read to her.

"If you have pulled this card, you can be sure that some kind of medicine is on its way—and it may or may not be to your liking. Whatever the medicine is, good or bad, you can be sure it will make you laugh, maybe even painfully. You can also be sure that Coyote will teach you a lesson about yourself."

Izabel was starting to forget how sick the first reading made her feel.

"Coyote has many magical powers, but they do not always work in his favor. His own trickery fools him. He is the master trickster who tricks himself. No one is more astonished than Coyote at the outcome of his own tricks. He falls into his own trap."

*This is the killer*, Izabel thought. He was the coyote influencing her life.

"And yet he somehow manages to survive. He may be banged and bruised by the experience, but he soon goes on his way to even greater error, forgetting to learn from his mistakes. He may have lost the battle, but he is never beaten."

But this she wasn't sure about. *Things don't typically end well for a serial killer, do they?*

"As Coyote moves from one disaster to the next, he refines the art of self-sabotage to sheer perfection. No one can blindly do themselves or others in with more grace and ease than the holy trickster."

*Yes*, Izabel thought. *Yes.*

Maris skimmed down the page. "Here," she said. "Snooze time is over. Watch out. Your glass house may come crashing to the ground at any moment. All your self-mirrors may shatter."

*That took a turn.*

Maris's finger kept moving. "And this: Go immediately beneath the surface of your experiences. Ask yourself what you are really doing and why. Are you playing a joke on yourself? Are you trying to fool an adversary? Is someone tricking you?"

But Izabel heard, *Are you in danger?*

And as if Maris could answer an unasked question, she read, "If Coyote is approaching you from the outside, beware of this master of illusion. Coyote may put you in his spell and take you to a briar patch to pick berries. It will be a painful lesson for you if you follow him."

Izabel didn't know—was staying in town the equivalent to following him? And what would the briar patch be? And what would be the berries? And would they be sweet? Worth it in some way? And didn't she come into this reading not believing any of this?

Maris closed the book and said, "I think this means, for you, that you must be tricky. If you are going somewhere, tell people you are going somewhere else. You must deceive, in order to protect yourself and your family."

That reading made sense. Izabel quickly chastised herself for reading it the wrong way, for reading potential in the killer, potential for her own life.

"This card can also mean do not take yourself so seriously. Sometimes you're wrong."

Izabel felt sick again.

"Our hour's up," Maris said. "And it looks like you need to go home."

Izabel nodded.

"It was nice to meet you."

"You, too," Izabel said.

Maris followed her out, all the way to the doors of the spiritual center, and she waited there, behind her, not saying anything, watching until she got safely into a car.

AT HOME, CAMI was eating cut-up grapes on the couch, watching a cartoon called *Glitter Force*, where teenage girls change into superheroes and collect pieces of something magical that will one day form into something magical enough to save everything.

"Hi, mi amor," Izabel said to Cami.

"Hi," she said, smiling but not taking her eyes off the screen.

Kaito came out of his machine. "How was it?" he said.

"We should leave," she said.

"The cards said that?"

"More directly than I could have imagined."

"Go cards!"

"Yeah," Izabel said.

"Aren't you happy?"

"I am. I just don't understand why you are so sure and the universe is so sure, and I am unsure. Why can't I be sure?"

He hugged her. "I don't know."

"Do you mind if I go out tonight?"

"Out where?"

"Maybe a drive. Kind of like saying goodbye before we leave. If we leave. If we get approved."

"We'll know soon," he said. "Do you think it's safe to go out?"

"I'll be in a car the whole time," she said. But she remembered how scared Maris seemed to be, so certain she was in someone's crosshairs.

"I guess it's fine," he said.

"Okay. After dinner then? After I put Cami to bed."

Kaito agreed and went back to his office. Izabel sat down with Cami on the couch and took a piece of one of Cami's grapes.

"Hey!" Cami said, teasing her.

Izabel laughed.

Cami squinched up her eyes like she was mad, and Izabel squinched hers right back. They stared like they were about to battle, in a cartoony way, like they were in one of Cami's shows. And then they smiled at each other.

"You know, raisins are made from grapes," Izabel said.

"No," Cami said.

"Yeah, they are!"

"No way."

"Haven't I been telling you the truth for a lot of years, gurisa? Where's my credibility?"

In a whisper Cami said, "But this time you're not."

Izabel laughed. "I'm going to show you a video. You want to watch a video?"

"Yeah," Cami said.

Izabel found a time-lapse video of grapes drying into raisins, and Cami watched it, the beginning at least. She stopped paying attention as soon as the grapes ever so slightly resembled raisins. "Cool," she said.

"Can you trust I will tell you the truth now?" Izabel asked.

"Yes," Cami said, holding the *s* like a hiss, eyes back on *Glitter Force*.

"Thank you." Izabel took Cami's hand and kissed the sticky palm of it.

At 5 p.m., every device in the house dinged. It was the email that they'd been waiting for. Izabel let Kaito be the first to read it.

"We're approved!" he yelled. He grabbed up Cami and jumped around with her squealing in his arms. His excitement and his relief were contagious and Izabel jumped with them.

"What's approved?" Cami asked.

"We're moving, baby," Kaito said.

"Moving where? I don't want to move."

"No, it's a good thing. It's exciting. We're going to have so much fun," he said.

"Like a vacation?"

"Yes! Like a vacation."

"Because I don't want to move."

"Then think of it like a vacation."

"But it is a vacation. We are not moving."

"We are moving," Kaito said, "but—"

"No!" Cami yelled and squirmed out of his arms and ran under the kitchen table, where she often went when she was upset.

Then every device in the house dinged again. Izabel looked this time. It was the News app—a statement about the precautions the town was taking to ensure everyone's safety. Izabel tapped into the app and the main page was already filling with stories about how few people had been approved, all the statistics and the demographics of the approvals.

"Come out, pumpkin," Kaito said.

It was one of the rare days that Izabel was glad the air was toxic. A day when, in the old world, there would have been riots. Or at least police in riot gear. Police, threatening people with their own violence—a kind that was ready to meet nonviolence, ready to meet panic.

"No!" Cami yelled. "I'm a moon child and I'm going to be taken back to the moon kingdom!"

Izabel looked away from the tablet and back at her family: Cami under the table and Kaito crouching down, trying to negotiate with her.

He said, "But that means you must have done something terrible in the moon kingdom and you were sent here as punishment. And you've never done something terrible."

Cami spit on the floor. "I spit on the floor," she said. "That's terrible. I've done terrible stuff."

Izabel and Kaito tried not to laugh.

"That's gross, honey," Izabel said.

"What about all those suitors that wanted to marry you, my beautiful moon daughter?" Kaito said.

"They were all fakes! They couldn't even get me the branch with jewels on it!"

"That's true," Kaito said.

"They stole a branch and I heard them do it and I knew we were being followed!"

"That's a different story," Izabel said.

"Oh, yeah," Cami said.

"In that story," Izabel said, "the daughters keep leaving. They find a new kingdom. Maybe this is the part of your story where you find a new kingdom."

"Maybe," Cami said. "Can I have a tissue?"

Izabel gave her a tissue and watched Cami wipe her spit back and forth on the floor.

## CHAPTER THIRTEEN

In the car, Izabel pushed down her mask. Instead of selecting a destination, she pressed the icon to program a route. She traced her finger through the streets of the hypercontrived town, along the edge of the concrete slab they all lived on, as close as the car would get to it, then by the solar field to the west, the warehouses, the porting station, and then back, weaving through the streets of houses that radiated to the east, until she would arrive home again.

An alert came up on the screen. She would need to change the air filter herself on a route this far. *Do you feel comfortable doing this on your own?*

She checked that there was a new filter ready for her. Then she pressed *Yes*.

The car began the journey through the silent town and its lit domes. When she reached the edge of the slab, she saw the robots that tended to it. Someone like her husband was manning each one, patrolling, stepping off the slab and cutting back the plants. And the plants—they grew thicker and thicker on the earth they'd laid claim to.

She was glad she didn't live too close to the edge, where she could hear the whirring blades of the robots, the mechanics of their moving bodies.

Going past the refrigerated warehouses, she imagined the activity inside. She'd seen pictures where the people were bundled for winter temperatures, then covered in vinyl suits, then aprons on top of those, hairnets and gloves. They cut fish into neat serving sizes.

She knew there were incentives for those jobs, so people wouldn't only take the basic income, but she wondered if the incentives were worth it. She thought about the propaganda of the new world— that we must work together to succeed, that we all depend on each other. They were convincing slogans. They seemed wholly true not too long ago.

And incentives were better than the alternative, better than taking these jobs out of desperation and still not being paid enough to do them.

Izabel tried to imagine a woman who took a warehouse job because she wanted the most elaborate house she could have. She imagined that every week she saved her extra money, and then every year, she had something remodeled, something tiled, fixtures of gold, an indoor infinity pool dug into the concrete slab, if that were allowed.

Then she imagined a woman who had a plain house, but so many children, every one of whom she dressed in velvet and silk, in shirts with intricate beading along the collars and cuffs and hems.

She imagined that, on the weekends, the woman dressed herself in wedding dresses covered in Swarovski crystals, like the ones Izabel saw on *Say Yes to the Dress*.

She could imagine a dozen women and how they might spend extra money on frivolity and extravagance. How they might create their lives to resemble something entirely out of place in the new world.

AT THE CAR park, she paused the car. It prompted, *Do you want to get out here?*

*No*, she pressed.

She watched all the automated things the cars did, covered, but outside. They went through the car wash, they pulled into spots, they plugged in. A robot rolled up next to them and changed their air filters. This one was not manned by anyone. It was a programmable action. But there was always at least one person in a dome alongside them all, watching live feeds from different angles.

Izabel thought that job must seem pointless. But maybe they were doing more than Izabel knew. Maybe they monitored diagnostics on each car. Maybe they called any cars that needed repairs into the garage. Though that person would not be the repairman. That was another person. Every differently trained person of their town.

She told the car to continue, and it headed east. The rows of homes discomfited her. They always did. She watched them intently, as if one might move.

The rows were interrupted now. The four houses that were destroyed by the killer were in various stages of reconstruction, or, more accurately, removal and replacement. She recalled the images from the news—the red dots over the felled homes tricked one into thinking that the lots were greatly overwhelmed by a *thing*, when actually they were holes in the once uniform street.

And then she saw him.

KAITO HAD PUT Cami to bed, but she was rustling now. He sat beside her and put his fingers on her head.

*"He is out again,"* she said.

THE CLOUDS AND the pollen-filled air washed out the moonlight that would have flashed against the knife, but Izabel could still make it out. And if she hadn't been able to, the action of his body—lifting himself, and his arms, landing his clenched hands on the plastic of the dome and dragging them down—it was unmistakable.

Izabel acted without thinking. She paused the car. The prompt came up asking if she wanted to get out, and she pressed *Yes*. She pulled her mask over her face and ran out, waving her arms, screaming without opening her mouth too far, as she'd learned to do with a mask tight to her chin.

The killer stepped back from the torn opening he'd made. His suit covered every inch of his body; its plastic mask obscured his face. Izabel didn't think about what to do. She didn't think about whether she could tackle him, hurt him, delay him in some way. Instead, she climbed through the hole and into the house.

Inside the alarm was blaring. A man was collapsed on the floor. He was the first thing she saw. Her breathing was already becoming difficult. She kneeled and shook him, but he didn't move. Then she saw, a few steps behind him, a woman, and then their teenage daughter.

CAMI BEGAN TO shake under her father's hand. *"Your mother is there. Your mother is with him."*

"Cami, please wake up," Kaito said.

"Where's my mom?

*"She is with him.*

"She's home.

*"She is not home."*

"Please, Cami, please," Kaito pleaded. He hit the emergency button on his tablet.

IZABEL SHOOK THE woman next, and she woke up. Izabel was beginning to cough. She thought she and the woman would work together to pull the daughter to the safe room. Instead the woman reached out for Izabel's mask. She scratched Izabel's face. But the woman's grasp, her aim, everything was not as strong as it could be, and Izabel pulled herself away. She backed up and watched the woman struggle, scared to approach her. Izabel's cheek stung.

The woman passed out again, but Izabel kept her eyes on her. She moved to the daughter and pulled her toward the front of the dome. Izabel was coughing harder.

Izabel dropped the plastic down and turned on the emergency air filter. It filled the small space with noise but did not turn green. She pressed all around the edge of the plastic to make sure the seal was good. She tried to calm herself.

That's when she heard the voice over the intercom. The woman's voice wasn't as controlled as it was during the small fault at Izabel's house—maybe it had started that way, but now the woman was crying between asking, "Is anyone okay? Please respond." Izabel tried to respond but her voice was too hoarse. "Is anyone okay?" the woman asked again. "An ambulance is on the way."

Izabel managed to say, "I'm here," but the woman couldn't hear her.

"Is anyone okay?"

The sirens came closer to the house. Izabel's vision was growing blurry. Her cheek still hurt. When she wiped at it, her hand came back into focus streaked with blood. She had almost passed out when the EMTs pulled her and the girl out of the room, placed them on spine boards, connected their masks to oxygen tanks.

Izabel watched the emergency lights flash red and white against the millions of specks of pollen in the air.

As they neared the ambulance, she saw that the car she'd come in was gone. She knew what had happened. The killer had taken it. And he wouldn't have reprogrammed it. He would have let it ride out to *her* destination. He would have, for at least a moment, sat outside her house.

Adrenaline rushed through her body. She thrashed around on the board, yelling for them to check on her family. They gave her a sedative, and her limbs felt heavy.

Izabel watched the EMTs rouse the girl. They asked the girl if she knew who Izabel was. The girl turned and looked at Izabel and shook her head. The girl looked so much like her mother.

"I can explain," Izabel said, still hoarse.

"We're just EMTs," said a near-boy. His nametag read AN.

The memory of leaving the woman on the floor replayed in Izabel's mind and she began to panic again. Was she supposed to have given her mask to her? Was she supposed to have died and let this girl have her mother? Was she supposed to have left Cami like that? Her eyes scrambled and she tried to sit up again.

"We will restrain you if we have to," An said.

Izabel screamed and began to cry. They gave her more of the sedative.

As she fell asleep she said, "I saw the killer." Everyone heard that.


WHEN SHE WOKE up in the hospital, it was hard to open her eyes. She lay there, listening, and she thought she was dreaming when she heard Kaito.

"Why can't we go in?" he said.

"I'm sorry, but the police need to speak with her."

"I understand that, but why can't we be with her until then?"

We. He was saying *we*. He had Cami with him. They were both okay. If this were only a dream, it would be a cruel one.

"Isn't she a witness?" Kaito asked.

"No. She's being treated as a suspect."

"A suspect? Cut the crap. Let us in there."

"I can't allow that."

"I want to talk to someone who can." Kaito sounded angry. "I want to talk to someone!"

"You two should go home," the officer said.

Izabel opened her eyes and screamed. It was the only sound she could muster as she watched the uniformed officer blocking Kaito and Cami at the door. The officer turned to look at her, and then he turned away again. He asked for a nurse.

Izabel found her voice and, as loud as she could, she said, "Not our house. Not our house."

"We'll wait here," Kaito said back, over the officer's shoulder.

"Not our house," she repeated.

"We'll be in the waiting room," he said.

She nodded.

"Do you want us to go now?"

She nodded again, even though she wanted to hold Cami more than she'd ever wanted to do anything before in her life.

When the nurse came in, it was Luis. Izabel tried to tell him everything—"I saw him and I tried to save them"—but it was hard to put her thoughts in order—"I killed a woman."

"You saved her," Luis said.

"No, not the girl. The woman."

"Oh," Luis said. "Maybe don't say that to anyone else."

Izabel nodded and tears were rolling down her cheeks and they stung in the cut.

"My skin is under her fingernails."

"You really need to stop talking now, okay?"

Izabel turned her head and the tears from one eye pooled on the side of her nose and the tears from the other eye rolled into her ear. She pushed her ear hard into the pillow and heard the water squish.

"Do you need more of the sedative?" Luis asked.

Izabel shook her head.

"Then you need to sharpen up or go back to sleep because they're going to be here soon."

"Who?"

"The police," he said.

"I need to talk to the police."

"I know, but maybe you should have a lawyer here."

"Do we still have lawyers?"

"Mmhmm," he said, adjusting Izabel's IV.

"Do you know any of them?"

Luis laughed.

Then Izabel thought of Andy and asked Luis to call her.

"Okay," he said.

"Why are you helping me?"

"You saved that girl," he said. "'The first survivor,' they're calling her."

## CHAPTER FOURTEEN

When Izabel woke again, it was to a fast-speaking woman. "Wake up, Izabel. I'm Inspector Paz. I'm here to talk to you and I don't like to waste time. Izabel, are you awake?"

"I guess so," Izabel said, because she felt like she could think straight now, and she recognized Inspector Paz from the news. The sedative must have worn off.

"I want to arrest you, but the local officers suggested I question you first."

"Arrest me?"

"Why not? Didn't you kill that family?" She sat back in a chair next to Izabel's bed, as if she were relaxed, asking Izabel these questions. "Didn't you kill all those families?"

"No. Of course not."

"I think you did. I have a theory. Most spree killers are men. You might know that. You don't need to be a detective to know that. But with the removed method of killing used here, I think it could be a woman. And then there you are at the scene of the crime."

"In the safe room. I made the safe room."

"Yes. Maybe you regretted it this time."

Izabel shook her head.

"You know what we're waiting on now? We're waiting for the doctors to clear you. Then you're coming to the station. And by the time we get you there, I bet we'll confirm that you got that scratch on your cheek from one of the victims."

"I did get it from her. I was trying to save her."

"She's dead."

"I can tell you what happened. I want to tell you everything that happened. My family needs protection."

Someone came to the door. "Step away from my client, please."

Izabel recognized Andy's voice.

Inspector Paz slapped both her knees and stood up. "Not a problem," she said.

"I'll need a word with her," Andy said.

"And I was leaving," Inspector Paz said.

As soon as Inspector Paz was out the door, Izabel thanked Andy for coming. "You okay doing this?" she asked.

"I'm not thrilled about it, but you need a lawyer."

"You don't think I killed anyone?" Izabel said.

Andy laughed.

BEFORE THEY COULD say much, a uniformed officer came in. His nametag read EVANS. He said the doctors had cleared Izabel, and he escorted them both to the station. None of them said anything in the car, but Izabel's thoughts were racing with everything she needed to say.

Officer Evans finally left Izabel and Andy alone in an interrogation room.

"We were approved for travel," Izabel said. "Kaito wants to leave. We're supposed to leave."

"Believe me, he's already told me. But they're not going to let you leave."

"Even once they realize I'm only a witness?"

"They'll need you as a witness."

"Is Kaito mad?"

"He's mad, and worried, too."

"Where are they?"

"They're at my house. He's watching Hestia while I'm here with you."

"I'm so sorry."

"What were you supposed to do? Not try to save that family? I'm surprised you didn't die doing what you did."

Izabel didn't say anything.

"You were incredibly brave," Andy said.

INSPECTOR PAZ WALKED into the room with Officer Evans, and they sat across from Izabel and Andy.

"I want you to start from the beginning," said Inspector Paz.

"I saw him from the car window."

"Before that."

"What?"

"Why were you in the car? Where were you coming from?"

Andy jumped in. "She doesn't have to answer that."

"It would help."

"I can tell you that it has nothing to do with your case," Andy said.

"Fine. Start when you saw him. What was he doing?"

"He was slicing the house," Izabel said.

"How?"

"You want me to act it out?"

Inspector Paz nodded once.

Izabel stood up, raised her arms fast, and pretended to land her hands, together, on a house and drag them through it.

"You look comfortable doing that," Inspector Paz said.

"This isn't a chance for you to antagonize her," Andy said.

"I'm doing my job."

"And if you want to learn what Izabel knows about the killer, then you better figure out another way to do it."

Inspector Paz threw her hands up, like she'd back off.

Izabel sat back down. "I got out of the car and ran over to him, throwing my arms around like this." She waved her arms.

"You don't need to act that part out," Paz said.

Andy shot her a look.

"Right," Izabel said. "And then I ran inside."

"Wait. How did you get past him?"

"He'd moved away and I just went to see if anyone was in the house."

"He didn't fight you? Why didn't he kill you?"

"I don't know."

"Okay, back up. What did he look like?"

"He was in a suit, one of those SCBA suits, an oxygen tank on his back. His face was behind the plastic, and it was too dark to make him out." In Izabel's memory, where the killer's head should have been, it looked like a black void, like outer space.

"The lights would've gone on in the house, when the house was damaged."

"Yes." Izabel's memory changed a little. A stripe of light bent over the plastic. "It only made a glare over the mask."

"Were his hands out?"

"No." But then she shook her head. "Maybe they were."

"Try to remember."

Izabel tried, and then said, "I can't remember."

"How tall was he?"

"Taller than I am. I don't know."

"How tall?"

"About six feet I guess."

"Unremarkable," Paz said. "Not so tall or short to notice."

"Yes."

"Weight?"

"Average."

"Did the suit pull on him?" Paz asked, gesturing across her stomach with both hands.

"No, I don't think so."

"So thin then?"

"Yes," Izabel said.

"Then what happened?"

"I ran into the house, and the three of them were on the floor. The man was closest to the door but I couldn't wake him. I went to the woman and she woke and went for my mask. That's when she scratched me. I went to her daughter."

"You left the woman when she was alive?"

"I didn't know what else to do."

"You could have saved her," Paz said.

"It didn't feel like I could."

"They all would have died," Andy said.

"You don't know that," Paz said.

"None of us can know," Andy said. "Can she keep going?"

"I don't need to hear more. You got the daughter, you put down the seal, you turned on the filter, they came and picked you up—we have the recording from emergency services."

"What about my family?" Izabel said.

"This thing about the car?"

"It wasn't at the house when I came out."

"We found the car back at the car park," Paz said. "It went exactly as you programmed it. Stopped at the house with the attack, went to your house, went back to the car park. We dusted for prints, hairs, anything. The car was clean. We don't know why it continued to your house, but it doesn't mean he took the car."

"Not even my prints were in the car?"

"You an inspector now, Izabel?"

"It's just, if someone wiped it down—"

"I know what it means," Paz said, "and I'm looking into it." She slapped her knees again as she got up. "We're done."

"What happens now?" Izabel asked.

"You're released."

"But we can't go home. It's not safe."

"I'm not sure anywhere in this town is particularly safe right now," Paz said.

"Our application was approved," Izabel shouted. "We can leave."

"That's been revoked."

"What? You can't do that!" Izabel said.

But Andy put her hand on Izabel's hand.

"They can?"

Andy nodded.

"It was amazing you got approved in the first place—the chances were so slim," Paz said.

"They want my husband at the training center in the capital."

"But they don't need him there. And I need you here."

"There must be a spare house," Andy said, "somewhere they can go."

"Or the house of someone who is leaving," Izabel said, as the idea struck her.

Paz looked surprised. "We can look into that." Then she looked at Andy. "For now, maybe she can stay with you?"

"Yes. She can. You can," Andy said.

"What about the girl?" Izabel said.

"Who?" Paz said.

"The girl I saved. What will happen to her?"

"I don't know."

"I . . . I will take her in."

"Izabel," Andy said. "That's a big thing to say."

"I'll find out," Paz said. And she left the room.

IZABEL DIDN'T LIKE being in the car. She knew nothing was wrong, but it was putting her on edge. It didn't help that Andy was so calm and quiet beside her, looking out the window like the rows of houses weren't unnerving, like there couldn't be a man between any two of them.

At Andy's house, Cami ran into Izabel's arms. "I missed you," Cami said. It was the first time she'd said that in a long time.

"I missed you so much." Izabel kissed her all over her face and neck until Cami wriggled free, laughing and screeching like Izabel was chasing her.

"Are you okay?" Kaito said.

"Yes," she said, though she could feel that wasn't true. It wasn't even noon yet and she had no idea how she would get through the day.

"Can we have a minute alone?" Kaito asked Andy.

"You can use my room," Andy said.

They all knew the walls were thin enough that everything would be heard, but the perception of privacy was enough.

"What is it?" Izabel said.

"I can't get over that you were out there. That you were near him. I should never have let you go out last night."

"I don't blame you."

"I blame us both!"

"What was I supposed to do?" Izabel asked.

"I don't know. And now we can't leave."

"They told me," Izabel said. When Kaito didn't say anything, she asked, "Do you blame me for that, too?"

"No, but I don't feel safe here and we were about to leave. We were so close."

Neither of them said anything for a minute. Izabel sat on the bed and Kaito paced in front of it.

"You know how I feel, right?" he said.

"I know how you feel."

"And do you really think he knows where we live?"

"They told you?"

"Andy told me."

Izabel started to cry. "I didn't think about that when I left the car."

"I know." He sat down beside her.

"I didn't think about how our address was in there." She was blabbering out the words now. "Or that he would take it."

He put his arms around her and she broke into sobs.

"I messed up," she said.

"But you saved that girl."

"Oh god, the girl," she said, nearly shrieking it.

"What?" he said.

"At the end of the interview with the police, I told them we would take her in."

"You what?"

"I should have asked you first. It was instinct or impulse or something."

"Jesus."

"I'm sorry."

He didn't say anything, but he didn't look mad. He looked at the corners of the room.

"She has no one," Izabel said.

He shoved his hand down into the air. "I'm thinking."

She waited. She knew not to push it.

## CHAPTER FIFTEEN

K aito got a call from work. "I don't have to go,"
he said.

"It's okay," Izabel told him.

So he went into town, to an office that had the machine he
needed for work. Izabel sat on Andy's couch, in Andy's living room.
Andy was with the girls in Hestia's room. Izabel could hear them
playing a board game, something about getting owlets back to their
nest before morning.

Izabel unlocked her tablet. She hadn't touched a screen since
being in the car last night. It made her feel sick touching it.

Cami ran out of the room and into the bathroom, smiling at
Izabel as she passed her.

Izabel opened her app, tapped *2017* again, tapped *About the Air.*

Today, we are proud to launch the #ToxicNeighbor campaign,
a Southwestern Pennsylvania citizen engagement campaign
that aims to build a new generation of clean air activists
while holding state elected officials and business leaders

accountable for the development of a massive, polluting petrochemical plant in Beaver County.

Emissions from this plant will contain a toxic mix of pollutants—particulate matter, sulfur dioxide, and volatile organic compounds such as acrolein, benzene, toluene and naphthalene—that exacerbate symptoms of asthma and cause cancer. It will be the largest source of volatile organic compounds in Southwestern Pennsylvania.

Tell Governor Tom Wolf, state lawmakers, local officials, and Shell leadership that Shell Global is a #ToxicNeighbor that is not welcome in our region.

Let your voice be heard. Sign the petition, share it with your network, and join the conversation on social media. We need all hands on deck. And we need you to take action today. Members of Southwestern PA communities must band together and refuse to become the next Cancer Alley.

Izabel's mother used to tell her that cancer was the most absurd thing about the time they lived in. That it was so deadly that it would kill countless people that they knew, and yet the inevitably of its cure was so clear, "to anyone worth anything," she'd say. "A disease like that can't go unsolved forever."

She'd describe a time when no one would die of cancer. When pediatric oncology wards would be distant memories and talked about like rooms of iron lungs and children's misshapen legs. "If anyone can't see that, it's a failure of their imagination." It was only a question of what would cure it—medicine, nanobots, stem cells, a virus.

"And then the budget comes out," she'd say, "and it's two hundred billion dollars toward the wars. Cancer continues."

Izabel wondered if her mother would like to see how it had turned out. That the incidence of cancer was lower, without cigarettes, with better food and water. But that it still killed people. That in this new world, cancer might have enough funding, but not enough scientists. That everything looked completely different all around her, like someone shook the world like a snow globe and said, *Rebuild*—but they left cancer in the mix.

Izabel imagined Cancer Alleys all over the world. And she wondered, would she always daydream about the apocalyptic worlds that the old world thought it was plummeting toward?

CAMI YELLED FROM the bathroom.

"What is it?" Izabel yelled back.

"I need help."

"You pooped?"

"Yeah."

Izabel put the tablet down. In the bathroom, she leaned Cami into her knees and wiped Cami's butt. Then she put butt cream over where she'd wiped. She lifted Cami off the toilet.

Cami pulled up her pants and ran out of the room.

"Don't you need to wash your hands?"

"I didn't touch anything!" Cami yelled back.

"Truth," Izabel said to herself as she washed her own hands. She looked at herself in the mirror—the scratch was scabbing over. And she was glad for the mark it made, that she didn't look the same as she had the night before. That her reflection suggested, if only slightly, that she was a changed woman.

ON THE COUCH again, Izabel fell asleep. She didn't wake up until Kaito got back. Cami yelled, "Daddy!" and ran to him for a hug. Andy and the girls had been having dinner at Andy's table.

Izabel sat up.

"Mommy!" Cami said and ran over to her for a hug, too.

"I thought you'd sleep through anything," Andy said. "The girls and I got my office set up for you all like a guest room."

"Thank you," Kaito said. "I'm going to put my things down."

"I'll follow you," Izabel said. She nudged Cami back toward the table.

In the office, a futon was folded out and fitted with sheets and a blanket. An old crib mattress was on the floor beside it with its own sheets and a patchwork blanket that looked like it had been passed down through generations.

Izabel said, "I just wanted to thank you for being there, at the hospital, when I woke up."

"Yeah, that was lucky," Kaito said.

"Yeah," she said. But it wasn't what she'd expected him to say. He would usually say, *Of course*, or, We wouldn't have *not* been there. "Wait," she said. "What do you mean?"

"Shit," he said.

"What?"

"I never told you. Things were so chaotic with you and the police."

"What? Tell me now."

"Cami did that thing where she was talking in her sleep again."

"About the killer? When I was near him?"

"Yeah. And she wouldn't stop shaking. It seemed serious. But then, not compared to what was happening with you."

"It was so bad you took her to the hospital?"

"She was screaming and she wouldn't wake up."

"What did the doctors say?"

"It stopped in the ambulance. They examined her and drew some blood. I described what she'd been like and the EMTs confirmed it."

"It's good they saw it."

"Yeah. And when they were done checking her out, she went back to sleep. The normal kind. We were waiting for the blood results when we heard about you."

"What's going on with her?"

"I don't know," he said. But he was making a face.

"What is it?"

"You're going to think I'm crazy."

"I won't."

"What if she's inspirited?" Kaito said.

"She's not inspirited."

He didn't say anything.

"Maybe we should take her to a therapist," Izabel said. "Maybe it's some kind of night terror."

"Yeah," he said. "That's a good idea."

But she could tell he was thinking of yōkai and old stories from his father.

The next day Izabel thought she'd be able to let Cami go to school if she went along in the car with her and Hestia. Andy said she'd go, too.

Everything went fine inside—putting on shoes and masks and backpacks. Even through the double doors, Izabel felt okay. But as Izabel got closer and closer to the car, she panicked. Her knees buckled and she dropped to the ground.

"Mom!" Cami said.

"Your mom is okay," Andy said, putting her body between

Izabel and the girls. In an extra-cheery voice she said, "You girls go to school now." She slammed the car door shut as soon as both girls were in.

As the car drove off, she grabbed Izabel's arm and put it around her shoulders. "You can do it," Andy said. "Back to the house now."

In the house, Izabel stayed on the floor near the door. Andy got a hand towel, ran it under water, and wrung it out. She brought it back to Izabel, got down next to her on the floor, and wiped the pollen off her knees.

Kaito came out of the bathroom. "Jesus. What happened?"

"She's not ready to go in a car yet," Andy said.

Kaito carried Izabel back to their futon and laid her down. "You're okay," he said.

"Will Cami be okay at school?" Izabel said.

"Of course she will be."

Izabel nodded. "I want her to come back."

"That's not what's best for her."

"I know," she said, teary.

He said, "What can I do?"

She shook her head.

He crawled into bed next to her and held her, and she fell asleep again.

WHEN IZABEL WOKE up, the house was silent and she was alone. Andy had left a note near her head. It read, "Working at the mall. Make yourself at home." She stayed in bed and tried her tablet again. It reminded her less of the car than the last time she used it.

She opened a sudoku app and set it to *Easy*. It took her about four minutes to finish a board. Between each board, there was an ad for another game. The first ad was for a game where you find hidden objects to solve a murder. An old woman was on the floor with a gunshot wound to the head. It was cartoonish but graphic. Izabel groaned and turned the screen away from her. But as she kept playing and the ad kept appearing, she got used to it.

IZABEL WENT INTO Hestia's room. There was a shelf filled with old books. People weren't supposed to have books anymore. Books collected and held dust, and so pollen. But Izabel missed books. She understood why Andy would have them.

Some of the books were a set about elements. Izabel pulled out the one about nitrogen. It made her nostalgic, holding the book, turning the pages. She slid her finger along the underside of an edge. A section of the book was about "Peaceful Explosions." It was a term for explosions not intended to do harm to humans. So blowing the tops off of mountains for mining—that was a "peaceful explosion." Even if it harmed humans eventually. Izabel put the book back on the shelf.

She spotted a toy that had rolled back under Hestia's desk. She bent down and bumped her head as she reached for it. She remembered her mother saying, "You always have to put your head lower than you think."

While her head was hurting, she wasn't worried about Cami being away from her. That was one good thing about pain.

IZABEL JUMPED A little at the sound of the doorbell. She stood next to the kitchen counter, her arms tense, while she told herself over and over that it was probably Andy. And it was.

Andy wiped off her shoes, left them at the door, and hung up her mask. "How was your day?" she asked Izabel.

"Good," Izabel said. "Sorry about this morning."

"Don't worry about it," Andy said.

"I can help with dinner tonight."

"Only if you want to," Andy said.

"Not really." Izabel laughed.

Andy laughed, too.

The doorbell went off again. It was the girls. Izabel saw their outlines in the space between the sets of doors. She heard the air rush over them and then they ran in holding hands. Each of them went to hug their mothers. Izabel felt like she was in a sitcom. But then she noticed Cami was upset.

"Oh no. What is it?"

"I can't tell you."

"Why?"

Cami shook her head.

"You can tell me anything."

Cami's eyes welled with tears.

"Are you worried I'll be mad?"

Cami nodded.

"I won't be mad. I promise."

Still Cami wouldn't tell her.

"What if I got you some juice?"

"Okay," Cami said.

Izabel lifted her up and put her in a chair at the table.

"I once did so badly on something at school and I was so upset," Andy said. "I told my parents and it made me feel better."

"Was it something like that?" Izabel said, handing her a juice.

"No," Cami said. She drank the juice.

Izabel sat down next to her and squeezed her arm.

"I once hurt someone at school, when I was your age. A boy kept chasing me so I twisted his arm. I twisted it until he cried, and then I cried, too."

Cami looked at Izabel like Izabel was a monster.

"Not something like that, huh?"

"No!" Cami said, like a fancy white woman going, *I would never!*

"You don't have to tell me," Izabel said, "but I want you to know you *can* tell me. No matter what it is."

After Cami had a snack, Izabel asked her again.

"I used a pen," Cami said, her face turning red.

"What?"

"I'm only supposed to use a pencil in class and I used a pen." Little tears rolled down her little face.

"Oh, mi amorcito," Izabel said. She pulled Cami into her stomach. All that torment over nothing. And Izabel, revealing herself, to everyone, to be a violent person.

## CHAPTER SIXTEEN

A few days later Paz called Izabel to tell her they could take the girl after the doctors cleared her. And Paz told her the girl's name so Izabel could finally stop calling her *the girl*. Jana Harb.

Izabel hadn't been able to bring herself to look at the news, to learn all the family's names, to see the pictures of them when they were not dying on the floor. And Kaito and Andy knew not to talk to her about it. Not yet.

Paz also told her that they'd know which new house they could move into by the time they came for Jana. But she added, "Even if you're being paranoid."

"Can I pick up her things?" Izabel asked.

"You mean go to my crime scene?"

"Yes," Izabel said.

"No, you may not," Paz said.

"Please."

"I'll see what *I* can do. But you are not allowed anywhere near that house."

"Okay," Izabel said. And she was embarrassed by the way she wanted to see the house again, not only to have clothes for Jana, but to be inside it, to touch the things she'd passed in the night, to see the knife's damage in the sunlight, when all the details of it would show.

IZABEL HAD MADE Cami an appointment with a therapist in her first days at Andy's house. She'd scheduled it ambitiously. Now that the day had arrived, it would be Izabel's first time leaving the house.

"You don't have to come with us," Kaito said.

"I do," Izabel said. "I can't stay in here forever."

They packed snacks for Cami in her little plastic containers.

"Would you blindfold me?" Izabel asked.

Kaito looked at her. "If that would help."

Both Izabel and Kaito were encouraged to be at the appointment, but, at least partly, Kaito didn't want to go. He didn't want to miss work. He was still holding on to the idea that if he made himself desirable enough, they would grant them permission to leave, despite the police's interest in Izabel.

Kaito tied a scarf around Izabel's eyes, and then he took hold of her arm. Cami held Izabel's other hand and together they walked her out to the car. Cami let go as she climbed in. Kaito put his hand gently on Izabel's head and she bent herself in, like she was getting into the back of a police car in an old television show.

"Do you want to take it off now?" Kaito asked, after he closed the door behind him.

"No," she said.

"How do you spell 'cliff'?" Cami said.

"'Cliff'?" Izabel said. "Like, 'Careful if you're ever near a cliff'?"

"Because there could be an avalanche!" Cami said.

"Because you could fall over the edge!" Izabel said. But she added, "Oh. I see. You're thinking of the bottom."

"Yeah."

"I was thinking of the top."

"You have to say, 'Be careful if you're ever near the *top* of a cliff.'"

"Yeah, I guess I'd have to say that," Izabel said. But she didn't think that was true. She was pretty sure everyone thought about being at the top of cliffs and not at the bottom of them.

"So how do you spell 'cliff'?"

"C-L-I-F-F," Izabel said. And before she knew it they were at the community center.

THE CHILDREN'S THERAPISTS worked out of the community center because the children were all familiar with that space. When Izabel took off her blindfold, she saw girls spilling out of a room in ballet slippers and leotards. She put the scarf in her purse.

There were only a few men around. Izabel quickly sized them up, canceled them out. *Too tall, too fat, couldn't be him.* She was doing better than she expected.

But then they turned a corner and Maris was there, down the hall, with a woman and two children. Maris's back was turned to them but Izabel recognized her immediately.

"Did you know?" Izabel said so loudly that all the children in the hall went silent.

Maris turned around.

"Did you know!" Izabel shouted, approaching her.

Maris shook her head. "I only read the cards."

"Bullshit."

"Okay, let's get to our appointment," Kaito said, getting his arm around Izabel's waist.

"No!" Izabel screamed.

Maris started to move away from her, further down the hall, hands on the backs of the children, pushing them along.

"You knew!" Izabel yelled after her. "You knew!"

Kaito picked Izabel up and kept going toward the therapist's office. Cami stayed near his leg. And Izabel kept screaming at Maris until she couldn't see her anymore.

IZABEL TRIED TO settle down in the waiting room. Cami rubbed her back and told her not to be sad. The rubs felt more like Cami was smushing a fly into her back, trying to kill it.

"Thanks, honey," Izabel said.

Then Cami crawled onto Kaito's lap and asked if she could play on his tablet. She brought up a game of monsters that needed to solve math puzzles in order to get monster snacks.

Cami got annoyed whenever Kaito looked away, even if she didn't need him for anything in the game. To her, it didn't count that they were together unless they were both looking at the same thing.

Izabel suggested Cami play with the zen water painting set that was on the table. Cami shook her head and turned her face into her father's neck. He reached his hand up onto her head and one finger slipped into her thin hair. Izabel imagined his hand with one less finger, his hand coming back out from Cami's hair, and that one finger soundly healed over at the knuckle.

So Izabel painted with the water. She wanted to use the least amount of effort, which led her to move only her wrist. Just lines at first, and then, as she continued, it looked like a tiger's stripes. Maybe that's how tiger stripes came to be, by some god's hands. And what those stripes resembled, the grasses and shadows of vines and trees and more grasses, those, too, made by more hands of gods, each seeking a bit of rest.

THE THERAPIST CAME out and brought them back into the office. She was especially kind toward Cami.

"You can call me Opa," she said. And then, looking at Izabel, "Does Cami know why we're here?"

Izabel looked at Kaito. "I'm actually not sure."

"Is it okay with you, if we talk openly in front of her?"

"Yes, definitely. We didn't mean not to talk to her about it."

Kaito nodded.

Opa looked back at Cami. "Do you know why you're here?"

"I've been sad in my sleep," Cami said.

"Are you sad when you wake up?" Opa asked.

"No."

"And is that how you two would describe what's been happening?"

Izabel started. "There's been a lot of sleep-talking, and then, only a few times, it's escalated."

Kaito continued. "The worst time, she was screaming and wouldn't wake up."

"And otherwise she's been easy to wake up out of it?"

"I think so," Izabel said. "When it was just talking, we didn't really try waking her. She always seemed to still be sleeping fine and, you know, 'never wake a sleeping child.'"

Opa laughed. "Understood. That's important."

Izabel was surprised Cami hadn't bothered them to leave yet. She must have liked Opa and her long black hair and her chunky necklace and bracelets and rings.

"So let's go back to when this started," Opa said. "Anything memorable that happened then?"

"We had a malfunction with the air filtration system at our house one night," Kaito said. "We ended up in the hospital and, while she seemed okay, they had trouble getting Cami to wake up."

"Did that scare you, Cami?"

"No," Cami said.

"And the sleep-talking started at the hospital?" Opa asked.

"No, right after," Kaito said.

"So when was that? An exact date would be good for me."

Kaito pulled out his tablet. "It was April eighth."

The adults paused a second. That was a date they all knew. That was the night of the first killing.

"Thanks," Opa said. "So you feel comfortable at the hospital, Cami?"

Cami shifted around in her seat.

"What's wrong with the hospital?" Izabel asked.

Cami grabbed Izabel's arm and hid her head behind it.

"Did something happen more recently at the hospital?" Opa asked.

Izabel and Kaito both realized it at once. Izabel said, "She saw me there."

"And there were police," Kaito added.

"I was the one who," Izabel struggled with how to say it in front of Cami, "saw what happened."

It was enough for Opa to figure it out. "Oh! Oh. You know, at the next session, I'd love to just see you, Izabel, and you, Kaito, together, and we can talk about that then. But right now I have one more question for Cami. You don't want to visit the hospital anymore?"

Cami shook her head.

"Okay, that's good," Opa said. "That's good for all of us to know."

Izabel kissed Cami's head.

"Let's go back further. Any health issues?"

"No," Izabel said.

"And with her birth?"

"All the way back, huh?" Izabel said.

Opa laughed. "It's good for me to know."

"Labor was slow, and they used Pitocin to further things along. They broke my water. Meconium was in the water so they started to move more quickly. Everything seemed fast from there." Izabel didn't like recalling Cami's birth and how scared she was that Cami would inhale the meconium. Her chest felt hot talking about it. She was worried she'd start crying, so she said, "But then she was out and she was healthy and so was I."

"So you were never separated from each other?"

"She slept in the nursery and then they brought her to me when she woke up to nurse."

"And you nursed?"

"It didn't go great at the hospital, but we settled into it."

"How long did you nurse?"

"About eight months."

"And you were able to hold her after she was born and stay with her mostly?"

"Yes. I mean—Do you have kids?"

"Yes," Opa said.

"Then you know. It's a lot of back and forth as they do tests at first, whatever that's called."

"The Apgar."

"Yeah, the Apgar."

"Anything unusual otherwise? Was she a good sleeper or never cried? Anything like that?"

Izabel laughed and felt a little calmer. "No, the normal bad-sleeper, good-crier," she said.

"And how is her sleep now, outside of the sleep-talking?"

"It's good, I guess," Izabel said.

"Does she go to bed at the same time every night?"

"Not too far off."

"How about in the morning—does she wake up at the same time?"

"Yes, for school."

"So she has a pretty scheduled day?"

"Yes."

"Even these last few weeks, with," she paused, "what's been going on with you?"

"We thought it would be good," Kaito said, "if something were consistent."

"You know?" Cami said.

"Yes?" Opa said.

"I don't close my eyes when I sleep."

"No?" Opa said.

"That's true," Izabel said, smiling at Opa, exaggerating a little, so Opa knew Cami slept with her eyes closed like every other child in the world. "Ever since she was little, she sleeps with her eyes open."

"Wow," Opa said. "That's very cool. Is there a reason you need to keep your eyes open?"

"No, that's how I work. Those are the ways of Cami."

"Oh?"

"Like the ways of the world," Cami whispered, "but 'of Cami.'"

"I get it," Opa whispered back.

It looked like Cami was doing some four-year-old version of blushing.

AFTER THE APPOINTMENT, Kaito wanted to go to work. "Can you make it back yourself?" he said.

"I think so," Izabel said.

"Without the blindfold?"

"Yeah."

"I can help with the blindfold," Cami said.

"That's okay, honey," Izabel said.

Kaito watched them go to a car, saying he would get the next one. Izabel pinched her fingernail into her thumb as they walked, to focus on that. In the car, she waved back at Kaito so he'd see she was fine enough.

Out of nowhere, Cami said, "I bet you would be super sad if I was defeated."

"Yeah, I would be. Super sad. All over."

"You don't have eyes all over."

"You don't need eyes to be sad. Being sad isn't only about crying."

"How would you be sad?" Cami said.

"My hands would shake and my stomach would hurt and probably my head would hurt, too."

"I bet your legs would shake."

"Yeah, my legs would shake, definitely."

"I bet you would put flowers all over my grave."

"Did you see that somewhere?"

"Yeah."

"Yeah, people used to do that. Do you want me to do that?"

"Mmhmm," Cami said.

"Okay. Any flower in particular?"

"Wait, you can't get flowers!"

"If that's what you want, I can get you flowers."

"And a grave?"

"Daddy's got a robot. We can make it happen. Anything you want."

"Are you going to have a grave?"

"No, I think I'll get all burnt up and you can keep me or spread me around somewhere. Do you know what I'm talking about?"

"Yeah." And then she didn't say anything else.

"Do you want raspberries when we get home?" Izabel asked.

"Yes!" Cami said. As if that had been a normal conversation. As if Izabel weren't holding down vomit.

## CHAPTER SEVENTEEN

The next time Paz called, it was to say that Jana had been cleared and Izabel had to come get her—now. Izabel was alone in Andy's house. Andy and Kaito were both out working. The girls were at school. Izabel hadn't left the house since the appointment with Opa. In her head, she'd been replaying her outburst at Maris for days. She texted Kaito to see if he could get Jana instead.

In the meantime, she threw on pants and put a bra on under the shirt she'd slept in. She checked her hair in the mirror. Kaito still hadn't responded. She told herself, *You can do this*.

She called a car and waited at the door with her mask around her neck. She checked that the scarf was still in her purse. The doorbell went off and she saw the car. *Run*, she thought. *Who cares*. She put her mask up and ran to the car, slammed the door shut behind her, tied the scarf around her eyes, breathed heavy in the backseat.

The car made a small *ding*. She lifted a side of the scarf. With one eye she saw that the screen was prompting her. She pressed *Hospital* on the list of common destinations.

PAZ WAS WAITING for her in the lobby and walked her to Jana's room. Paz wasn't saying anything, so Izabel didn't either.

In the room, Jana wasn't in a hospital gown—she was dressed like any preteen girl, jeans and a T-shirt, studs in her ears, little teal flowers. Her hair was pulled back in a low ponytail that looked perfectly combed. Izabel wondered if she'd spent time looking nice for her or if she always looked so put-together.

"Thank you," Jana said. Izabel wasn't expecting that. She suddenly felt a wave of guilt. She just wanted to say hello first. And honestly, she'd been preparing herself for the worst, for Jana to hate her for being so presumptuous as to volunteer herself and her family to take care of her.

Before Izabel could say anything, Paz asked her, "Where's the rest of your family?"

"Kaito's working and Cami's at school."

"We need them here so we can take you all to the new house."

"You didn't tell me that."

"We moved a lot around to make this happen," Paz said. "You still want this new place, right?"

"Yes," Izabel said. She turned to Jana, and said, "Sorry." Jana sat down on the bed while Izabel tried contacting Kaito on her tablet again, asked him to get Cami from school and get to the hospital.

Then Paz said, "There are forms you have to sign."

"Okay," Izabel said.

"They're not here. I'll walk you over."

This was not how Izabel wanted any of this to go. "Can Jana come with us?"

Paz looked at Izabel like she was nuts. "No. She'll stay in the room."

Izabel apologized to Jana again.

OUT OF THE room, Izabel was glad, at least, to not be smiling at Jana while she kept remembering how it had felt to drag her body across a living room floor. Izabel realized that her fingers must have left bruises on Jana's arms.

As Paz and Izabel walked through the halls, Izabel kept noticing the men around her, patients and nurses and doctors. In her head she went through them—*too short*, *too broad-shouldered*—ticking off each of them against her brief memory of the killer.

There were a handful of men she could not discount. *That could be him*, she thought, as a doctor passed. *And him*, she thought, as they walked up to a male nurse.

Paz said, "She's the one taking Jana. Do you have the papers for that?"

His nametag read MATT. He handed Izabel a clipboard and pen, and told her she could sit behind the nurses' station if it helped.

Izabel shook her head and began filling out the forms standing up. She felt like Matt was looking at her, and the longer he spent looking at her, the more convinced she became that he was the killer.

"Are you feeling okay?" he asked. "You look a little green."

THE NEXT THING she remembered, she was on a bed with smelling salts under her nose.

"That's it. Another big breath." It was still Matt.

She started to take in the curtained-off hospital bed. On her next breath, she coughed and coughed.

"There you go. That should do it." He smiled at her.

"You fainted," Paz said. "Why'd you faint?"

"Was I out a long time?" Izabel asked.

"No. This guy caught you before you hit the floor. He got the smelling salts. You're all caught up."

*Maybe he isn't the killer*, she thought. "Sorry. I guess it's a little overwhelming."

"We're not done yet. Can you handle the rest of the day?"

"Let me get her some juice," Matt said.

"I can handle it," Izabel told Paz.

"On the plus side, the more weak shit like this you pull, the more I'm starting to think you're not the killer."

"I'm not the killer," Izabel said.

Paz shrugged.

MATT INSISTED IZABEL go in a wheelchair until she left the hospital. When he went to look for one, she labeled him *too nonthreatening*. She knew that meant nothing—nothing about whether he was capable of killing privately, in some lonesome way—but it was enough for her to calm down around him.

As Matt pushed her through the hallway, Paz trailed behind, shaking her head. Around the corner came another nurse, pushing another patient, a woman who looked too cheerful to be sick. The nurses began chatting with each other. The woman looked familiar to Izabel but she couldn't place her.

She knocked her arm gently against Izabel's and said, "Check us out."

Izabel smiled at her.

But then the woman said, "Oh, sweetie. Oh, you saved something?"

"What?"

"Someone's very grateful that you saved something."

Paz told the nurses to shut up.

"Or someone! Is that what happened?" the woman said.

"You're Lucy," Izabel said. She started to remember all the things she'd heard about her—the woman who held séances at the spiritual center. The town medium. How she would brush into someone at the mall and tell them someone was thinking about them, adding some small detail, like a tattoo they had, so the person she was talking to got goose bumps, or burst into tears, or couldn't catch their breath.

"That's right." Lucy smiled.

Izabel felt disoriented. "Thank you for telling me," she said.

"Wait a second," Paz said. "Stop, just stop the chairs." She came around in front of them. "Who is this?" she asked, looking at Izabel and pointing at Lucy.

"It's Lucy," Izabel said.

"Lucy who? How do you know she saved someone?" Paz asked Lucy.

"She was on the news," Matt said.

"Not *that* part. That there were two survivors, yes. But that one saved the other, no. You," she said to Matt, "only know because you've been one of Jana's nurses."

"I didn't know it was a secret," he said, looking ashamed. "I told—"

"Did you tell this woman?" she asked.

"No," he said.

"Then, okay, shut up." Paz looked at Lucy. "How do *you* know?"

"Adira, the girl's mother, told me," Lucy said.

Paz kept looking at her as if she hadn't answered.

"Lucy is a medium," Izabel said.

"A medium?"

Lucy nodded.

Paz threw up her hands and started walking again.

"I can try and be in touch with her, if it would help," Lucy called after Paz. Then she turned to Izabel. "Now I know I can reach her through you. What's your name?"

"Izabel."

"Would you come visit me, Izabel?"

"In the hospital?"

"No, at the spiritual center. They can't keep me in here too long. I got dehydrated is all."

"Okay," Izabel said.

Paz was still walking away from them.

"We better go," Izabel said, looking up at Matt.

BACK AT JANA'S room, Izabel asked Matt if she could get out of the chair now.

"Are you sure you're feeling steady?"

"Yes," she said. "Look." She stood up and spun around.

Jana smiled.

"Let me know if either of you need anything," Matt said, leaving with the wheelchair.

"What happened?" Jana said.

"I fainted."

"Does that happen to you a lot?"

"That was my first time actually. Can I sit with you?"

Jana nodded.

So they sat together on the bed and waited for Kaito and Cami. They weren't ready to talk, but Izabel liked sitting beside her.

WHEN KAITO AND Cami came in, Cami was hiding behind Kaito's leg.

"This is Jana," Izabel said.

"We're so glad to have you," Kaito said.

"So glad," Izabel said, feeling awful for not having said it already.

"Cami, say hello," Kaito said.

Cami stayed hidden.

Jana said, "Hello, Cami."

Cami tried to push Kaito's knee out so she could peek at Jana between his legs.

"Okay, cut that out," Kaito said.

Paz asked, "Did you all bring your things?"

"No," Izabel said.

"What do you mean no? What was your plan?"

"I don't know," Izabel said. "You didn't give us much warning."

"Fine. Fine. We'll figure that out later." Paz grabbed a bag off the floor near Jana. "This is everything of Jana's that I could get for now. She went through it and we're good, so let's go. I have other things to do today."

They all went together toward the cars.

"Ready?" Kaito said.

They put on their masks. Jana's was covered in flowers—not in a tacky, young-girl way, no cartoonish daises, but in a bold print that Izabel imagined on old wallpapers and valences.

In the car, Paz used her police sign-in so she could put in an address without the car saving it. They drove to a road that looked like every other road of dome houses. But it wasn't a road any of them had lived on before, and they all seemed relieved at that.

Inside, Paz said, "This is it. Have a look around. Electricity, water, all of it is set up and being billed to a dummy account. If you have any problems—that have to do with me, problems I could actually help fix—feel free to get in touch. Otherwise I don't want to hear from you. I can't believe it's already two o'clock."

And with that, she left.

"I like her," Cami said.

THE HOUSE WAS still filled with things. Not the drawers in the bedrooms, but everywhere else. The closets were only half emptied, and what was left were gowns, suits, three-inch heels, and clutches. The rugs were beautiful, thickly woven, nicer than any rug their family had ever owned. Izabel found herself thinking, *It brings the room together*, like the agents said in the old real estate shows she watched.

In the kitchen there was an old stove that someone had refurbished. It was ruby red and all its doors were curved out like they were bread bins instead of ovens. Izabel imagined the metal sanders and the spray paint it took to make it look this good again, tools that people had to wear masks around, before people were always wearing masks.

The four of them walked through every room together, more quietly than Izabel expected. She thought maybe they'd be claiming objects and spaces, calling out and being silly. But it wasn't like a hotel, like vacationing with her mother, who would always claim the chair with wheels and then scoot around the room in it, showing it off, even taking it into the bathroom, raising it up to wash her hands without getting to her feet. Izabel would alternate between laughing and acting like she was embarrassed of her, even though she wasn't, even though no one else was in the room.

This place felt too much like someone else's house, like they were trespassers. And it was clear to all of them—this wasn't how people moved. This was how they fled.

IZABEL SET TO work with Kaito, taking the sheets from the beds, getting the loads going in the washing machine. They looked at the dishes and decided they didn't need to be washed. They looked at the pillows and wished they'd brought their own. They fluffed them, trying to rid them of the shapes of other people's heads.

There were a few empty boxes the last family had left near the entrance, and Izabel used them to clear the surfaces of picture frames, jewelry boxes, small vases—anything too personal left scattered about the house.

She started in what would be Jana's room, and when she was finished, she told Jana she could come and start unpacking her own things into it. Cami ran after Jana to help.

Izabel cleared Cami's room next, but they'd have to wait for their things before they could make it into a space for her. Izabel was sure Cami would give her a hard time about that later, but she also knew that she could be appeased, easily, simply, with chocolate and an apology and a plan to fix it.

It took the longest to clear what would be Izabel and Kaito's new bedroom. There were postcards and drawings hung on the side of an armoire, and empty spots where more precious pictures must have been. There was a faux tree covered in sets of earrings. Imagining the woman's ears made Izabel feel lightheaded. That woman's ears were soft and safe somewhere, unlike Izabel's family.

Until that moment, it felt like she was bringing her family to safety, with this safe house, a house the killer did not specifically know was hers. But seeing how scared this family had been, remembering the randomness of the killings, seeing the earrings left sparkling on the tree—Izabel fell with a thud, her back slamming into a dresser of drawers.

Kaito rushed in.

"We're not safe," she said.

"We are," he said.

She shook her head. She knew that he knew it, too. He'd wanted to go. He'd done everything right. And now, when her breaths were shallow and her chest hurt, Izabel felt she didn't deserve him. She didn't deserve any of them.

From the other room, Izabel heard Cami laugh. It was one of Izabel's favorite sounds, when someone else made her laugh. When Cami was having a moment of joy that Izabel was not a part of. When Izabel was in another room, having an entirely different feeling, like despair.

## CHAPTER EIGHTEEN

Kaito fed the girls salmon that he found in the freezer while Izabel took a shower and checked the house again for left-behind things that might trigger her in the morning. When the boxes were full, Kaito piled them in the utility closet where no one had any reason to look at them again. Paz wrote that their things would come tomorrow.

"Everyone full?" Kaito asked, over the sound of a children's television show.

Izabel peeked into the room and saw that Jana was leaning over to watch Cami's tablet with her.

"I want Mommy to put me to bed," Cami said.

"That's fine," Kaito said, "but that's not what I asked. Are you full? Are you ready?"

Cami nodded.

Izabel walked over to them, hair still wet, and scooped up Cami. "Of course I will put you to bed!"

Jana went into her room without a word. Izabel took Cami to the bathroom where Cami peed and brushed her teeth, and

Izabel put a little diaper cream around her anus that never stopped being red.

In bed, Izabel sang her a song her mother used to sing her, about baby chicks: "Los pollitos dicen, 'pío pío pío,' cuando tienen hambre y cuando tienen frio. La gallina busca el maíz y el trigo, les da la comida y les presta abrigo. Bajos sus dos alas, acurrucaditos, duermen los pollitos hasta el otro día."

"Will you kiss my head?" Cami said. "I'm scared."

"Why are you scared?" Izabel asked.

Cami didn't answer.

"I was scared of my house when I was little," Izabel said, which was true. She used to run up the stairs from her mother's basement as if the dark could bite her. And, more foolishly, as if some true danger couldn't reach her after she'd closed the basement door. "But this house is small," Izabel said. "I walked all over it." She got louder. "I looked in every corner." She threw her arms out and then put them, in fists, on her hips. "I'm aware and in charge of every inch of this house!" She kissed Cami on her head as Cami giggled.

But after Cami was done giggling, she said she was still scared. Izabel didn't know if it was because Cami's fear was that great, or because Cami doubted that Izabel had the control she purported. And Izabel was almost certain it was the latter. And Izabel resented Cami for a thought she only might be having. And she felt that resentment as she kissed Cami and held her until she fell asleep.

IZABEL WENT TO Jana's room next. Jana took out her earbuds.

"You holding up okay?" Izabel asked.

Jana nodded. "You?"

"Yeah."

Jana pinched her pajama pants. "The inspector didn't get any of my hijabs."

"Oh, honey, I'm sorry. We can go buy you some tomorrow."

"I don't like to go out without one."

Izabel thought of the scarf in her purse. "Would a scarf be okay? Until we buy one?"

Jana nodded.

"I was thinking about tomorrow," Izabel said. "Is there anywhere you're supposed to be?"

"Like school?"

"Yeah."

"My mother was homeschooling me."

"Ah, okay."

"Until I decide on an apprenticeship. There are some people that will take on a shadow as young as fourteen."

"So two more years."

"You don't have to do it," Jana said.

"No, I mean, I would be happy to—"

"There are tutors and stuff."

"There aren't a lot of children your age around," Izabel said.

"My parents called me a miracle."

"Yes."

"I guess I still am."

"Right."

They were quiet.

"I'm really sorry," Izabel said.

"I know," Jana said. "I mean, everyone is. Everyone at the hospital kept saying that."

"Yeah. But it's true. I mean, it's true from me at least. Really true."

They were quiet again, until Jana suddenly burst open. "I used to tell my parents that I thought something was wrong with me, because if I thought about terrible situations, like if me and another kid were kidnapped, and I could escape somehow, I'd save myself every time. And my parents were like, 'You're young,' or, 'That's how you imagine it, but it'd be different if you lived it. You'd make the right choice then.' But I knew I wouldn't. I knew it. And now here I am, like I chose to save myself and they died."

One second Jana's eyes were dry and the next they were filled with tears that streamed down her face.

"But you didn't choose it," Izabel said, sitting down on the bed.

"Maybe I did!" Jana said. "Maybe thinking that way *was* making that choice."

"No." Izabel wrapped her arms around her. "No, no, no," she kept repeating.

In the morning, Izabel got ready in their new bathroom. The sinks were shaped like seashells, carved into the vanity. Another odd throwback, like the kitchen stove. Izabel brushed her teeth, bent over, spit into it, and some of her spit splashed back directly into her eye.

"Shit," she said.

She cupped her hand and filled it with water, splashed it over her eye and forced herself to blink. She did it again and again until it stopped burning.

She looked at herself in the mirror. She covered the good eye and looked around with the bad. Everything was fine and in focus. Her face was wet. The front of her hair was wet, which made it look like her hair was thinning. And maybe it was.

From the other room, Kaito yelled that they were ready. They were taking Jana to a tutor she'd seen once or twice before, then dropping Cami off at school, and then seeing Opa, just the two of them.

IZABEL WATCHED OUT the car window. Finally she was feeling comfortable in cars again, if she looked far enough away. She thought, if she was feeling up to it, she would go to the mall after their appointment.

"Can they bring my workstation to the new house?" Kaito asked.

"They can bring you a new one," Izabel said.

"Why not mine?"

"Because he could be watching our old house, following people from it."

"And by *he*, you mean the killer?"

"Yes," she said.

Kaito sighed.

"Look," Izabel said, "you don't have to be worried about it. I'm glad you're not, honestly. Because we'd both be a wreck if you were. But you have to respect how I'm feeling about it."

"I do," he said. "I'm doing that."

"I know," she said.

"I'm fine with it," he said. "I just wanted to ask."

"Isn't working at the office going okay?"

"It is," he said.

Izabel realized this whole ride she'd been looking at those trees on the north edge of town that Cami was always waving at.

OPA STARTED THEIR session by asking them about recent changes in Cami's life. "A move? A new sibling?" she said.

Kaito laughed.

"Sorry," Izabel said. "That was just a little too," and she touched her nose.

Kaito explained: "We just moved and we just took in a girl."

"And this is when the behaviors began with Cami?"

"No. She started sleep-talking weeks ago. The move and Jana, that's all this week."

"Okay, let's work up to that. Were there any changes to Cami's life around the time that the sleep-talking began?"

"We told you about the hospital that night," Izabel said.

"I don't mean that. I mean, changes with her school, any other parts of her schedule, if she lost anyone she was close to, if you got a pet."

"So you think," Izabel said, "there's a chance this has nothing to do with what happened at the hospital that night?"

"Yes," Opa said. "That's what I'm here to sort out."

"I can't think of any changes," Kaito said.

Izabel was still trying to take it in—that there might not be one singular moment when she'd failed her daughter, which led them here. And for a second that felt amazing. But then she realized how, maybe, she'd failed her daughter countless times.

"Can you describe what your typical day might be like?" Opa said.

Izabel took a deep breath. "We wake up, she eats, she goes to school, she eats again when she gets home, we go out for the afternoon somewhere, we come home, and we all have dinner together."

"And have the teachers mentioned anything to you about her behavior or any changes at school?"

"No."

"But she likes school?"

"Yes, definitely."

"And she gets along well with her teachers?"

"Yes. One day they sent her home with a medal they cut out of paper that said she was the puzzle master."

Opa smiled at them. "What's bedtime like?" she asked.

"We usually all get ready for bed together," Kaito said. "We sort of get her ready first and then she plays on our bed until we're ready, too."

"Does she sleep in your bed?"

"No," he said. "One of us, usually Izzie, takes her to her room and lies with her until she falls asleep."

"And what time is this?"

"It's a little different every night," Izabel said.

"About?"

"I guess around ten."

"And does she stay asleep in her bed all night?"

"Most nights," Kaito said.

"And if not, is she coming to you, or is she crying until you go to her?"

"She used to cry until we went to her, but now she comes in," he said.

"And when did that change?"

"Maybe a year ago," he said.

"When is she getting up in the morning?"

"Around eight," Izabel said.

"And Kaito, you're already up for work?"

"Usually," he said.

"Have you woken up by then, Izzie?"

"Kaito is the only one who calls me that," Izabel said.

"I'm sorry," Opa said. "I didn't realize."

"It's okay."

"Izabel then?"

Izabel nodded.

"Would you two be up to implementing a stricter bedtime routine for two weeks and seeing how that goes?"

"What would it look like?" Izabel asked.

"Like, 7:45 is bath time, 8:30 is a snack, 8:45 is time to brush teeth, 9:00 is a story, 9:15 is a song and a snuggle, 9:30 is bedtime."

"I don't like to bathe her every day because her skin dries out."

"No, of course, whatever works for you. What's important is that you pick the times of things, write it out, share it with me, and then follow it for two weeks very strictly."

"We can try that," Kaito said.

"He says that, but a lot of this would fall on me and I'm not sure Cami would really respond to that kind of schedule."

"We don't have to start there," Opa said.

"I can help with this," Kaito said.

"For two weeks? Every night? Your job doesn't work like that."

"But it seems like a reasonable first step, doesn't it? She's not asking us to remake the world."

Izabel shot him a look, and then said to Opa, "She's been doing so much better since the move. Maybe we don't need to be making more changes right now."

"For her or for you?"

"No. No, I'm fine."

"It's a legitimate reason to not make these changes—if you've had too much change lately, Izabel."

Izabel's breathing quickened. She couldn't answer.

Opa walked over to her desk, opened a drawer, grabbed a paper bag, and brought it to Izabel. "I want you to breathe into this for me," she said.

Izabel leaned forward and did what Opa asked. She felt Opa put her hand on her back.

"She passed out at the hospital the other day," Kaito said.

"Okay, that's okay," Opa said.

Izabel's cheeks felt so hot that she thought her tears would feel cool running down them.

"Have you considered seeing a therapist, Izabel?"

She lied, shaking her head.

"Would you like to see one? I could recommend someone."

She shook her head faster.

"Would you like to see me?"

That made Izabel stop. She took the bag away from her mouth. "I would see you," she said.

"Okay, great. So here's what I'll say. Kaito, you take over bedtime and follow a schedule and monitor it. If there are nights you can't do, that's fine. Izabel, if it falls to you, you do whatever you want. All that matters is that everyone is sleeping. The next time you come in, I want to see Izabel and Cami together. And the time after that, I'll see only you, Izabel. Does that all sound good?"

They both nodded.

"And what if it happens again, with Cami?" Kaito said. "Do we wake her up?"

"No," Opa said as she wrote something on a pad and ripped it off. "Izabel, this is a medicine that I want you to carry around with you. You feel one of those panic attacks coming on again, you take it."

"Okay," Izabel said.

"It's dissolvable so you don't need water to take it."

"Thank you," Izabel said.

"If you find you need it more than twice a day, call me."

"Thank you," Kaito said.

"Can you two talk to each other about this anxiety?"

Neither of them even moved to nod.

"Try your best." She smiled at them.

Back in the car, Kaito held Izabel tightly under his arm, but he didn't say anything.

Since Izabel and Kaito first got together, as gentle as Kaito was, Izabel knew that he would hurt anyone who ever hurt her. He would be violent, fierce, and quick about it. He was a vengeful person, an honorable one.

But what she understood now—in the car, his arm squeezing her, the town quiet and sterile, the far trees the only swaying, moving things in sight—what she understood was that she didn't know what it was that, for him, constituted her being hurt. Because she'd been hurt plenty of times, and he'd never done much.

She thought he'd have to find her dead somewhere to raise that kind of response in him, from him, in order for him to become the person that she always knew he could be.

## CHAPTER NINETEEN

After dropping Kaito off at work, Izabel did go to the mall. She filled the script for Niravam that Opa had written her, and with the new pills in her bag, Izabel went to the privacy pods. There was Sasha behind his desk. And there was Patrick again in the waiting room. Both of them were the approximate size and height of the killer. She wanted to take one of the pills, but she didn't know if she'd fall asleep or not be able to get herself home. She sat down as calmly as she could.

Patrick seemed to light up at the sight of her. "How've you been?" he asked.

"Fine," she said. And maybe she said it a little coldly because she was tense, alone in a room with two men, two men who fit the description.

Patrick couldn't hide his response to that coldness—he looked disappointed.

So she added, more warmly, "How about you?"

"Good," he said. "I guess you didn't get approved for travel either." But something in the way he said it sounded rehearsed.

"It's a long story," she said.

But he didn't ask for the story. He said, "Need some time again today?"

"I do," she said. "And you're working again?"

"Yes," he said. He tapped his briefcase with his foot.

And then Sasha called her name.

"Me?" she asked, thinking he'd call Patrick first, and looking back at him.

Sasha nodded.

"It's fine," Patrick said.

So Izabel went back, and in the pod, she began to write.

Dear Killer,

Here are the things I've imagined I will do to you once we catch you: I will stand over your body and laugh. I will raise one bent leg onto your body like you are a land I have discovered. I will pee on you. I will kick you until you are dead. I will choke you until you are dead. I will punch your face, but not until you are dead, and I will watch how your face swells.

She shredded it.

Dear Killer,

Here are the things I couldn't do to you even though I hate you: I could not have you open your mouth and rest your top teeth on a hard surface and then stomp on your head so that your teeth break.

And maybe that's it.

She shredded it. And then she wrote to Cami again.

Dear Cami,

If the killer kills me and not you, there's a lot I need to tell you. Like how I've learned, with men, it's better to overemote. My boyfriends didn't believe I was sad unless I was crying. All the ways I'd taught myself to be guarded in my life—the ways I was taught not to be emotional if I wanted to be taken seriously, if I wanted to be given roles of authority—they didn't work in a relationship. I had to be two different women. I had to be different women all the time.

She wrote another.

Dear Cami,

I want to tell you about the ways lovers can hurt you, because it's unlike the ways anyone else can hurt you, the ways I've hurt you. Take this as an example: Once, a gnat flew toward my eye, would've flown into it, but I closed my eye in time. Not on purpose—you couldn't time something like that—but by luck, by blinking. And in raising my eyelid again, I killed the gnat. I want to emphasize the ease of the progression of actions. You will feel as fragile as that, in love with another person, and that is how the other person's strength will feel, as violently overwhelming as an eyelid to a piece-of-shit fly.

She touched the soft black walls of the pod. She remembered how Jana was using her scarf as a hijab. On her tablet, she wrote Jana, asking her to meet her at the mall's food court after tutoring.

She wrote Cami one more letter.

Dear Cami,

Your abuelita once yelled, "I will not be your American!" at the mail. She tore up a letter about a preapproved credit card and shoved the pieces into the recycling. I thought I'd have to teach my future children about credit cards and debt and the American that America wants you to be. I would have taught you to yell, "I will not be your American!" when we looked at tuition costs for college. But I don't have to teach you about any of those things. There is, though, this feeling still, that we should yell. There's this broken idea of citizenship.

The light went on. She folded up the letters to Cami and put them in her purse next to the last one she'd written. She couldn't believe, with everything that had happened, the papers in her purse had been left reasonably undisturbed.

NEXT IZABEL FOUND the sandwich-maker Cami had mentioned in her dream. She knew right away he wasn't the killer. He was an older man, with a broad build. She ordered a grilled portabello sandwich. And because he wasn't the killer, she took her time watching how he cut the bun, how he shuffled along the counter, watching all the ways his body moved, all the ways that the killer's body did not.

As she ate her sandwich, she opened her News app, still set to *2017, About the Air.*

What are Spare the Air days?

Air quality in the Bay Area can be unhealthy at times throughout the year.

Spare the Air Alerts are called when ozone pollution is forecast to reach unhealthy levels. Ozone, or smog, can cause throat irritation, congestion, chest pain, trigger asthma, inflame the lining of the lungs and worsen bronchitis and emphysema. Long-term exposure to ozone can reduce lung function. Ozone pollution is particularly harmful to young children, seniors and those with respiratory and heart conditions.

When a Spare the Air Alert is called, outdoor exercise should be done only in the early morning hours when ozone concentrations are lower. Residents are encouraged to reduce air pollution every day by rethinking their commute and avoiding driving alone. . . .

The Bay Area Air Quality Management District is the regional agency responsible for protecting air quality in the Bay Area. For more information about Spare the Air, visit www.sparetheair.org.

The Air Quality Management District sounded like it could be a place for people to live in the sky. Izabel wondered how high they would need to go to be outside of the pollen's reach. She imagined the thin air making her tired. She imagined coughing up blood into the snow. But they would need to go higher than mountain-tops. She'd heard rumors that people were still living on space stations. She didn't know much about that. People hardly talked about space anymore. She missed that kind of human ambition.

WHERE IZABEL RETURNED her tray, there was a new poster up. A Norwegian troll. Under it was written GUARDIAN OF CORPSE-FJORD, SWALLOWER OF HEAVEN'S WHEEL. When Izabel imagined swallowing heaven's wheel, she could feel it large in her throat.

Jana came up behind her and Izabel jumped.

"Sorry," Jana said.

"No, it's fine," Izabel said. "How'd tutoring go?"

"Good," Jana said.

"It will work? To keep going to her?"

"Yeah."

"And we can work on other things, too," Izabel said.

"I know," Jana said.

"Are you hungry?"

"No, I'm good. Kaito packed me a lunch."

"Really?"

Jana nodded. "I ate it in the car."

"Okay. Let's go shopping then," Izabel said.

Jana smiled but didn't move. "Will someone recognize me?" she said.

Izabel hadn't thought of that. The police had kept Izabel's picture out of the news, but when the news had posted pictures of Jana's parents, there were a few with Jana there, smiling between them.

"I don't think so," Izabel said. "If they do, what do you want me to do?"

"Deny it," Jana said.

"I can do that."

With that they headed into the store. While Jana looked at hijabs, Izabel looked at prayer books and rugs and incense.

"Do you need a prayer rug?" Izabel asked.

"No," Jana said. "I don't pray."

"Okay," Izabel said.

"Do you think I should pray?"

"I don't know," Izabel said. "I don't pray."

"What religion are you and Kaito?"

"I sometimes identify as Jewish, I guess. Kaito might identify as Buddhist. He used to. Neither of us practices anything."

"Okay," Jana said. She went back to looking at hijabs.

Izabel wondered if Jana's parents used to pray and how often, if either of them performed the adhan. But she didn't want to upset Jana by asking her about them.

Jana held up a hijab. "This one."

"Beautiful," Izabel said.

AT HOME, AT their new home, their things had arrived. Izabel started to go through them, setting up Cami's room before Cami got home from school. She put out her xylophone, her puzzles, her box of LEGOs, and her magnetic drawing board.

But Cami didn't notice when she came back. They'd given each kid a toy at school. A timer to brush your teeth by. It lit up and a played a little song that was exactly 120 seconds long. Cami ran to show it to Jana first.

"Wow," Jana said.

"Mommy?" Cami said. "Can we play with your makeup?"

"Sure," Izabel said.

Cami took Jana's hand and Jana looked nervously at Izabel.

"She only likes to play with the brushes," Izabel said.

Jana mouthed, "Oooh," and followed Cami into the bathroom.

Izabel started to figure out dinner. In the fridge there were lots of condiments and a few pieces of fruit that were going bad. But the freezer was full of frozen meals. She found four boxes of pad thai with tofu.

Kaito came home and collapsed on the couch.

"Do you need anything?" he asked.

"I'm okay—you can rest for a bit. Pad thai good for dinner?"

"Yes!" he said.

They could hear Cami in the bedroom telling Jana, "That brings out your eyes," and they both laughed.

"Ugh," Kaito said.

"What?"

"Nothing. My arm fell asleep." He draped his arm over his face. "I think that how crappy our bodies are is good evidence for evolution versus creation."

"Like that our legs fall asleep on the toilet?"

"Exactly," he said. "*And*, if there was a god, the eighth day would've been toilets and soft toilet paper and other items of convenience."

"Definitely. And antibiotics."

"Yeah. You're right. Eighth day, medicines. Ninth day, items of convenience."

"Got it."

"I would've been a decent god," he said.

"You would've been a great god," Izabel said. And he fell asleep.

By bedtime the toy was broken. The song would stop but the light wouldn't turn off. After everyone was asleep, after Izabel turned off the light in the bathroom, she saw its light there on the countertop. She wondered if it was bright enough to be seen through the plastic windows of the dome. And would the killer see? And would the killer come? She put the toy in a drawer.

Sometimes she thought she drew him toward herself, with her dread of him.

## CHAPTER TWENTY

Early in the morning, Paz called and said Izabel had to come in to the station. She didn't tell her why, even when Izabel pressed her. Kaito yelled from bed that he didn't like it. Izabel knew Paz could hear him, but she didn't say more. She only insisted that Izabel come in.

Andy was already there when Izabel arrived. When they saw each other, they hugged for a long time.

"I'm sorry we had to leave so abruptly," Izabel said.

"Don't worry about it," Andy said. "How's the new house?"

"It's good," Izabel said. "How's Hestia? How are you?"

"We're good. House is a little lonely without all of you."

"Please. I'm sure you're glad to be rid of us. It was too much, all of us in there."

"Yeah, you're right." Andy smiled. "Do you know what this is about?"

"No," Izabel said.

"Anything new happen?"

"Not with us."

Officer Evans showed them back to an interrogation room.

"Is this really necessary?" Andy asked.

"I was told to bring you in here," he said, and then he left.

"That's a good sign," Andy said.

"What?"

"He wouldn't leave the room if you were a suspect again."

"Would they have let me come here without a police escort if I were a suspect again?"

"Maybe not. But now we know for sure."

Paz came in.

"Hello, ladies. I couldn't tell you why we needed you here in case you refused, and this is coming from higher up. Not from me. Higher up." She raised her eyebrows at them as if she were making an important point.

Izabel and Andy nodded.

"Good, so Lucy is here and you're going to meet with her and I'm going to take notes."

Izabel snorted.

"Don't do that. You believe in this shit."

"You don't."

"I *certainly* don't, but we don't have much to go on here and she keeps calling."

"Why does Izabel need to be here?" Andy said.

Paz shook her head and held out her hands. "Lucy says she needs to be here so here she is." She was gesturing at Izabel and looking at Andy. "Are you going to be a problem?"

"I'm never a problem," Andy said. "Are you recording this?"

"We want to record it, yes," Paz said.

"No. You can take notes, but you can't record it."

"Fine."

"Do you need anything?" Andy asked Izabel.

"I'm okay."

"I'll get some waters in here," Paz said.

PAZ CAME BACK with Lucy and four bottles of water. Izabel opened hers immediately, focusing on it instead of Lucy.

"It's good to see you." Lucy smiled. "Adira, the girl's mother, keeps coming to me since we met."

Izabel looked up at that. "We're taking good care of Jana."

"She knows."

"Why do you need me here?" Izabel asked her.

"She's more clear when you're here."

Izabel nodded.

"I asked you to come see me," Lucy said, putting her hand on Izabel's hand. "You said you would."

"I haven't had time yet. I didn't know it would help with this."

"It might not."

Paz blurted out, "You have been calling every day—"

Lucy slid her elbow gently into Paz's arm and Paz stopped.

"The mother would be most clear with Jana here, but that can be difficult for a child. I thought you'd prefer this."

Izabel nodded again.

"Let's start," Paz said.

"She wants me to say she's sorry. She won't say anything else until she knows she's said that."

"Why's she sorry?" Paz asked, turning on her quick.

"That's not for you," Lucy said. "Have you heard it, sweetie?"

"Yes," Izabel said. She wanted to reach up and touch the mark left on her cheek, but she didn't.

"Then I'm ready to start," Lucy said. "I'm going to hold your hand, Izabel, and I want you to keep your eyes closed. Inspector,

I'm going to count backwards from ten and then I want you to ask me questions as if I'm Adira, as we discussed. Okay?"

Lucy counted backwards from ten, and Izabel focused on the feeling of Lucy's hand as she kept her eyes closed.

"What can you tell me about the person who cut through the house?" Paz asked.

"It was a man."

"Can you tell me anything about the man?"

"He was taller than Mohamed."

"Your husband?" Paz rustled through some papers. "Your husband is five eight?"

"Yes."

"So five ten maybe?"

"Yes."

"Did you see his skin?"

"He was a white man."

"Did he say anything?"

"He cursed when the woman showed up."

"What did he say?"

"I don't want to say it."

"Please," Paz said. It was the nicest Paz had ever sounded.

"Cunt."

"Did he have an accent?"

"No."

"A low voice, or high?"

"Normal."

"Was there anything unusual about him?"

"He did not run away."

"Why was that unusual?"

"I thought he would run. Perhaps he couldn't."

"What do you mean?"

"The suit he was wearing. It looked heavy."

"Did you see any marks on him, any tattoos?"

"I'm not sure."

"Did he smell like anything?"

"Yes."

"What did he smell like?"

"I don't know."

"But something?"

"No. It was her. She smelled."

"Who?"

"The woman who saved Jana."

"What did she smell like?"

"She smelled like sandalwood."

"But was there another smell?"

"I don't think so."

"Okay. Did you see what he used to cut your house?"

"Yes."

"Can you describe it?"

"A knife. It was long, a little curved."

"Was it sharp on both sides or just one?"

"One."

"Was there anything near the handle?"

"Serrated near the handle."

"On which side?"

"Both sides."

"You're sure?"

"Yes."

"Was there anything unusual at the tip of the knife?"

"No."

"Was there anything unique about the handle?"

"I don't know."

"Is there anything I should have asked you about the knife?"

"No."

"Did you see where he went after?"

"He went toward the street."

"After that?"

"I heard a car door."

"Do you know where he went after that?"

"No. I stayed with Jana."

"Is there anything I should have asked you about the man?"

"No."

"Was the woman who smelled like sandalwood involved?"

"Inspector," Andy snapped.

"No. She saved Jana."

"But before that?"

"Inspector!"

"No."

Lucy counted up to ten and Izabel opened her eyes.

Andy looked pale, sick even. She looked at Izabel so intensely that Izabel felt small and lost and large and powerful all at once. Andy asked her, "Are you okay?"

"I'm fine," Izabel said. "That was amazing. She knew so much."

"That was you," Andy said.

"What was?"

"That was you. You were talking. You said all that."

"No," Izabel said.

But Paz was looking at her strangely, too.

"No," Izabel said again.

"It's okay, sweetie," Lucy said.

"I thought it was you," Izabel said.

"I helped."

"I didn't say you could do that," Izabel said. She pushed her seat back from the table. "I didn't say you could do that."

"We needed the information," Paz said.

"You knew? You knew she was going to do that?" She stood up and kept backing away from them.

"She told me what she thought might happen," Paz said.

"It might not have happened like that," Lucy said. "It could have been me."

Izabel's back hit the wall. "But it wasn't! Why didn't you tell me?"

"You might not have come, dear," Lucy said.

"We needed the information," Paz said again.

Andy was up now. Izabel turned her back to them. Andy rubbed her arm.

"Did you know?" Izabel whispered.

"No," Andy said. "I didn't. Come back to the table."

"Can she leave?" Izabel said, referring to Lucy but not looking at her.

Paz said, "*You* can leave."

Before Izabel could respond, Andy said, "Let's go."

They went to the main doors and Andy pressed two buttons to call for two cars. "I'm sorry—should I have called for one? You can come with me."

"No, it's fine. You go home. I'll go home."

"You're okay?" Andy asked.

"I feel okay."

Andy still looked sick.

"Tell me what it was like," Izabel said.

Andy looked at her like she might say too much.

"Tell me."

"It was the weirdest shit I've ever seen."

"I heard everything. I didn't think it was me talking."

"It didn't sound like you."

"It didn't?"

Andy shook her head.

"Are you scared of me?"

"No. No!" Andy squeezed Izabel's arm. "But I am scared right now."

"It was scary."

"It was a little scary."

A car pulled up.

"You can take it," Izabel said.

"Are you sure?"

Izabel nodded. She wouldn't tell Andy, but she was going back in. She wanted to see Lucy again. She wanted to understand what had happened. She was worried Jana's mother was in her somehow, that she was inspirited.

"Call me, okay?" Andy said, slipping on her mask.

"I will," Izabel said.

As Izabel walked back toward the interrogation room again, Officer Evans followed her.

"You can't go back there, ma'am."

Izabel put up her middle finger over her shoulder and kept going. She knocked on the interrogation room door.

Paz opened it, but someone else was in the room with her and Lucy now. Paz walked out into the hall and closed the door behind her. "What is it?"

"I tried to stop her," Officer Evans said.

"I've got her from here."

"I need to talk to Lucy," Izabel said.

"Not right now."

"Yes, right now." Izabel got louder. "I need to talk to her right now."

Paz took Izabel's shoulders and pushed her into the nearest room.

"You don't need shit from her right, *right* now. She's in there with my boss and I need you to pull yourself together."

Izabel was shaking. "Fuck you."

"You better remember who you're talking to."

Izabel started looking around the room Paz had pushed her into. It was an arms room, and there were guns, lots of guns—handguns tagged on a table, rifles upright in a rack. Izabel started to panic. "I'm not okay," she said.

"You're fine," Paz said. "You're more than fine. You were already my only witness, and now, with all that shit that just came out of *your* mouth, it doesn't matter how Lucy explains it, you're my star witness."

Izabel shook her head. "No, I'm not."

Paz grabbed Izabel's head with both hands and held it still. "Yes. You are."

There was something tender about having her head in Paz's hands, even if it was also shockingly intimidating. And then they both heard someone yell for Paz. She let go of Izabel and stepped one foot out of the room.

In those seconds, Izabel grabbed a handgun and put it in her bag.

Paz yelled, "I'm coming," and came back to Izabel. "Look, my boss wants to meet you. I said, *No, another day*, but now you're still here. Christ. Can you do this?"

"I have a medicine in my purse I'm supposed to take."

"Then take it."

"Now?"

Paz nodded.

Izabel took out the bottle, pushed down the child lock, took out a pill, shoved it in her mouth, and let it dissolve on her tongue. "Oh no," she said.

"What?"

"It tastes like orange," Izabel said. "I hate orange."

"You've never taken one before?"

Izabel shook her head.

"What if it makes you all loopy?"

"I don't know."

"You're a mess," Paz said.

Izabel didn't say anything. She focused on her breath and how horrible the medicine tasted. It felt like it was sliding into that space between her back molars and her cheek. She ran her tongue back there. It felt like her mouth would taste bad forever.

"Better?" Paz asked.

"I don't think it works instantly," Izabel said.

"I'm walking you in there and they're going to make a fuss and you are going to act like the hero you are."

"I'm not—"

Paz yelled, "Are you listening to me, Izabel!"

"Yeah," Izabel said. "Yeah, I'm a hero. I'm your witness."

"Good," Paz said. And they left the room and all the guns in their matte metals.

## CHAPTER TWENTY-ONE

After the police station, Izabel needed to talk to Kaito. She went to the offices where he'd been working. She asked for him at the desk and the man asked her to sit. His nametag read ARNOLD. His shoulders were too slender for him to be the killer.

She sat, put her purse on the floor, took out her tablet, and saw the gun. She wondered what Arnold would do if he knew she had a gun in her bag. At her feet, she made sure the bag slouched closed.

In her app, the 2017 news coverage had been about *the fires* for days. The fires are controlled. The fires are out. New fires are beginning. The conditions are dry and windy.

Izabel's mother hadn't told Izabel about the fires of 2017, the maps of smoke, the evacuations, the number of missing, the number of dead. But her mother didn't know that the world was about to end in disaster—one that left all the houses standing. No one surviving or not surviving in swimming pools. Maybe if her mother had known, then she would have told Izabel about disaster all the

time. How it affected people. How it continued past any one particular event.

Some of the news stories were about how there weren't enough
masks, there weren't the *right* masks for the poor conditions, for all
that smoke. There were so many pictures of the world left behind,
the fields of ash.

These pictures suggested yet another possible apocalyptic world
to Izabel, one that maybe they were still continuing toward, but to
which no one had arrived yet. They had arrived at this apocalyptic
world too quickly. It had won the race.

She read an article about the proposed cleanup. There were so
many organizations involved—the Federal Emergency Management
Agency, the California Department of Toxic Substances Control,
the California Department of Resources Recycling and Recovery,
and the California Department of Public Health. They had a
plan, in theory, but the state of things couldn't be evaluated. They
couldn't begin until all the fires were out.

Izabel almost enjoyed the story—the nonsolution solutions,
everything always impossible and continuing anyway.

She read an article about the ash itself. The people digging
through it with their bare hands. The chemicals that can pass
through skin. The hazard. They wrote about how the rains hadn't
come, but how, when they did, the ash would run into watersheds.
The ash-filled rains would run into the yards of homes where families thought the fire had not touched them. The fire would touch
them this way.

If old homes had asbestos shingles, that was in the air now. That
old *now*, which Izabel relived alongside her life.

"It'll be another minute," Arnold said.

Izabel imagined the people wading through the ash. She imagined it giving way under people's feet like a fine sand, like quicksand

maybe, if it were deeper. She could see the masks on their faces, the large plastic glasses over their eyes, makeshift protection pieced together from a hardware store. Socks pulled up over the cuffs of their pants. Scarves around their necks maybe. All of them sweating through their search. What would they keep anyway, of what they found in the ash? And could they trust it? To be clean and safe?

Suddenly Izabel remembered her mother running her nails through Izabel's hair when she was checking her for ticks. Izabel loved when she did that. She wanted her mother to run her fingers through her hair more often. Thinking back, Izabel didn't know why she didn't just ask her. *She would have done it*, Izabel thought.

But she knew what she'd really wanted was for her mother to *want* to touch her more. That same test Izabel used to set to her boyfriends when she was young, waiting for them to know what to do. She didn't do that with Kaito. She told Kaito what she wanted and he did all of it, any of it, remembered to keep doing it, without her asking again. In this one way, she'd taught herself how to be happy.

When Kaito finally came out, he spoke quietly. "What are you doing here?"

"I had to talk to you," Izabel said.

"What is it? What did Paz want?"

"Lucy was there."

"The medium?"

Izabel nodded. "She contacted Jana's mom."

"Holy shit."

"She contacted Jana's mom *through* me."

"What do you mean?"

"I mean, I talked, but Adira was the one who was speaking."

"What?"

"I don't know. I thought I was listening to Lucy. I didn't know I was doing it."

"Are you okay?"

She shook her head, and Kaito held her like he had in the car. And then he said, "Was it helpful? To the case?"

"I think so," Izabel said, though she didn't want him to be considering the *value* of what had happened.

"That's good then, right?"

"What if she's in me?" she said.

"Jana's mom?"

She nodded.

"No! She's not."

"You think Cami is inspirited. Why not me?"

"You're not. She's not in you. I promise."

"You promise?"

"Yes," he said, with a single, sharp nod. And he said it so definitively, this man who believed in ghosts and spirits and monsters, that Izabel accepted that she was herself and herself alone.

AFTER DINNER, JANA volunteered to do the dishes, and Izabel watched her and wondered if she was beginning to feel like part of the family.

Kaito took Cami to do the new bedtime routine. It was going well, but they weren't sure if it was changing anything. She was still sleep-talking, but nothing upsetting.

Jana rinsed the dishes and put them in the dishwasher. She filled it differently than Kaito and Izabel did, with the plates bent toward the middle on one side and the other, instead of all lined up in the same direction.

"Thank you," Izabel said.

"No problem," Jana said. She dried off her hands and, since Izabel was still there, she came back to the table.

"Do you like it here?" Izabel asked.

"Yeah, it's cool. Do you like it?"

"Yeah."

"What was your old house like?" Jana said.

"More of the standard-issue stuff. We had a tiled shower that I loved."

"Different from this one?"

"Yeah, different colors, and textures. But I like this one, too."

"But it's not yours."

Izabel nodded and Jana picked at her nails.

"What about your old house?" Izabel asked.

"My parents had a lot of tapestries, I think you'd call them."

"Do you want one here?"

"No," she said. "I like how this is new for all of us."

"Me too."

Jana looked down at the table. "I can't have a friend over, right?"

"What do you mean?"

"It's like, a secret, where we live."

"Oh, yeah. But we could meet somewhere. Or you could go over their house. Do you . . . do you have a boyfriend or girlfriend?"

"I didn't mean"—Jana shook her head—"about anyone in particular."

"Sorry. I didn't want to embarrass you."

"It's okay. You didn't. No, I'm . . ." Her eyes filled up with tears.

"What is it?" Izabel reached her arm over the table.

"Is it a secret because he still wants to kill me?"

"No, no, honey. It's because I'm a witness. They're protecting me."

"He *might* still want to kill me."

"No—"

"He knows I survived."

"He does, but they said it's all been random. Your family wasn't targeted."

"But they don't know that. They don't know that for sure."

Cami screamed in her room.

Jana rushed to her, a step in front of Izabel.

"It's happening again," Kaito said.

*"He's out,"* Cami said. And then she shouted, "I don't want to talk about him!"

"She's talking to someone," Jana said.

"It sounds like that but we don't know. It might be a night terror," Izabel said.

"Her eyes are closed."

"Yeah."

"I used to get night terrors, and my parents told me about them. They said my eyes were open. I wasn't awake and I didn't recognize them, but my eyes were open."

"We took her to the doctor and they said she's fine," Kaito said.

"Okay, so she's fine *and* she's talking to someone," Jana said.

*"He's on the street where you lived,"* Cami said.

"Who is?" Jana asked.

"We don't know," Izabel said.

"Near my old house?" Cami said. "I want to go back to my old house. I don't like it here. I miss my house.

*"You can't go back there.*

"I know. My mom told me that."

"Maybe you should go to bed, Jana," Izabel said. "We'll stay with her."

Jana got up, but she said, "I want to stay with her, too. I can sleep in here."

"She'd keep you up," Kaito said. "You need to sleep." He looked at Izabel. "Everybody needs to get some sleep, yeah?"

"Oh, yeah, yeah," Izabel said. "I'll get ready for bed, too."

As she was walking Jana out of the room, Cami said, *"He's doing it again. They're going to die."*

Jana stopped. "What did she say?"

"Don't say that!

*"I'm sorry, Cami. They're defeated.*

"No." Cami started crying.

"Why is she saying that?" Jana said.

"I don't know," Kaito said.

"Wake her up!" Jana said.

"They told us not to," Izabel said, holding Jana back from the bed. "But we used to, and she never remembered. She doesn't know. She's only sleeping."

"That's stupid. You sound stupid. You can hear her, can't you?"

"Please, Jana. There's nothing we can do."

Jana dropped to the floor.

"What would you have us do?" Izabel pleaded.

"I don't know," Jana said.

"It might be nothing," Izabel said.

"It might be nothing," Jana repeated.

"Let's get you to bed now," Izabel said.

Jana got up and left the room without her.

Kaito whispered, "We'll know in the morning."

But Izabel didn't respond. She went to her purse, touched the tip of her middle finger to the gun's grip, and then she stuck one of the orange-tasting pills on her tongue.

JANA RAN INTO their room in the morning. It was the first time she'd come in while they were asleep. "Izabel!" she said. "Kaito!" She was holding a tablet.

"What is it?" Kaito said.

"He did kill again last night. Is this your old street? Is this where you lived?" she asked, crawling onto the bed to show them.

Kaito said, "I don't have my contacts in—give it to Izabel."

Izabel looked at it. Her voice came out gravelly: "It is." She sat up and took a drink of water. It was the house to the right of theirs. They knew them. They were a couple about their age. They had twins, a little older than Cami. Two boys. Not identical. One came out looking like the mother and one the father. The mother had told Izabel that twins ran in their family, and she cried talking about her twin uncles, who had died when the trees turned.

"So Cami wasn't dreaming," Jana said.

"We don't know that," Izabel said, still sounding hoarse.

"But she said—or whoever she was talking to said—he was on your old street and he killed them, and he did. It's right here."

Kaito and Izabel didn't say anything.

"Call the police!" Jana said. "Call Inspector Paz!"

"And tell her what?" Izabel said. "My four-year-old dreams vague details of the attacks?" It came out meaner than she meant it.

Jana started to cry. "You have to do something."

"If it were information we could call in, we would," Kaito said.

"Last night she said which street!"

"But that was the first time," Kaito said.

"Wait," Jana said. "You knew about my family? Is that why you were there?"

"No," Izabel said.

"Don't lie to me!"

"I'm not lying." Izabel's voice was clearing up now. "That was by chance. I was out. Kaito was at home with Cami."

"And Cami," Kaito said, "mostly just screamed, because Izabel was there, and she thought he was going to kill her."

"We don't know that," Izabel said.

"How many times has she done this?" Jana asked.

"We're not sure," Izabel said.

"Every time?"

"Not the first one," Kaito said.

"Then, then"—Jana started to cry harder now—"you could've stopped him before he got to my family."

"We couldn't. She's asleep. She doesn't know what she's saying," Izabel said.

"And who would believe us?" Kaito said.

"I believe it! I believe her!"

"Why are you all yelling?" Cami said at the doorway. "Did Jana sleep in here? I thought we all had to sleep in our own beds."

Jana wiped the tears off her face.

"She didn't sleep in here, mi amor. We were just talking," Izabel said, patting a spot on the bed.

Cami climbed up. "Slumber party!" she said.

Kaito smiled at her.

"Do you remember anything from last night?" Jana asked.

"Daddy read me the book about the animals who wouldn't try sushi."

"I mean, during the night. Do you remember anything?"

"When I was sleeping? How could I remember that?"

"Not even a dream?"

"Nope," Cami said. "Did you have a dream?"

"No," Jana said.

"You see?" Izabel asked.

Jana lay down between them all with her face down in a pillow, and Cami copied her.

## CHAPTER TWENTY-TWO

I t was clear to Izabel and Kaito that killing their neighbors was a message to Izabel, for her.

They called Paz and she said, "I know that. You think I can't put two and two together?" But she also said, "Still, could've been random."

Izabel wasn't sure if Paz had said that for Izabel's sake, to calm her, or because of the police's liability around the whole mess, but Izabel found herself repeating it to herself. *Still, could've been random.*

That morning Izabel had to take Cami to therapy. She checked her tablet for alerts. Hickory and alder trees were peaking, it said.

Kaito stopped Izabel before the doors. "Thank you for making us go to Andy's, for not letting us go back for anything." Cami hugged his leg. "I didn't get it," he said. "Not all the way."

Izabel would've stood on her toes and kissed him if her mask wasn't already on. She touched his arm.

As they walked out to the car, she held Cami's little hand and muttered into her mask, "Could've been random. Could've been random."

CAMI WAS HAPPY, and happy to be seeing Opa again. She spent the car ride looking out the window, pointing at trees.

"What kind of tree is that?" she asked.

Izabel leaned over. "That one is a maple tree."

"What kind of tree is that?"

"Also a maple."

"That one?"

"That one, too. All the ones that look like that."

"That one?"

"Ask me about one that doesn't look like that, and I'll tell you what it is."

Cami looked around.

"That one!"

"An evergreen."

"That one?"

"Let's do something else," Izabel said.

Cami plopped down on the seat.

"Why don't people talk about trees?"

"You know why."

"I forget."

"I've told you how your abuelita died. You remember?"

"Yes. She couldn't breathe. That's why our masks are important."

"Yes. And the trees are why she couldn't breathe."

"And flowers."

"Yes, lots of plants. But mostly the trees."

"I still like trees," Cami said with her head down.

"Of course you do. I still like trees. They didn't do it on purpose."

Cami stopped and looked at her mother the way she did when she was deciding whether Izabel was telling the truth. "Yes, they did," she said.

"No, honey."

"Yes! Mom!"

"Okay, okay. I'm sorry. Okay."

The two of them looked out of the windows. Pollen had dried around tracks of water all over the car, from when it was washed. Little imperfect yellow outlines.

"If they did it on purpose," Izabel said, "then I don't like them."

Cami didn't say anything.

OPA GOT THEM from the waiting room and brought them into her office. "How are you two doing?"

"We're good," Izabel said. She put her bag down next to the chair, making sure the gun didn't show. It hadn't left her bag since the station.

"And you, Cami?" Opa said.

"Great!"

"Great!" Opa said back, spreading her arms. "We have a lot to do today. Want to know why?"

Cami nodded.

"Today is all about you."

"Okay!" Cami said.

"I want to start with an exercise and then I'm going to ask you a lot of questions and we'll color a little. Does that sound good to you?"

"I like to exercise," Cami said.

"Not that kind of exercise, more like an activity."

"But you said exercise."

"It's actually another definition of exercise."

"Oh, I know about that. A teacher at school likes to say 'neat,' but it doesn't mean she wants us to clean up."

"Exactly right. Just like that. Okay, are you ready to get started?"

Cami nodded.

"You're going to start by putting your hands together like this." Opa put her right hand on top of her left hand, leaving a little space between them, resting them in her lap. "That's your elevator."

Cami put her hands out and looked in her elevator.

"Now I want you to put your elevator in your lap and imagine you're inside it with a friend—anyone you like."

"Should she close her eyes?" Izabel asked.

"Up to her," Opa said. "Have you picked someone, Cami?"

"Yes."

"What's your friend's name?"

"It doesn't have a name," Cami said.

"It?"

"It's my tree friend."

"Cami," Izabel started.

"No, it's okay. Your tree friend is great. If you can imagine the tree small enough to fit in your elevator. Can you do that?"

Cami nodded.

"Okay, now I want you to take a deep breath in, and as you do, your elevator is going to move up your body to the top of your chest."

Cami took a big breath in and the elevator flew up to her chin.

"That was great. Very good. But I think we might have scared your tree friend, you know? Because trees aren't used to moving very much, are they?"

Cami shook her head.

"So now I want you to do a long breath out and as you breathe out, I want you to move your elevator back down to your lap."

Cami breathed out and lowered her hands back down, slower this time.

"Great. Now I want you to do it a few more times. When you breathe in, take your elevator up. When you breathe out, take your elevator down. And try to go nice and slow and steady."

Cami very carefully raised and lowered her elevator and it almost lined up with her breathing.

"Izabel, why don't you put your hands around Cami's hands and try to match your breathing to hers."

"Okay," Izabel said. She turned toward Cami and put her hands below and above Cami's hands. Cami looked right into Izabel's eyes, taking the exercise very seriously. Izabel smiled at her, and then she tried to match Cami's little breaths.

Izabel breathed in through her nose, and when she breathed out, she closed her lips some and sort of blew the air out. She didn't realize she was doing it until Cami imitated her. Cami's big breath in, through her nose, drew her nostrils in and changed the shape of her cheeks. When she blew the air out, she pursed her lips into crinkles.

Izabel's face started to feel hot. Cami was so cute and sweet and earnest. Izabel wasn't sure she'd done anything as earnestly in her whole life.

Opa stopped them. "That was perfect! What a great job. And now that's something you can do at home whenever you want. Do you remember what we were going to do next?"

"Questions and coloring," Cami said.

"That's right. Good memory!" Opa brought out a few sheets of paper that all had the same outline of a thermometer. It was numbered one through ten. "Do you know what this is?"

"No," Cami said.

"We used to use thermometers that looked like this to measure how hot something was, or someone. Have you had your temperature taken at the doctor's?"

"It didn't look like that."

"Right. This is what they used to look like, but now they have newer ones that are safer. But this is my special thermometer and it measures how scared someone is feeling. I'm going to ask you some questions about things in your life and I want you to point at a place on the thermometer. If it was something that you don't feel scared about at all, you would point to one. Like, your elevator, how do you feel about that?"

Cami stood up and pointed to the one.

"Perfect."

"Now if it was something that scared you, the most scared you've ever been, then you'd point to ten. And how about if you were just kind of scared? Where would you point then?"

Cami pointed to the four.

"Yes! Okay. Are you ready to get started?"

Cami jumped around saying, "Yeah, yeah, yeah," on each jump.

"Alright," Opa said. "You might have to think about these, so you'll want to stay still, okay?"

Cami stopped jumping.

"How do you feel about your mom?"

Cami pointed to the one.

"How do you feel about your dad?"

She pointed to the one again.

"How do you feel about Jana?"

She pointed to the one again.

"How do you feel about your teachers at school?"

She pointed to the one again. "This is a lot of ones," Cami said.

"That's good," Opa said. "Is there anyone in your life who

makes you feel scared? At school or at home or some place I haven't mentioned?"

"No," Cami said.

"Okay, good. So back to our thermometer. How do you feel about your new house?"

Cami pointed to the three, and then the six, and then the four. "I'm not sure."

"That's okay. I'm going to get another one of my doctor's tools." Opa brought out a very large, circular magnifying glass with a wooden handle, like in a cartoon.

"Oooh," Cami said.

"I'm going to start down at your toes and move this all over your body, and I want you to let me know if that's somewhere that you feel scared, okay? Will you sit down for me?"

Cami sat back down and Opa put the magnifying glass over one of Cami's feet. When Opa leaned over, her necklace hung away from her body and her hair fell forward over the sides of her face. Cami batted a piece of Opa's hair.

"Cami!" Izabel said.

Cami pulled her hand back.

"It's okay," Opa said. "Cami, when you think about the new house, and you feel scared, do you feel scared here?"

Cami shook her head.

Opa moved the magnifying glass up to her knee. "How about here?"

Cami shook her head again.

"You know what? This might work better if you hold the magnifying glass. Do you think you can do it?"

Cami nodded, and she took the magnifying glass from Opa.

"Why don't you start at your fingers and move up your arm?"

Cami did and then she held it over her chest.

"Any of those spots feeling scared?"

"No," Cami said, bending her head down to look through the magnifying glass.

Then she got to her stomach and stopped.

"Is that where you feel scared?"

Cami nodded.

"Okay. That's good to know. Let's put the magnifying glass down and we'll use it again if we need to. I have another thermometer question."

Cami jumped to her feet again.

"How do you feel about the hospital, Cami?"

Cami pointed to the ten.

"Wow, that's really scared. Should we use the magnifying glass again?"

"Yeah," Cami said, already sitting down, sticking her hand out for it.

"So let's start at your belly this time, do you still feel scared there?"

Cami nodded.

Opa moved the magnifying glass up to her chest.

Cami nodded again.

"What about up here?" Opa said, moving it over Cami's forehead.

"Yeah," Cami said.

"Do you know what you can do when you feel scared? You can get out your elevator and move it up and down, like we did earlier. That will help you feel not-scared because it calms down your chest and your head."

"And my belly?"

"When your chest and your head feel better, your belly usually starts feeling better after that. The next time you come back, we're going to play with toys, but can I give you a little homework?"

"Yeah."

"I want you to take this sheet of paper with my special thermometer on it, and draw something that you think is scary and then color in the thermometer for what scary level it's at. Does that sound fun?"

"Like a monster?"

"Yup. Do you like monsters?"

Cami nodded and jumped again.

"Me too," Opa said. "Izabel, would you mind staying after? I can have someone take Cami to the play center, if that's okay."

"Yes, yes, yes," Cami said.

"Okay," Izabel said.

Opa called someone on the phone and a nice woman came up and took Cami out of the office.

## CHAPTER TWENTY-THREE

Once Cami left, Opa said, "You haven't called to set up an appointment for yourself."

"No," Izabel said.

"I have time now."

"I don't know."

"I saw the news," Opa said. "I know this is difficult."

"It was our neighbors."

"Your old neighbors or your new neighbors?"

"Old."

"This is why you moved?"

"Yes."

"So this is a sign that he doesn't know where you are now? That your move worked?"

"Yes."

"But you feel guilty."

"I do."

"He might have killed twice as many families by now if you hadn't come across him that night. You probably saved people."

"I wish I'd killed him."

"Would you have been able to kill him?"

"No."

"Then what's the point of wishing that?"

"I just wish I had."

"I wish I knew who he was so I could stop him."

"But you didn't have the chance."

"*You* didn't have the chance! Because you were in his proximity doesn't mean you had the chance."

They didn't say anything for a few seconds, and Izabel didn't like pauses like that. "I'm scared for Cami," she said.

"I think everyone's scared for everyone right now. The whole town is scared."

"It doesn't feel like that."

"No? All these people applied to leave and then some left. That was because of fear for their families and themselves."

"But being here. Day to day. Everyone's going about their lives. There's no big change. It's minor. It's a shift more than a change."

"Haven't you talked to people about it? I've talked to people, and there seems to be a change in them and how they're feeling."

"I think that's more about how much they want things to have changed. They want us to have had a real, robust change in response to violence, to the return of violence, but there hasn't been one."

"Why do you think that is?"

"That doesn't matter."

"It matters to me," Opa said.

"I haven't thought it through. I'm talking shit."

"Then think it through. Take a minute."

But Izabel didn't actually need a minute. It rushed out of her:

"Maybe because there was more violence around us to start with than people realize. What the trees did, and are doing, can be seen as violence. Sickness is a violence. Death is a violence. Murder—criminal violence—it's not so different."

"Okay, so if that's not enough to have made a change, but I'm saying that I see a change, what's that from?"

"Maybe that's because of the violence of randomness."

"Were you scared of that?" Opa asked.

"I was, but not as much. Not as much as everyone else was. Not as much as I should've been."

"Why is that?"

"I don't know. Randomness is chaos, which is inherent to the universe and we survive it everyday, killer or not."

"Does it bother you that it didn't seem like people realized how violent it was *before* the killer started killing people?"

Izabel hung her head, shook it like she was shaking something out of her hair. "Yes," she said.

IZABEL PICKED UP Cami at the play center. They'd given her a Pokémon card of Scatterbug and she was so delighted by it. "Do you want to go to the mall?" Izabel asked.

"Wait, Mom," Cami said. "Watch this."

So Izabel watched as Cami shook the Pokémon card over her head. Then she brought it back down and looked at it, disappointed.

"I thought it would change. Maybe I didn't do it right."

"Why did you think it would change?"

"Will you shake it, Mom? Super fast?"

"Sure, I will. But it's not going to change."

Cami waited while Izabel shook it as fast as she could over her head.

"See?" Izabel said.

"Someone at school said they did."

"Maybe they were talking about how Pokémon evolve?"

"Yeah!" Cami said.

"But the cards don't change."

"Oh," Cami said, her face fallen.

"Let's go to the mall, okay? And we can look up what Scatterbug evolves into in the car?"

"Can we look it up first and then go to the mall?"

"Yeah," Izabel said. She brought it up on her tablet. Scatterbug evolved into Spewpa, which evolved into Vivillon.

"Vivillon is super pretty," Cami said.

"I really like Scatterbug. I think Scatterbug is probably the best card ever."

"It's not even evolved!"

"I know. But that's how I feel." Izabel smiled at her.

Cami was on the verge of understanding what Izabel was doing—this sort of exaggerated falsity, about a trivial thing, to cheer a child—but only on the verge.

At the mall, they got a snack. Near them, on the wall, were two posters. One was for a community theater group that was holding auditions for *The Music Man*. Izabel wanted to pull it off the wall and show it to Opa, like a kind of proof of how unconcerned everyone was. The other was a new monster poster—an Oni this time, one horn coming out of its head, and wearing a tiger's pelt over its penis, if a penis was even what it had between its giant legs.

"Is that the Oni that Momotarō defeated?" Cami asked.

"I don't know," Izabel said. But for the first time, Izabel didn't resent the image, and its intrusion into the public spaces of her life. She thought that, maybe, the artist wasn't trying to scare people, but only trying to understand, to understand the monstrous and the grotesque, the aberrant and the inexplicable.

Izabel played a Match 3 game on her tablet while Cami slowly ate a banana. The ads that came up during this game were for playing slots. And the slots were Pompeii-themed. To get a jackpot, you matched erupting volcanoes. Izabel was part of one catastrophic event mocking another.

"Mom!" Cami said.

"Yes!" Izabel said.

"If I were a snake Pokémon, my snake attack would be *very much hidden venomous bigger.*"

"Wow, that's a cool attack."

"Yeah."

"Are you done with that banana?"

"Yeah," Cami said, and she put the end of the banana in Izabel's hand. It was warm, and Izabel had to pretend it didn't disgust her, and then she had to decide whether to eat it or throw it away.

Izabel put it in her mouth and immediately regretted it. Cami was already playing a game with her hands, so Izabel spat the banana back out into a napkin.

One of Cami's hands said to the other, "I made you!"

Izabel raised an eyebrow at her.

"Don't look at me," Cami said, in an old-school Batman voice. "Only I can look at me."

Izabel laughed, but Cami kept her face serious.

When they were done in the food court, Izabel dropped Cami off at the mall's daycare, and she went to the privacy pods. Sasha was the only one there and Izabel was glad she didn't have to make small talk with anyone.

In the pod, she began to write.

Dear Cami,

I used to hold my breath going past graveyards as a child. Not just me. Kids did that, as a game. Even though some graveyards were too long for it. A kid at school said you got a wish afterwards, if you could do it, but that didn't seem right. Another said it was about bad luck or good luck. To me it seemed respectful, and that was enough. Your dad and I once talked about it and he said, the way he heard it, you were supposed to hold your breath past a graveyard until the first white house, so you didn't breathe in a bad spirit. I think I've breathed in a hundred bad spirits.

She took another piece of paper.

Dear Cami,

During the Turning, they didn't have drills at schools, to go to the gym, or wherever the best air system was. They should've been that prepared, but they weren't. It was hard to imagine the children dying by mass suffocation, in a kind of poisoning—though, as a Jew, of course I had imagined it.

She took another.

Dear Cami,

I thought you would grow up spending a lot of time looking out windows and asking me questions about animals and what it used to be like. I was going to tell you about birdcalls and squirrels and stopping to look at caterpillars and accidentally racing crickets that didn't know how to get out of your way on the sidewalk. But that's not what it's like with you at all. And I think I'm grateful for that.

Izabel shredded all of the papers at once, and she left before her hour was up.

NEXT SHE TOOK herself to the acupuncture clinic, like a series of privacy pods itself, but with white walls and more settings for the lighting. In the waiting room, Izabel walked to the sign-in desk. The man there was so tall that he couldn't be the killer. He didn't wear a nametag and Izabel was relieved not to know another man's name.

"Can someone see me today?" she asked.

"Do you have an appointment?"

"No. I was hoping you could fit me in."

"Let me see." He messaged someone with his tablet. Someone messaged back. "Room four," he said.

"Thank you," Izabel said.

In room four, Izabel took off her shoes and lay down on the bed. The acupuncturist came in, a very tall woman who Izabel hadn't seen before. Izabel wondered whether she was married to the receptionist and if they had very tall children together.

The woman took Izabel's left hand in a handshake with her own left hand and used her right hand to feel the pulses in Izabel's left wrist, focusing on a pulse along Izabel's radius. Then she walked around the table and felt Izabel's right wrist.

"Sit up," she said. "And turn."

Izabel put her legs over the side of the bed and rested her feet on a stool.

The woman lifted Izabel's shirt. "Round your back," she said, and Izabel did.

The woman followed her fingers up Izabel's spine, down Izabel's spine, up again, stopping at a certain vertebra, moving out from there, placing a needle to the left and then to the right of it. She placed eight needles in total.

"Lie down on your side slowly," the woman said. And as Izabel did, the woman met her head with two pillows. Then she moved a long pillow between Izabel's knees and put a blanket over her legs.

"Thank you," Izabel said.

"Twenty minutes," the woman said, and she left the room.

Izabel thought about the killer. She thought about Kaito and Cami and Jana. She thought about what Opa had said. She thought about Andy and Hestia. She thought about swimming. She thought about the man who made sandwiches.

The woman came back in, looked at her back, said, "You're still making work of them," and left again.

Within seconds, the left side of her back seemed to blossom into chills. She wondered if any one pin was the center of it. The chills moved out in waves. And then the right side of her back went, too, and the chills moved up to her shoulders. The waves grew stronger and more uncomfortable. As she considered if she should yell out about them, they settled, and Izabel fell asleep.

"Good," Izabel heard the woman say.

Izabel opened her eyes.

"Sit up."

Izabel did and the woman removed the pins.

"You need a few more points," she said. "But I'll only touch them."

"Okay," Izabel said.

"Lie back." The woman felt Izabel's wrists again and then set about her body. She touched a point on Izabel's ankle, on the side of her foot, on the top of her head. "Do any still hurt?"

"My head," Izabel said.

She touched the point on her head again with the needle. "Better?"

"Yes," Izabel said, surprised.

"A point of disharmony," the woman said.

## CHAPTER TWENTY-FOUR

Izabel picked up Cami from the mall's childcare and brought her home. They said hello to Jana, who was studying at the table. But Izabel wasn't all the way pleasant with either of the girls. She didn't feel like herself. She needed to talk to Paz.

Izabel gave Cami a bowl of graham crackers and put on *Miraculous* for her, a French television show about a girl who turns into Ladybug, a ladybug-styled superhero with a weapon that resembles a yo-yo but that no one calls a yo-yo.

Izabel slipped into her bedroom and called Paz. She didn't even say hello to her. She asked, "Didn't you have surveillance on our old street?"

"I can't comment on an ongoing investigation," Paz said.

"What?"

"I can't comment."

"But before—"

"You're in a different position now, Izabel. Look, do you need something?"

"No," Izabel said.

"Then I have work to do." She hung up.

Izabel came back out to the living room, still not sure how she was feeling, and very sure she didn't want to do the self-reflection needed to figure it out.

"Snuggle?" Cami said.

Izabel sat next to her on the couch and Cami snuggled into her. Izabel spaced out to the same sequence of music, over and over, each time the girl turned into Ladybug. The spot on her head still hurt. She rubbed it. She lay down, sleepy, bending her legs to fit on the couch. Cami moved to sit behind Izabel's legs, like Izabel had created a tiny wall, a fort, for Cami to hide in.

CAMI TRIED TO wake Izabel when she was thirsty. Before Izabel had opened her eyes, Jana said, "You could've asked me for that. You didn't have to bother your mom."

"Sorry," Cami said.

Izabel heard Jana open the fridge and pour the juice and bring the cup over to Cami. She heard the same show still on. She thought about how she could fall back to sleep, sleep the whole afternoon away, but she wanted to be able to fall asleep that night, to feel tired, like a normal person.

She opened her eyes, reached for her tablet, and sat up.

"You are awake!" Cami said.

Izabel didn't want to talk yet, but she kissed the side of Cami's head.

In her app, she left it on 2017, but then she tapped *Infamous*. The first headline was "Serial Killer Fears: Area of Tampa on Edge After 3 Killings." She felt the start of a panic attack in her chest. The article named the victims, their ages, and the dates they were shot. It described how the community was responding, how bus routes had been changed, the extreme degree to which police presence was heightened. Even the FBI and ATF had come to help. The article ended with a quote from a woman who heard gunshots. No conclusion after that. Nothing.

She wondered if it helped them, all the officers on the streets—if that could really make a killer stop, disappear. And if he disappeared, then what? She could look that up. Find out if they caught him. But she liked how, twenty-five years ago, Tampa was right where her town was now.

Before the end of the article, it mentioned that the mayor didn't use the term *serial killer*, but that the police chief did. It didn't explain why. Izabel thought about looking that up, too, but the semantics wouldn't do her any good.

The app had a link to a video: the residents of Tampa, marching and chanting. "Whose streets?" The volume came on too loud. "Our streets!"

"What's that?" Cami asked.

Izabel turned down the volume as fast as she could. "Nothing."

"It looks like a parade."

"Yes." She tapped back to the home screen. "You want to look at something on here with me?"

"Yeah."

"What do you want to look at?"

"Trees."

Izabel moaned.

"What? I like them."

"I know. It's fine. What should I look up?"

"A pumpkin tree!"

"There aren't pumpkin trees."

"But pumpkins are a fruit. They have seeds inside."

"Pumpkins grow on vines. I can show you orange trees or apple trees?"

"Okay."

"Okay, which?"

"Orange trees," Cami said.

"Together, they're called an orange grove."

"Is it called an apple grove?"

"No, that's an orchard."

"Have you been to one?" Cami asked.

"Not a grove, but I went apple picking in an orchard when I was little."

"When you were four?"

"Maybe. And when I was a little older than four."

"Five?"

"Yeah." Izabel laughed. "Maybe five."

"Do maple trees grow fruit?"

"No. We called their seeds whirlybirds."

"Why?"

"I'll show you that, okay?" Izabel pulled up a video of maple seeds floating to the ground. "We used to pick them up and break them down the middle, and peel them open and stick them to our noses."

"That's silly."

"Very silly."

"What about evergreens?" Cami asked.

"They drop pinecones."

"What do other trees drop?"

"Acorns and walnuts," and Izabel tickled her as she said, "and monkey brains!"

"Monkey brains?!"

"I don't know why we called them that. I'll show you a picture of those, too."

When Cami saw, she said, "Brains aren't green! They're pink."

"Yeah, you're right."

"Do walnuts hurt when they fall out of a tree?"

"They do. My neighbor, when I was growing up, had a walnut tree. They'd pay me to go around and collect as many as I could in a bucket."

"How much?"

"A dollar."

"That's not a lot."

"It's not nothing."

"Is that what Daddy does?"

"Sometimes, yeah. He harvests all sorts of fruits and nuts and vegetables and pumpkins."

"Pumpkins?"

"Yeah."

Izabel laid her head back and closed her eyes again. She wondered why no one in their town had organized some sort of march through the mall, a chance to yell, *Whose streets? Our streets!* in unison. It made her think that more people were like her than she'd thought—a little hopeless and a little tired.

THAT NIGHT EVERYONE but Cami was on edge as bedtime approached, all waiting to see what would happen, what Cami might say in her sleep.

Cami bounced around the living room. "Daddy told me they used to name streets after trees!"

"That's true," Izabel said.

"Do you want to hear some?" Cami said. "Poplar, Sycamore, Spruce, Chestnut."

"Wow," Izabel said.

"Have you heard of all *those* trees before?"

"I have actually."

"Have you seen them?"

"I don't know."

"We should draw pictures of trees!" Cami said.

"It's getting late, honey."

"Just one!"

"Okay," Izabel said. "Everyone get your tablets. But then bed, Cami."

"Yes!" Cami said.

They all sat down at the table with their tablets and styluses. "Let's draw a sycamore," Cami said. "Set a timer, Mommy."

"Okay, two minutes?" Izabel said.

"Yes," Cami said.

"Should I bring up a picture?" Kaito asked.

"I need to look at it," Jana said.

Cami was already drawing.

Izabel drew a picture of a tree that was leaning over, with a face, a big open mouth, and it had vomited. The vomit was mid-air. She wrote SICK-A-MORE above it.

The timer went off and they all stopped.

"Eww!" Cami said, looking at Izabel's.

"Get it?" Izabel said. "*Sick*-a-more."

Cami let out a big laugh. "I get it! Because it's sick!" And she let out another big single laugh. It made everyone else laugh.

Then they all made a fuss over Cami's drawing. Izabel wasn't sure how big of a fuss to make over Jana's picture, even though it seemed exceptional to her, the detailing of the branches in and out of clumps of leaves.

Cami told her twice: "You're really good at drawing, Jana! You're really good at drawing!"

"Okay, time for bed now," Izabel said. And Cami didn't argue this time. And they went to get ready.

When Cami was asleep, and Kaito had gone to bed, and Izabel had returned to the kitchen to unwind with an old episode of *What Not to Wear*, Jana came out of her room.

"Hi, Jana," Izabel said. "You okay?"

"I want to sleep with Cami tonight," Jana said.

"Sleep or stay up worrying?"

"I think I'd stay up either way."

"You won't wake her?"

Jana shook her head.

"Then I don't see why not," Izabel said.

Jana hugged her before she'd finished.

Izabel held her and said, "You have to figure out a way to get some sleep, at some point, even with everything that's going on."

Jana pulled back and said, "I will."

Izabel kissed her on the forehead as she let go of her, and then she immediately worried she'd crossed a line they'd never discussed.

## CHAPTER TWENTY-FIVE

Jana fell asleep despite herself. The night was quiet. No rain or wind. When Cami began talking, it stood out clearly, but still everyone slept.

*"He is out again,"* she said. *"He is near where you live."*

"I don't want to talk about him. I want to know if you've ever broken something."

Jana began to wake up.

*"Broken how?*

"Like dropped something and it broke into pieces.

*"No, I haven't. Cami, this is important."*

Jana rushed to Izabel and Kaito's room. She shouted, "She's doing it again," but she didn't stay as they woke up.

Back in Cami's room, Jana heard, *"He is only one street away, one closer to where the sun rises."*

Jana grabbed her mask, ran to Izabel's purse, grabbed the gun, and ran out the doors of the dome.

Izabel ran out of her room when she heard the sound of the doors. She heard Cami still talking. Kaito was a step behind her.

"Call Paz," she told him.

"Where's Jana?" he asked.

"I'm going to get her—call Paz."

Izabel put her mask on and ran out the door. "Jana!" she yelled. Her voice was easier to hear than she thought it would be.

"He's only one street away," Jana yelled back. She was fast, cutting between houses. Izabel could just make her out in the dark. She saw the gun in her hand.

Izabel followed her. The concrete was rough against her bare feet. "We can't be out here this long in these masks. You know that. Jana!"

And then Jana froze, ahead of Izabel, in the middle of the street. She raised the gun.

"What are you doing?" Izabel said, out of breath. But then she saw him, too. He was between two houses on the other side of the street, not moving. He had heard them. He was looking back at them.

"I'm going to kill him," Jana said.

"If you miss, you'll rip through a house and kill a family yourself," Izabel said, finally reaching Jana, standing behind her.

Jana lowered the gun a little, then raised it again. "I have to try."

Izabel started coughing and couldn't stop, but she shook her head. Jana and Izabel both started to cry because of the pollen.

"We've been out here too long," Izabel got out between coughs.

Jana stomped her foot quickly as if she were stamping out a small fire. She put the gun in Izabel's hands. "Then you do it," she said.

But once Izabel had the gun, she picked Jana up off the ground and ran with her.

Jana began kicking. She screamed, "We have to go back! He was right in front of us!"

Izabel held her tighter. Her eyelids were starting to swell. She lined herself up with an opening between houses and closed her eyes as she ran. Then she opened them and lined herself up again, closing her eyes for the longest stretches she could.

"No!" Jana sobbed.

Izabel made it back to the house, and she put Jana's feet on the ground without letting go of her. The gun was still in her hand, but only because she didn't know what else to do with it. She couldn't imagine the killer getting ahold of that, too.

Kaito rushed out of Cami's room with her in his arms. Cami was holding onto his neck and Izabel couldn't tell if she was awake or asleep. She'd been crying—Izabel could make out that much.

Izabel pulled Jana into the front room while Kaito grabbed things from the kitchen. He put Cami and a bottle of water and a hand towel on the floor next to Izabel and Jana, who had finally given up fighting Izabel and was slumped against her. Then he pressed the button, sealed the plastic sheet, and turned on the filter.

They moved Jana's head back, took off her mask, and poured water over her eyes. Izabel took off her own mask and held it high while Kaito poured water over her eyes, too.

The filter finally turned green.

Kaito poured water on the towel and used it to wipe off Jana as she curled her body away from them. There was pollen in her ears, in the creases of her neck and eyelids, all over her hair.

Izabel gestured to Kaito to get her own hair, too, and he did. The towel was yellow now. And they heard the sirens coming.

"Cami said you saw him," Kaito said.

Izabel nodded.

"She said you had a gun, but I didn't believe it until I saw you with it." He looked at it behind her now.

Izabel nodded again.

"Can you talk?"

She shook her head.

"Are you okay?"

She nodded, but also shrugged, because she didn't really know.

"Did he follow you?"

She shook her head and began to cry again, because she didn't know that either.

"I called Paz and she said she would come, and Cami said a car was coming, but she was getting more and more upset, and then she said you were coming back, and she hasn't said anything since."

Izabel ran her hand over Cami's hair. She was waiting to hear the rip of their house's plastic, from the killer having followed her, but instead the people from the ambulance rushed in.

The EMTs got them all into the ambulance. Izabel recognized them both, Uzair and An. The family was quiet as the men worked together to get oxygen masks on Izabel and Jana. At the hospital, they took them to the basement, cut them out of their pollen-stained clothes, showered them, and got them into hospital gowns, the same way Izabel and Kaito used to do with survivors coming to the hospital.

Upstairs, they were placed in adjacent beds and nurses took over. They squeezed a serum into Izabel and Jana's eyes and told them they wouldn't be able to open them for at least an hour. Next the nurses placed soft gauze over their closed eyes and wrapped it tight to their heads.

The nurses told them about the doses of albuterol they were giving them to open up their airways, that it could make them shake.

Kaito kept saying that he was there with them as he held their hands.

Next Izabel and Jana were given IVs, "to make it easier," the nurses said, "for any further steps." The first step was to give them antihistamines. The nurses said it could make them feel drowsy. Izabel fell asleep thinking about how she couldn't hear Cami in the room.

## CHAPTER TWENTY-SIX

Izabel woke up when a nurse was taking the gauze off her eyes. Kaito was there, smiling at her, bleary-eyed.

The nurse led her through a quick eye exam. Izabel held a small piece of black plastic over one eye and then the other.

Then the nurse went over to unwrap the gauze from Jana's head.

"Where is Cami?" Izabel asked. Her voice was hardly there.

"They took her from me," Kaito said. He started to cry. "They said it was protocol."

"What?"

"I think they're going to take Jana, too. We're in a special area now, for pollen exposure. But once she can be moved."

"No," Izabel said hoarsely. "No." She tossed her head. "I want Cami."

"I know," he said. He knew she was still waking up. He held her hand until she got her bearings.

She wiped her tears away. "Why?" she said.

"They said it's about child endangerment."

"The gun?"

"Yeah," he said. He leaned down and lowered his voice. "Where did the gun come from?"

"I took it from the police station."

"Why? Why would you do that?"

"It made me feel safe."

"I wish you'd told me."

"Me too," said Izabel. "But I didn't bring the gun out there. Jana did."

"How? Did you tell her about it?"

"No. I didn't know she knew about it."

They didn't say anything for a minute. They watched Jana taking her eye exam.

Then Izabel said, "I'm sorry."

"You stopped him," Kaito said.

She didn't understand.

"He didn't kill anyone tonight. You saved a family, and we're all okay." He squeezed her hand.

A doctor came over. DR. MAZUR—his nametag hung on a lanyard. He was the exact size and shape of the killer. Izabel tried not to focus on that. She tried to be rational. She told herself, *If he was the killer, he wouldn't be back at work so fast.*

"Jana's eyes are seeing well," Dr. Mazur said. "She's out of the woods for any other repercussions from prolonged pollen exposure. We're going to move her to the children's wing. Someone will be in touch with you soon about when you can see her."

Izabel and Kaito nodded, knowing the gravity of what had happened, but Jana yelled out, "I want to stay with them."

Dr. Mazur said, "That's not possible—"

"I want to stay with them. I won't go with you!"

"Please," he said. "We're only following the protocols set in place."

"Get a woman," Izabel said, realizing Jana had noticed it, too, how Dr. Mazur's outline matched the one they had seen between the domes.

Kaito understood somehow. He stood up. "Our daughter would be more comfortable with a woman nurse or doctor. This has nothing to do with you, but with what's best for her. She won't protest again if you get a woman."

Dr. Mazur looked at Jana, and she nodded. So he left.

Izabel said, "We'll come get you soon."

"You're not mad?" Jana said.

Izabel shook her head.

Kaito said, "You were very brave and I'm proud of you. But next time we work together."

A few women staff members came in and wheeled Jana off in her bed.

IZABEL GOT DRESSED. She and Kaito were asked to wait in what looked like a break room, with a table and chairs and a small fridge.

When Paz came in, Opa was with her.

"So you call me in the middle of the night," Paz started, "and tell me the killer is near your house, that your wife and Jana are out in the street somewhere, and I come out in a car and see you, Izabel, sprinting through the street, carrying Jana over your shoulder back toward your house. So I circle the block and I see him. Well, I can't believe it. Same suit you described, everything. But I haven't got backup. I hadn't put it all together, in the middle of the night. And I follow him the best I can, but as I can't get out of my car for too long, he eventually loses me. I'm beating myself up about this, mind you. I'm pissed off. And then I hear about all of this"—she gestured at the space between Kaito and Izabel—"and how there's a *gun* involved and I have to get child services involved. And lo and behold, I call child services and you're already seeing one of their therapists. Yeah. So now Opa's here with us. Thanks for coming, Opa."

Opa nodded.

"That was *my* night," Paz said. "Now I want to hear about yours. From the beginning. From earlier than that. From whenever you think is the right place to start. That's the part I want to hear it from."

Kaito said, "It seems like our daughter sleep-talks about the killer."

Paz smiled. "Yeah, I was wrong. Okay. We're not going to start there. Where'd you get the gun?"

"I took it from the police station," Izabel said.

"What's wrong with your voice?"

"I was outside too long."

"Chasing the murderer?"

"Chasing Jana."

"Yeah, chasing Jana who was chasing the murderer. So you took the gun from the police station. I guess I'll find that out soon enough when they run the serial number. Hell of a shit storm that's going to be. Thanks for that. Why'd you take the gun?"

"I don't know."

"Was it to kill him?"

"I guess it was to be able to kill him if I saw him again."

"You think you can recognize him?"

"No. But I'd be able to kill him if he came to my house."

"So your whole family would die, but you'd get your last shot in. That kind of thing?"

"Yes."

"Your voice is shit. When will it come back?"

"I don't know."

"The doctors didn't say?"

Izabel shook her head.

"Are your children safe, at your house, with you two?" Paz asked.

"Yes," Kaito said.

"I think I should ask the questions regarding that," Opa said.

Paz ignored her. "Did you know about the gun, Kaito?"

"No."

"Then you can't say, can you?"

"He might know where we live again, now," Izabel said.

"So you want me to use police resources to have you moved again? Because you keep magically crossing paths with the killer, even though you have no idea who he could be?"

"I'm not saying that," Izabel said.

"Which part?"

"I'm not saying you should move us again."

"What?" Kaito said.

"You should use me as bait," she said.

"We haven't talked about this," Kaito said.

"The rest of my family could stay at Andy's house."

"No—" Kaito said.

"Just you?" Paz interrupted.

"Just me."

"You can't decide where the girls will be staying," Opa interjected sharply. When she spoke again, her voice was softer. "I'm going to be interviewing Jana and Cami and making a determination about whether there is a concern about their welfare. I will also be interviewing each of you separately."

"Tell me again, the bit about your daughter's dreams," Paz said.

"She sleep-talks about the killer," Kaito said.

"What's that like?"

"Her eyes are closed and it sounds like she's holding a

conversation," he said. "Recently, she's been saying details about where, exactly, he is."

"That's how you knew where he was?"

"Jana heard Cami and ran out into the street to look for him."

"You knew about other attacks?"

"Kind of. Vaguely. Except the one before this. That time she said he was near our old house."

"You didn't call me then?"

"We didn't know what to say. It sounded ridiculous."

"It does sound ridiculous." Paz tapped the table. She turned to Opa. "I want the girl in a sleep study."

"I'm not sure—"

"I want her in a sleep study *tonight*, and I want you there observing."

"Okay," Opa said.

"And any specialist you think you need with you."

"I'll see to it."

"I have to go. I'm going to interview Jana before Opa does. I want to stop seeing you two, but it doesn't look like that's going to happen anytime soon, does it?"

"She's a minor," Kaito said. "Don't we have to be there?"

"Not when there are concerns for her safety," Paz said. And she left.

Opa said, "I'll let you observe my interviews with the girls after I'm done interviewing each of you."

"What's the sleep study like?" Izabel asked.

"We'll put a few sensors on Cami to monitor her as she sleeps. We'll also watch her and record her. You can sleep in the room with her, either of you."

"Even if we're found unfit?"

"Yes. If you're not there, and she has trouble sleeping, that could throw off the study. Unless Cami doesn't want you there, but I have a feeling that isn't the case."

"You don't think we're dangerous?"

"I think that if you are dangerous, it's not in a way that Cami would recognize."

"I love her. We love them both."

"You haven't known Jana very long at all," Opa said.

Izabel thought about that. She said, "Sometimes love is a decision."

Opa nodded.

"I told you things in confidence," Izabel said.

"I know. Maybe I shouldn't have offered to be your therapist." Opa took a big breath. "We're getting ahead of ourselves."

## CHAPTER TWENTY-SEVEN

Kaito and Izabel were brought back together again after their interviews. They were put in a room with a one-way mirror and a speaker so they could watch Opa with Cami.

Izabel wanted to know how Kaito's interview went, if they were asked the same questions, if he lied at any point. But that's not what Kaito wanted to know.

"You want to be bait?" he said.

"I don't *want* to be bait, but I want him caught. And it makes sense, doesn't it?"

"Can't they figure this out without us?" he said.

"I don't know."

He turned to watch Opa.

"Are you going to let me do it?" Izabel asked.

But he didn't respond. He watched Opa and Cami playing with LEGOs at a small table in the other room. There were a lot of hospital-related figurines and tiny hospital beds and what looked like a metal stand with a bag of fluids, except it was all gray, all just shapes, not discrete from each other. And then there were police figurines, EMTs, an ambulance. And there were superheroes, too, like Superman. And plenty of people not dressed like anything in particular. There was even a playground set that looked like something they had at home.

Opa asked Cami to put together the scene that scared her, and then Opa moved behind her.

"I'm going to tap on your shoulders, if that's okay."

"That's okay," Cami said.

As Cami built the scene—laying a woman in the hospital bed, putting police in a circle around the bed, putting two more people outside that circle of police—Opa tapped on Cami's shoulders, one after the other, perfectly rhythmic, perfectly paced, all her fingers out, and the flat of her middle finger doing the tapping.

"Can you describe the scene to me?" Opa said.

"It's my mom."

"Which one?"

"In the bed."

"Are you there?"

"That's me, and that's Dad."

"Why are you all the way over there?" Opa asked, still tapping.

"The police said we couldn't see her."

"Was your mom asleep or awake?"

"She looked hurt."

"If you could've changed that scene, any way you like, with any of the LEGOs here, how would you change it?"

Cami didn't pick up any of the superheroes. Instead she built something. Opa kept tapping as she put a few brown blocks together and then a few green blocks on top of them. It was a little tree. She placed it inside the ring of police and put the figurine in the bed on top of the tree. Then she jumped the tree outside of the ring and put the figurine of Izabel down next to Cami and Kaito.

"Does that feel better?" Opa asked.

Cami nodded.

"Can you do your elevator breathing again, Cami?"

Cami put her hands in her lap and started moving them up and down with her breath. Opa kept tapping for a few of her breaths. Then she stepped back around and sat in front of Cami again.

"Thanks for playing with me," Opa said.

"I like playing with you."

"I like playing with you, too. Can I ask you a few questions?"

"Okay," Cami said.

"Do you feel safe at home?"

"At my new home or my old home?"

"At your new home."

"Yeah."

"Do you feel safe when you're with your parents?"

"Mmhmm."

"Do you feel safe with Jana?"

"Jana is nice. She plays with me."

"Does everyone at home seem happy?"

"Yes."

"No one seems extra sleepy or grumpy?"

"No."

"Do you know anything about guns, Cami?"

She shook her head.

"Do you know why you're at the hospital today?"

"No."

"Remember you told me you've been sad in your sleep?"

Cami nodded.

"That happened again last night."

"Am I sick?"

"I don't think so," Opa said.

"Then why am I at the hospital?"

"We have better tools here, which can help you, Cami. Tonight you're going to sleep here and I'm going to watch you and make sure I can help you, if you feel sad again."

"I don't want to sleep here."

"What if your mom can sleep here with you? Then would it be okay?"

"Can I see my mom?"

"Very soon."

"And my dad? And Jana?"

"Everybody. Very soon."

Cami nodded.

Opa left and a nurse went in. Cami smiled at the nurse even though she was someone she'd never met before, even though she was a complete stranger.

THE CONVERSATION WITH Jana went differently. They didn't sit at the table and play with toys. They sat in regular chairs, and Jana seemed torn between acting engaged and dismissive.

"I want to go back to Izabel and Kaito and Cami," Jana said.

"Can you tell me what it's like living with them?"

"It's nice. They're nice."

"Do they drink alcohol or do drugs around you?"

"No."

"Do you feel safe with them?"

"That's kind of a trick question because I don't feel safe anywhere right now. That doesn't have anything to do with them."

"That's fair. Let me ask then, do you feel comfortable with them?"

"Yes."

"No one has touched you inappropriately?"

"No."

"No one has hurt you in any way?"

"No."

"What about the gun?"

"What about it?"

"How did you know about it?"

"I saw it in Izabel's bag."

"She didn't show it to you?"

"No."

"Did Cami know about it?"

"No."

"Did you feel more safe with a gun in the house or less safe or the same?"

"More safe."

"Is that why you didn't tell anyone about the gun? You wanted Izabel to have it in the house even though it's against the law?"

"Yes."

"Do you know about Cami's sleep-talking?"

"Yes."

"Have you seen her do it?"

"Yes."

"What do you think about it?"

"I think she's talking to someone."

"Who?"

"I don't know."

"Not her parents?"

"No. Someone who knows things no one can know."

"Like where the killer is?"

"Yes."

"What do you think about that?"

"It doesn't make any sense."

"Does it make you scared?"

"Kind of."

"Does it make you scared of Cami?"

"No, she's just a kid."

"Do you have any thoughts about how she might be having these conversations, or why?"

"I know nobody else thinks she's having them, which makes you all pretty stupid."

Opa smiled. "What do you want to happen next, Jana?"

"I want to go back to Izabel and Kaito and Cami."

"And what then?"

"I don't know. Go back home."

"Izabel and Kaito are worried the killer saw where you live, when Izabel carried you back to the house."

"I should've shot him," Jana said quietly.

"Really?" Opa said. "It's a big thing to kill another person. That stays with you for the rest of your life."

"I wouldn't feel bad about it."

"Maybe not. But you'd remember it."

Jana didn't say anything.

"Do you think Cami is safe with Izabel and Kaito?"

"Yes."

"Do you think Cami is safe with you?"

"Me?"

"You're telling me you wouldn't feel bad about killing another person."

"A murderer! Who is terrorizing a whole town!"

"I know that. But I'm asking you to consider, are you a person who is safe for a child to be around right now?"

Jana's eyes looked around her body, at her left arm, her right leg, her right knee. "I'm good with Cami. I'm good—"

"I don't mean to upset you," Opa interrupted. "And I don't think you would be a bad person if you couldn't be around Cami right now. You suffered a tremendous trauma. It's hard to come out of that and be—" But Opa didn't name anything in particular. "I think you're right. I think your relationship with Cami is a good one. She speaks very highly of you."

"If we can't go home, where do we go after this?"

"Izabel wants you all to stay at a friend's house while she acts as bait for the killer."

"Like a trap?"

Opa nods. "What do you think of that idea?"

"I want to be there."

"She doesn't want you to be."

"Why?"

"Because it would be dangerous."

"I don't care."

"Are you partaking in any reckless behaviors, Jana? Drinking? Drugs? Unprotected sex?"

"No!" Jana said. "I don't care about that stuff."

"What about smaller things? Taking a car to the wrong place? Spending too long outside? Cutting yourself?"

"No."

"Because your behavior the other night was reckless toward your own safety, and then you put Izabel's life at risk."

"I didn't want her to follow me."

"I know that, but she did." Opa paused. "Do you want to hurt yourself?"

"No. I only want to hurt him."

"So you don't think you'd partake in any behavior that would put you or Cami at risk?"

"No, never Cami. I wouldn't." Jana's face was turning red.

"I know you don't like these questions, Jana, but do you understand why I have to ask them?"

Jana nodded. "Do Izabel and Kaito not want me back? Is that why you're asking me?"

"No," Opa said. "Not at all. They want you back very much."

"They already had to move once."

"They're not thinking about that. It's my job to think about that. They just want you back."

Jana couldn't look at her.

"I have to write up my report, and the police will have a say in what happens next, but I'm recommending you be put back into the care of Izabel and Kaito. They'll come to your room shortly."

"Okay," Jana said. But she didn't look okay.

OPA CAME INTO the room with Izabel and Kaito.

"She needs to be on suicide watch and you need to start bringing her to therapy after we release her. I don't know why they didn't tell you that straight off."

"Okay," Izabel said.

"I don't think it's safe for her to be around Cami yet," Opa said.

"She wouldn't hurt her," Kaito said.

"Not intentionally," Opa said, "but she could. Especially if she thinks Cami can lead her to the killer."

"I don't understand," Izabel asked. "How can we have them both but not have her around Cami?"

"While Cami might be released into your care soon, Jana will have to stay here a little longer. And in the hospital, they'll have to be in separate rooms. You can visit them together or split up or trade off, whatever you want to do. You'll have complete access to both of them until someone says otherwise, but I don't think they'll go against my recommendation."

"Thank you," Izabel said.

"We'll start the sleep study after dinner," Opa said. And then she left.

Alone again, Kaito said, "I didn't think they could take them from us. I didn't think, coming in last night . . ."

"They're not going to take them from us," Izabel said, firmly, like it was a truth that was so clear and obvious that she could wear it on her finger like a ring.

## CHAPTER TWENTY-EIGHT

When a nurse brought Cami into the room for the sleep study, Izabel was already there. Cami yelled and ran into her arms.

"Mi amor," Izabel said.

"I want to go home."

"They told you we're going to sleep in here."

"I don't like the hospital. I told you. I told you *and* Opa."

"I know you did, but this is important. And look how cool it is in here." She put Cami down at the table next to the bed. On it was a plastic port with a dozen wires. They ran into a drawer. Cami followed them with her fingers where she could.

Izabel started to ask the nurse, "Do you think—"

"You know," the nurse interrupted, "they've already started recording in here, so we better get started."

Izabel stepped back from her, understanding how careful she would need to be.

"Cami," the nurse said, "let's sit you up on the bed, okay?"

Cami let the nurse pick her up and place her on the side of the bed. Izabel sat down beside her.

"We'll start with this. It goes around your finger like a Band-Aid."

Cami moved her hand away from the nurse. "My Band-Aids have robots on them," she said.

"Ah, I like robots."

"Does it hurt?" Cami said in her little voice.

"No, not at all. And it doesn't have robots on it, but it does glow."

"It glows?"

"Yeah, can I put it on and then you'll see?"

Cami put her fingers under her thighs.

"You have to let her," Izabel said. "What if we made a deal?"

"Like for lollipops?"

"Yes, for lollipops."

"Can I have one now or do I have to wait until I wake up?"

Izabel looked at the nurse.

"I can find a lollipop," the nurse said. "Let's get this on first. Then I'll get one."

"A red one?" Cami asked.

"I'll see what I can do." The nurse winked at her as she said it.

Izabel wasn't sure Cami understood winking, but Cami took out one of her hands, and the nurse put on the oxygen monitor.

"See? It doesn't hurt."

"I don't like it," Cami said.

"But now I can go get a lollipop," the nurse said, "if you keep it on."

"Okay," Cami said, wriggling her body, as if that would help her with the tug it made.

Izabel stood up to talk to the nurse in a hushed voice. "Did they bring any of my things from our house? I always have a red lollipop in my purse."

"I don't know, but I'm sure I can find one. You think that'll do it? We have a lot more of these things to put on her."

"Can we do them once she's asleep?" Izabel said. "In that first hour, nothing can wake her."

When the nurse came back with a red lollipop, Cami let her put bands around her chest and stomach, but she still complained about the oxygen monitor. The nurse moved it from her finger to her toe, and then put a blanket over Cami. They could all see it glow under the white blanket, like a lost ship.

The nurse sat down in a chair and pretended to fall asleep.

Cami finished the red lollipop and handed the sticky post of it to Izabel. She said she didn't like the monitor on her toe either. Izabel told her the nurse was asleep so they couldn't move it. And Izabel began to sing, "Los pollitos dicen, 'pío pío pío.'"

Cami fell asleep, and the nurse went back to work, placing electrodes on her face and chest. She used a paste to stick a few onto Cami's head, parting her delicate black hair. The last thing the nurse did was place a small plastic tube under Cami's nose, with a plastic prong at each nostril.

"What do all these things do?" Izabel asked.

"I have a handout about it if you want."

"No, it's fine. What do I do?"

"You try to get some sleep. That chair I was in reclines into a bed. Or a bedlike chair at least."

"I've been in them before," Izabel said. "Thank you."

"Opa is watching," the nurse added as she left the room.

Izabel lay back in the chair and opened her app. She wanted to see how twenty-five-years-ago Tampa was doing with their killer.

The top headline for the day was "Tampa Mayor on Mystery Killer: 'Bring me his head.'" The article was filled with more of the mayor's quotes, and Izabel liked how passionate he was. Another article had a video of surveillance footage of the suspect flipping an old flip phone. Another was about a $35,000 reward for information leading to an arrest.

Old Tampa was still in the shit, too.

Opa came in and said, "I noticed you still aren't asleep. Do you want me to give you something?"

Izabel said yes.

IZABEL HAD A dream about a wedding that Andy was about to have. But even in the dream Izabel knew Andy wasn't getting married. Worse, Izabel's mother was there, and Izabel knew that couldn't be true either.

And Izabel, being the kind of woman she was, she couldn't just enjoy it, dreaming of her.

Andy asked Izabel and her mother to bring these old antique bells out from the kitchen and over to the ceremony, to place one under each chair, so everyone could ring them during the kiss. Izabel didn't tell her how horrible that would sound. She kept trying to take the bells outside for her.

But that's all Izabel did, the beginning of the action, over and over, the kitchen table still covered with bells.

She didn't know why her mother wasn't in the kitchen helping her. She found her at a desk where she'd taken piles of papers, bills, mail, and she was organizing it all. Dream-Izabel couldn't believe it. She yelled at her mother, "What are you doing? Why are you doing that?" Even though non-Dream-Izabel didn't care what her mother was doing.

Her mother insisted she was doing it *for* Andy.

Izabel said they were supposed to be carrying the bells. Her mother rolled her eyes, as if Izabel was ridiculous for not seeing which was the more important thing to do.

Izabel was so upset with her, but she was more upset with herself, for arguing with her mother when all non-Dream-Izabel wanted to do was hold her.

Dream-Izabel went back to the kitchen and put more bells on a tray.

By the time Izabel got to the ceremony, it had already started. She couldn't believe she'd missed so much of her friend's wedding. She tried putting the tray down without making a sound.

She was lowering it as slowly as she could when the dream was suddenly over. Her mother was gone again. Opa was there, waking her.

"What's happened?" Izabel asked. "Where's Cami?"

"She's with Kaito. We let you sleep in. Seemed like you needed it."

It was hard to open her eyes. "Why do I feel like this?"

"Could be what I gave you to help you sleep. Have you ever taken something for sleep before?"

Izabel shook her head.

"You'll feel fine soon."

"Did it happen again?"

"What?"

"Did Cami talk?"

Opa sat down in the chair across from her. "Yes. A whole conversation about the hospital, and how she didn't like the thing on her toe even though 'it looked really cool.' Her words."

"And?"

"And all her readings are normal. Breathing, normal. Sleep cycle, normal."

"So what's happening to her?"

"I don't know. I often seen this sort of imaginative play when a child is awake, but never asleep."

"We don't know what to do."

"I think the work we're doing together is important. She's definitely been traumatized by some of the things she's seen and heard."

Izabel didn't say anything.

"So have you. And so has Jana."

"I'll start bringing Jana. I didn't realize how bad it was."

"She doesn't have to keep staying with you. It's incredible what you've done, taking her in, but you have to do what's right for your family."

"She's our family now."

"Okay. I only wanted to say it out loud in case you needed to hear it."

Izabel wanted to say more, to tell her off, maybe, or at least to explain it better, this thing Opa didn't seem to understand, about how Jana was part of Izabel's family, about what that meant to Izabel. But Izabel was too tired. And then she remembered the dream. She remembered how close she was to holding her mother again. How she'd yelled at her instead. She started to cry.

"What is it? What's wrong?" Opa said.

"I had this dream."

"That can be a side effect of the pill I gave you, too—vivid dreaming."

"I didn't like it."

"If you were to keep taking it, that side effect would go away."

"I don't want to take it again."

"I know, but you might change your mind. I can take you to your family now, if you're ready. Inspector Paz is coming back soon to talk to you."

Izabel stood up and felt woozy.

Opa said, "Can I tell you what I think?"

"About what?" Izabel said, unsure she wanted to hear anything Opa had to say after the last twelve hours they'd had together.

"About your idea," Opa said. "Your trap."

"Oh. Sure," Izabel said.

Opa clenched and unclenched her jaw. "I want you to do it."

"That's not what I thought you would say."

"It's not what I should say, professionally. The psychologist in me says you should be careful of actions that give you a perceived sense of control. That control is often false and relying on it can be dangerous. When you find out that control isn't real, you can feel more out of control than you did before. That's a moment that can break you."

"That's comforting."

"But," Opa grabbed Izabel's arm, "as someone who lives in this town with her family, her children, your idea sounds like it could work. We need something that works right now."

It was the first time Opa and Izabel had touched. Izabel realized how few people she came into skin-to-skin contact with anymore. Not like in high school, when she held her friends, when they sat under each other's arms, heads in each other's laps, running their fingers through each other's hair. Touching people was part of becoming an adult, but then it was given up in adulthood. It seemed unfair and illogical.

Izabel put her hand on Opa's hand. "I'm going to do it," she said.

## CHAPTER TWENTY-NINE

Paz brought Andy with her to the hospital. They took Kaito and Izabel to a room where they could talk.

"We want to move forward with your plan," Paz said, "if you're still willing. Andy's reviewed the paperwork. Waivers, et cetera, waiving all liability in the case of injury or death."

"What?" Kaito said.

"It's standard," Andy said.

"No," Kaito said.

"You can't do this unless you sign," Paz said to Izabel.

"And if something happens?" Kaito said.

"Obviously the goal is that no harm comes to Izabel or to anyone on my team."

"I'm okay with it," Izabel said.

"Why? Why are you okay with any of this?" Kaito said.

"Because we could catch him," Izabel said. "Don't you think we could?"

"I don't know," he said. "Are you going to tell us more details?"

"We'll make a show of Izabel going back to your old house, put it on the news and everything—'the woman who faced the killer.' Really piss him off. We've already cleared the houses around yours. There will be a suited team in the house next door. There's already a full suit waiting for Izabel at the house."

Nobody said anything.

"Is there something else?" Paz asked.

Izabel shook her head.

"Jana's not going to like this," Kaito said.

"Can I say something?" Andy said. "Not as your lawyer? This isn't a good idea."

"You're the one who said we can't live in fear," Izabel said.

"This isn't about fear. This is about a crap plan that provokes a killer."

"By this time tomorrow we should have the killer in custody," Paz said.

"You've been here for weeks," Andy said. "You don't have leads? You didn't have a plan before this?"

"Not one that would work this fast."

"Andy, it's fine," Izabel said.

"What about Cami?" Kaito asked Paz.

"What about her?" Paz said.

"You need Cami for the plan," he said. "Somewhere you can hear her and be in touch with your team, with Izabel."

"No," Paz said.

"He's right," Izabel said.

"Have you both lost your minds?"

"Let's take her to Lucy," Kaito said.

"For Christ's sake," Paz said.

"You know what Lucy's capable of," Izabel said. "You know as well as we do."

"We have a lot to do today, you know?"

"Jana needs to be there, too," Kaito said.

"Why?" Paz asked.

"I won't sign it unless we all go," Izabel said.

Paz let out a strange sound, like she was yelling with her mouth closed. "Okay!" she said.

"Andy," Izabel said, "can you draw up something about how nothing we say at Lucy's can be held against us?"

"I can do it on my tablet as we head over."

"I hate all of you," Paz said.

THEY TOOK TWO cars to the spiritual center. Paz with Izabel, Kaito, and Andy. Opa with Cami and Jana.

When they arrived, they went straight to a conference room. It had a long table, the kind Izabel had seen in old FedEx commercials with people sitting around it, smiling at Xeroxed pie charts.

"I'm sorry to show up like this," Izabel said when Lucy came in.

"It's okay," Lucy said. "This is important." She looked around and waved at the children. "Hello, everyone."

They all sat down at the table. Izabel smiled at Jana and Cami. It felt good to finally have her family together again.

Lucy sat next to Cami. She asked her, "Can I hold your hand, little one?"

And Cami nodded.

"Do you know how to take deep, slow breaths?"

"Like your elevator," Izabel said.

Cami pulled her hand back again and showed Lucy the elevator.

"That's perfect," Lucy said. "Do you think you can do it with only one hand so that we can keep holding hands? Your hand is just so cute and soft."

"My mom says that, too."

"And she would know, wouldn't she?"

"She grew me in her belly."

"She sure did."

Cami gave her hand back to Lucy and then went back to focusing on her elevator.

Lucy closed her eyes. No one said anything. Then Cami stopped moving her elevator.

"Hello," Lucy said.

*"Hello,"* Cami said. *"I'm sorry I haven't been able to help more."*

"What's your name?"

*"I have been called Elm."*

"Like the tree?" Lucy said.

*"Yes."*

Izabel cut in. "You're Cami's tree friend?"

*"Yes."*

"Christ," Paz said under her breath in a laugh.

"In that group of trees north of town?" Izabel asked.

*"Yes."*

Kaito said, "You're a kodama."

*"I have been called that, too,"* Elm said.

"How are you inside Cami?" Izabel asked.

*"One night, I woke in her, but I am also where I always am."*

"Can you leave her?" Kaito said.

*"Yes."*

"No!" Jana said.

"I didn't mean now," Kaito said.

"We need your help," Izabel said.

*"I'm sorry I haven't been able to help more,"* Elm said again.

"We are setting up a trap for the killer tonight," Izabel said. "It would help if you can tell us what direction he's coming from, and when he's close to the house. Our old house. Anything else, Paz?"

"I'm not participating in this."

*"I can help,"* Elm said.

"Thank you," Izabel said.

"But please don't mention Cami's mother," Kaito said. "Cami's only ever been annoyed when you talk about the killer. But when you mention how close he is to her mother, she becomes upset, uncontrollable."

*"It felt necessary to warn her."*

"I understand that. And thank you. But tonight it won't be necessary. We understand that Izabel will be in danger. We are taking precautions. Do you understand?"

*"I did not mean to upset Cami."*

"It's okay."

*"I care for her."*

"She likes you, too," Izabel said.

*"I can help."*

"Can I go now?" Paz asked. "Come back to the hospital when you're done here. They can reach me. The press conference is at seven o'clock. Sun's setting around eight. Andy, you're with me."

Paz and Andy got up. Andy kissed her own hand and waved it at them.

Izabel kept going. "The tests at the hospital say that Cami is still sleeping normally, even with all of your conversations. Is that true?"

*"I don't know."*

"Are you having conversations during the day?"

*"I talk but she does not respond."*

"Do you . . ." Izabel didn't know how to phrase it. "Do you really like talking with her so much? She's a four-year-old girl."

*"I do."*

"How old are you?"

*"I am two hundred years old."*

"Whoa," Jana said.

*"My species has been on the planet for twenty million years."*

"Are you a boy or a girl?" Jana asked.

*"I am both."*

"Can you be in my head?"

"Jana!" Izabel said.

*"I don't know how,"* Elm said.

Then Izabel remembered. "Cami said the trees did it on purpose, ten years ago. Is that true?"

*"The Earth was dying."*

"Is it true?"

*"It was the step we could take."*

"You killed millions of people."

*"Yes."*

"Why do you care, then? About this man?"

*"Further deaths are unnecessary."*

"That's it?"

*"I feel guilt."*

"Do trees feel things like guilt?"

*"Yes."*

"Do all the trees feel guilty?"

*"No."*

"Why not?"

*"The Earth thrives again."*

After a long pause Izabel said, "Then I'm glad that you are the tree Cami knows."

OUTSIDE THE CONFERENCE room, Opa pulled Izabel aside and apologized to her. She said, "I thought she was having trouble sleeping."

"How could you have known what was happening?" Izabel said. "I still can't believe it."

Opa lowered her voice. "I would try . . . I would try not to let too many people know about it. The science community—they don't talk about it, publicly—but they're starved for information, and a way to move forward, instead of in response. The link Cami has might look like that way forward."

Izabel felt the new threat to her daughter as sharply as she'd feel a knife. And then Izabel caught sight of another poster just behind Opa's head. The poster was of a yōkai she recognized— rokurokubi—a woman whose head traveled as she slept, her neck stretching, her head causing mischief, attacking animals, drinking lamp oil. In the poster, she was smiling, and Izabel had to turn away.

BACK AT THE hospital, Paz arranged to have Kaito and the girls sleep over again, this time together in a room. Officer Evans would stay with them, with a radio, a direct line to Paz. Izabel signed the waiver and then excused herself to the bathroom. There was still time before the press conference.

She walked further than she needed to, so she could relax in a private bathroom—she remembered where all the private ones were on that floor. She tried not to think of all the people who had thrown up in there, or had diarrhea. Instead she thought about all the women who had to juggle wipes and a cup for a urine sample, who chose to put the cup's lid on the edge of the sink or on top of the toilet paper dispenser, who wondered what counted as contaminated and what didn't.

She wasn't ready to go back and be brave, braver than a regular woman who sometimes got bacterial vaginosis. *I'll be that brave person starting at seven o'clock*, she thought. *Not before then.*

She leaned against the wall by the sink. She needed to know what happened in Tampa, she decided. She didn't open her app; she searched *Tampa, serial killer, 2017, arrested*. His face came up. He was caught after someone saw a gun in his bag at work.

# CHAPTER THIRTY

Paz looked Izabel over before the press conference, and she nodded, to herself it seemed. Then she looked Izabel in the eye and said, "Incite him."

"How?" Izabel asked.

"Make him sound weak. Call him names. We're not sure what sets him off so we'll have to try a little of everything. Mention his mother if you can."

"His mother?"

"It's usually a trigger."

"But—"

"Look, if it doesn't come up, it doesn't come up. I'm just saying, if you have the opportunity, mention his mother. Or something about his abilities as a lover."

"I'm going to sound insane."

"Insane is fine."

"I don't like blaming mothers."

"Well, look, we'll go back in time and give everyone access to birth control and abortions and great parents so that no one keeps secrets or has a kid they don't want and then we won't have all these papers about kids and their twisted relationships with their mothers, but until we get a time machine, this is what we've got." Paz adjusted Izabel's shirt. "You ready?"

"I guess," Izabel said.

PAZ GAVE A statement addressing, broadly, what had happened in Izabel's first encounter with the killer. She had told Izabel that they would focus on that and not mention the second time if they didn't have to. Then it was Izabel's turn at the podium.

"Can you tell us, in your own words, what it was like when you saw him?" a reporter asked.

"I didn't think. I stopped the car and got out, ran up to him, and then went into the house through the tear he—his knife had made."

"Did you see the knife?"

"Yes, and I described it to Inspector Paz."

Paz nudged her.

"It was large, like he was compensating for something."

One reporter laughed a little. Izabel felt ridiculous, but Paz looked pleased when Izabel glanced back at her.

"What did he do when you ran up to him?" another reporter asked.

"Nothing."

"Nothing at all?"

"No. And, uh, I thought he was a coward."

"Would you have fought him?"

"Yes," Izabel said, and that felt true.

"Could you have overpowered him?"

"Probably not."

"How large is he?"

"Taller than me." Then she added, "But not very tall."

"Did he say anything to you?"

"No."

"Did you say anything to him?"

"I don't think so, but I don't remember."

"Why haven't you said anything about this until now?" another reporter called out.

"The police asked me not to while they continued their investigation."

"Then there's been some development in the investigation?"

"You would have to ask Inspector Paz."

Inspector Paz came forward again. "I can begin taking questions now if you're done asking questions of Ms. Kalloe."

Everyone shook their heads and waved her off.

"Did you see his face?" someone asked Izabel.

"No."

"What was it like to save the girl?"

"It was hard. She had passed out. I could feel myself having trouble breathing."

"Where were her parents?"

"Near her."

"Were they already dead?"

"Yes," she lied. "I think so. She was the only one I knew I'd be able to move."

"Where is she now?"

"Again, you would have to ask Inspector Paz."

Paz leaned forward, and they all shook their heads again.

"Have you tried to contact him?"

"I don't know how."

"Has he tried to contact you?"

"Not that I know of," she said, but she thought about her dead neighbors as she said it.

"Would you contact him if you could?"

"Yes." She took a breath. "I would tell him he's a piece of shit and I bet he has a terrible mother who raised him to be a piece of shit."

Paz stepped in front of her. "Okay," she said. "I think that's enough questions for now."

"Izabel, where are you going now?" one reporter called out.

Izabel looked to Paz, and Paz nodded.

"I'm going home," Izabel said.

As IZABEL LEFT the room, she heard Paz fielding questions about the investigation. Officer Evans took Izabel to the front doors, where they waited for a car.

"What if he wants to come in here," Izabel said, "and stab me before I even leave?"

"That's why I'm here."

"Are you worried about that?" She was pacing, but Officer Evans stood perfectly still.

"No. He hasn't been able to kill anyone face to face, and from what I've read, that's not an easy escalation to make."

"You've read up on this stuff?"

"Yes. I think I've read everything in the online library that Paz highlighted as relevant for us."

"I didn't know she'd done that."

He nodded and looked at his watch again.

"Do you want to be an inspector?" she asked.

"That's the plan," he said.

"Will you be coming with me for the car ride?"

"No. You'll get in the car and go to your house alone. Everyone's in place."

"Okay," Izabel said. She tapped her right heel against the front of her left shoe. She was scared. She was not the brave person she thought she would be, could be.

A car pulled up for her.

"Good luck," Officer Evans said.

In the car, Izabel couldn't stop fidgeting. She opened her app, kept it on 2017, and tapped on *International*. She scrolled through until she found the headline, "AH-CHOO." The article was about a new political campaign in Japan, "The Twelve Zeroes," and one of its promises was to "Zero hay fever." Izabel tried to imagine allergies being a main concern of a political party in the US in 2017 and she almost laughed.

Near the end of the article was a paragraph that made her dizzy. They had been trying to make pollen-free trees, with, as the article said, "some success." That sounded like a myth. Like a fantasy. She felt like if she opened her mouth to exclaim about it, her voice would come out in squeaks. She searched for evidence of pollen-free trees online.

She found a lot of old gardening websites about making your garden asthma-friendly. Discussions of low-pollen trees, trees with their pollen stored deep in showy flowers that relied on cross-pollination from bees and birds, instead of the wind. And then, on one old website, she found this: "A pollen-free tree to avoid allergies has been made, *AgraFood Biotech* 127 (26 April 2004), 25."

*2004*, she thought. *Holy shit.* For a second she wanted to scream about it—*The answer is in a lab somewhere! Let's find it! It's the solution! We're saved!*

But then she admitted to herself that she didn't know what

would've happened to the world if they'd tried something, if they'd made some grand gesture of felling forests and planting all new trees. The disruption to the $O_2$ and $CO_2$ levels in the air, to the animal habitats, to the food chains.

And still all the mold, still all the grasses and weeds.

With what she knew now, with Elm, maybe the trees would have only moved up their plan. Maybe Izabel wouldn't have ever been born. Maybe Izabel would have been a young child and she would have died in the Turning. The killer, too. Maybe none of this would have happened. Right now, part of her wanted that.

When she looked up from her tablet, her eyes had trouble focusing on the street. But then she saw it—her old house. Next to it was the empty lot of her neighbors.

IT STARTED TO rain. Izabel didn't know if that would affect Paz's plan, or if it would affect how well the Elm tree could see the killer. But they'd already done it. They'd set everything in motion. And now the sun was going down.

INSIDE THEIR OLD house, their home, Izabel expected to see swirling pollen, as if they'd deserted it and it had become untended—a wasteland of sorts. But it hadn't. Scheduled maintenance of their house had taken place as it did to every building in every thriving town of the new world.

Izabel got into the suit they'd left her. She tried the mask on over her face, then pushed it up and left it on top of her head. She walked around her house pretending she was walking on the moon. It felt as strange as that, to be home again.

She got a beer out from the fridge and sat on the floor. She loosened the straps on the oxygen tank so it could rest on the ground to the right of her, and then she leaned back on the fridge.

As she got near the bottom of the beer, as she had to tilt her head back more, she kept knocking the mask on the fridge. *Ding. Ding.* Izabel laughed to herself. She turned, pulled the straps, and the oxygen tank climbed up her back.

She went to her bathroom and took out a bag of makeup. She spilled it out on the counter and leaned her tablet up against the mirror. She pulled up an old makeup tutorial video called "Perfect No Makeup Makeup." She put a drop of foundation on the back of her hand, and then, dabbing her finger into it, made spots on her cheeks and forehead. She took a sponge and pushed it softly into her face. She sat on the toilet, closed her eyes, finished her beer, and pushed and pushed the sponge.

When she opened her eyes, the color was almost consistent over her face. Not around her eyes, or her hairline, and she'd forgotten to go over her neck at all. The video had gone past the foundation now, past the bronzer and blush. The woman in the video was rubbing her finger into something white and then rubbing it under the ends of her eyebrows. Izabel didn't have anything white.

She was tired of the video anyway. She wiped off the foundation with wet cotton pads.

## CHAPTER THIRTY-ONE

"*A car is approaching from the east,*" Cami said, asleep in the hospital, Kaito and Jana awake beside her.

"Do we tell them that?" Jana asked.

Officer Evans radioed it to Paz.

"Approaching where?" Cami asked.

"*That's not important. Only that it approaches.*"

"Is it him?" Jana whispered in Cami's ear.

"I don't think Elm can hear you," Kaito said.

"Raisin, raisin, raisin.

"*Why are you saying that?*

"Because I'm a raisin and it's raisin language.

"*Ah, it's a strange language.*"

"Cami is a goof," Jana said.

Kaito nodded.

"*The car is stopping at the house,*" Cami said.

"Izabel," Paz's voice came out of the speaker of Izabel's tablet.

Izabel jumped. She was back on the kitchen floor having a second beer.

"Can you hear me?" Paz said.

"Yes. What did you do?"

"We hacked your tablet. I told you about this part of the plan, didn't I?"

"I don't think so."

"I think I did."

"Have you been listening to me this whole time?" Izabel said.

"We have."

"Shit," Izabel said under her breath.

"I'd recommend you stop drinking. A car is coming up to your house. Your daughter warned us."

"Who cares about a car?"

"You're the one who wanted me to take your daughter seriously, right?"

"You're right. You're right." Izabel pulled her oxygen tank tight to her back again and got up. She looked out the window that faced the street. "What do I do?" she said.

"Whatever you feel comfortable doing. I just wanted you to know that we're listening. We're here."

Izabel saw the car stop. The doorbell went off. A man got out. He was wearing a regular mask over his mouth and nose. He was about five foot ten, with brown hair, only a few inches long and very neat around his ears, like he'd come from a haircut. Izabel ran over to the door. He raised his arm, a single wave to her, like she knew him, like he only needed the slightest gesture to say hello.

She pressed the button to open the outer doors. She let him in.

*"I DO NOT want to alarm you, Cami.*

"Raisin!

*"Raisin, this is a message for your father.*

"Okay.

*"The man is not dressed how he is normally dressed. He might not be the man. But he has gone into the house. He has gone in through the doors."*

Officer Evans began to call it in.

"Why are you telling them?" Kaito said, standing up. "They must already know. Why isn't Paz updating us?"

"Do you want to hear from her or do you want her to do her job and protect your wife?"

Jana took Kaito's hand.


WHEN THE MAN was in the house, he took off his mask and Izabel could see it was Patrick, from the waiting room of the privacy pods.

"Nice suit," he said.

"Thanks," Izabel said. She looked more closely at him than she ever had before. He was younger than she'd realized. He was clean-shaven, but he looked like he needed to shave often to have that level of smoothness.

"Why are you here?" she said.

"What you said today—it was an invitation, wasn't it?"

"No," she said.

"My mistake then." He put his mask in his back pocket. "How long until the police arrive?"

"Should I call the police?"

"Please. Don't pretend."

"Minutes," she said.

"A lot can happen in minutes."

"*THE POLICE ARE leaving the house next door,*" Cami said. "*They are going into the house.*" She rolled over in her sleep.

PATRICK RAISED HIS hands into the air when the police came into the house. Izabel raised her hands, too, but she wasn't sure why.

"You're under arrest on suspicion of the murders of Peter Coughlan, Karen—"

"Do you have an arrest warrant?" Patrick said.

"Yes," Paz said.

"Without a name or even a description?"

"Yes," Paz said, "we do. Now shut up and let me finish."

Izabel stepped around all the cops and went back into her bedroom as Paz said the names of all of Patrick's victims. She tore off the suit and lay down, face down on the bed, how the girls had.

An officer came in. "Are you alright?"

"Yes," she said into the pillow.

"I radioed to your family that you're okay."

She turned her head. "Thank you."

"I can take you to the hospital now, if you're ready."

She rolled over and sat up. "Can they come home?"

"As far as I'm aware."

"Does everyone at the police station know about me and my family?"

"Yes." The officer smiled.

Izabel nodded. "I have to talk to my husband and kids about which house we go to, so let's go to the hospital." She got up, grabbed a sweater out of the dresser, and started to leave the room. But then she stopped. The officer almost walked into her.

"What is it?"

"Are you sure it's him?" Izabel asked.

"It's not as clear as we'd hoped it would be tonight, is it?"

"No," she said. She couldn't believe she was here, in a moment where she wished a man had made more of an effort to kill her.

BACK AT THE hospital, she hugged Jana and Kaito, and then she fell asleep as soon as her head hit the pillow next to Cami.

IN THE MORNING they talked about their options. Cami insisted that she wanted to go back to the old house, so Jana agreed that she would go and look at it. Kaito seemed happy about that plan, too. Izabel thought about Patrick, waving at her as he walked up to the doors.

But Opa wouldn't let Jana leave until she took her for another interview.

While they waited, Izabel played hand games with Cami, every one she could remember—*Bubble Gum, Bubble Gum*; *Down by the Banks*; *Patty Cake*.

"Again," Cami said.

"I can't."

"I'll play with you," Kaito said. "Take off your shoes and socks."

Cami tilted her head and raised her eyebrows to show her skepticism.

*Where'd she learn that?* Izabel thought.

"Go ahead," Kaito said.

Cami took them off, and he sat her beside him and took her feet in his lap.

"This little piggy went to market . . ." he began.

"Why to market?" Cami said.

"Just listen," Izabel said.

WHEN OPA AND Jana returned, Opa said Jana was doing better, but only because Jana was sure they'd caught the killer. Opa said, "If we're wrong . . ."

"I understand," Izabel said.

"You can take her with you, but only if you or Kaito can be with her at all times."

"We can," Izabel said.

"Do you understand the gravity of this?" Opa said.

Izabel said, "Yes," even though she didn't know if she did.

What else could she say?

HOME AGAIN, IZABEL sat on the couch as Cami pulled out toys to show Jana. Kaito went to check on his machine. She heard it hum. She kept looking toward the doors, to where Patrick had stood. Where they'd stood together. Close enough to touch.

Izabel got up to make dinner.

Jana told her that she liked the house, that it reminded her of her old home, but not too much. Because of Kaito's office in the third bedroom, the girls would be sharing a room. Jana said she liked that, too. Izabel thought about how the girls would probably only be happy sharing a room for another two years or so. But that seemed like a long time right now.

Paz told them she would set up cameras outside the house, and would drop off suits for all of them, just in case. She also told them, over and over, she had her guy. Izabel caught herself looking at the doors again.

During dinner, Cami asked Kaito to tell them a story.

"Which one?" Kaito asked.

"All of them!" Cami said. "One hundred! Until the ao andō appears!"

"No, baby," he said. "You don't want the ao andō to appear."

"What's the ao andō?" Jana asked.

"A ghost!" Cami said. "She's got long hair, and claws!"

"Seriously?" Jana said.

*"Speak of the devil and he will appear,"* Izabel said.

## CHAPTER THIRTY-TWO

The next morning started off normally enough. Cami went to school, Jana went to see her tutor, Kaito retreated into his office, the news was triumphant, and Izabel collapsed onto the couch, picking an episode of *Doctor Who* to watch. *Is this my life now?* she asked herself. *Is this my life again?*

But before it had even reached 10 a.m., Paz called Izabel and Andy down to the station. Izabel couldn't help but feel a bit of a thrill.

AT THE POLICE station, while they waited for Paz, Andy leaned in close to Izabel and said, "I can't believe it."

"It didn't go like we thought," Izabel said.

"Not that. I can't believe a tree has been in Cami this whole time."

"Haven't we seen each other since then?"

"No!" Andy said. "And I wanted to stay. I wanted to be at the press conference, too, but Paz said you needed to appear to be alone. You know you're not alone, right?"

"Yeah," Izabel said. If she were alone, she wouldn't be in this position. No one would care about her and she wouldn't care about anyone else, and she could've died in her bed one night in a torn-up house, or not.

"What are you going to do?" Andy asked.

Before Izabel could respond, Paz came out to them. "I thought you two would come back. You don't know your way around here yet?" She waved for them to follow her. "Here's the deal. He told us where he lived pretty quickly, which we knew wasn't a good sign, meant he'd cleaned up."

"Where does he live? To the south?" Andy said.

"Yeah. How'd you know that?"

"It just explains why the elm tree couldn't see which house he was going home to."

"Okay, you're gonna have to cut it out with all that."

Andy didn't say anything.

"So we need the knife. Oxygen tanks. Anything to connect him to the murders."

"Why are you telling us this?" Izabel asked.

"He says he'll talk to you."

"Shit," Izabel said. "Maybe lead with that, Paz."

"Why else would I call you in?"

"What about the suit?" Andy said.

"We found pieces that could have been put together to be the suit, but none of them are so unusual for a person to own nowadays. And it's smart that he didn't hide it. He can't get rid of all of the DNA that's probably on it. It's easier to explain away why he owns those things." She looked at Izabel the way that she used to, when she was considering whether Izabel was guilty. "How do you know him anyway?"

"The privacy pods. We ended up waiting for them together sometimes."

"Small town," she said, satisfied. "So will you talk to him?"

Izabel looked at Andy. She tried not to react. All she wanted in the world was to go in there with him. But she didn't know if it was to talk to him or strangle him or slam his head into the table. *What would I do if given the chance?* she thought.

Andy said, "If she wants to, then as long as nothing can be held against her—I want to amend the deal we had, to extend to this interview." Andy pulled out her tablet.

"Yeah, sure," Paz said. Then she turned to Izabel. "Well?"

"I'll do it," she said.

"Okay. I have to give you some more details of the case then. And I've got an NDA for you to sign."

Paz got her tablet out, and Andy and Paz exchanged theirs. Andy looked the nondisclosure agreement over. "Fine," she said. So Izabel signed Paz's tablet, and Paz signed Andy's.

"We think we tracked down the knife based on your description, and if we're right, it's a knife that was made for pilots—so they could cut themselves out of planes. He could've bought it online, but my guess is that it was passed down through his family. That it has some significance to him. So get him talking about his family. We're tracking down friends and colleagues now and bringing them in for interviews. If you can get more names, we'll bring them in, too. We can't find anything about what school he went to or how he survived the Turning. But more info is bound to come in."

"What's his job?" Izabel asked.

"He's a graphic designer, picking up contracts here and there."

"So he didn't *need* to meet anyone in person."

"No, and he hasn't recently. But a few years ago, when he was building his portfolio, he was meeting with clients. One of them might remember something."

"Is he dating anyone?"

"Look at you, little detective," Paz said.

"Shut up," Izabel said back.

"Based on an app we found on his phone, he's been dating, but no one person seriously."

"Any overlap with who he killed?"

"Not that we've found, which might mean that kind of motive is out. So we need another motive—something less direct, but still something a jury will understand. If you can find anything special about the dates of the murders, the people, the locations of the houses—"

"I don't remember any of that information."

Paz handed her the file that had been sitting on the table, and Izabel opened it. The first page had a list of the dates of each murder, and beside each date were corresponding names. The second page was a map with the dates beside each marked location. The third page was a blank map. Behind that were pictures.

"No," Izabel said when she saw the first picture. "I can't look at these."

"Then don't. But keep them in case you need them. I want to know if he's racist, homophobic, transphobic, if he doesn't like animals, if he doesn't like big business. Hell, if he doesn't like apples, I want to know about it. We'll put a bud in your ear and we'll be able to talk to you with that."

"Okay."

"And we have robots looking for the knife in case he threw it off the edge of the town, but it would be great to narrow down *that* location."

Izabel looked at her and said, "You know I can't get all this."

"I know," Paz said. "But you'll get something. Just keep him talking. We can hold him for two more days."

"Wait, what?" Izabel said.

"I'm filing for an extension, but without more evidence, I can't hold him past that, and he knows it. That's the clock he's playing out."

"Does Andy come in with me?"

"She doesn't need to. He's lawyered up so you won't be in the room alone with him. And Officer Evans will be in there, too, standing by the door."

"Do you want me to come in?" Andy said. "I might know his lawyer."

Izabel nodded.

"One more thing," Paz said. "Don't ask a question you don't feel comfortable having him ask back. It's the most common instinct he'll have, to flip the question instead of answering. And if you don't answer, he won't either."

"Okay," Izabel said.

"Wait, *this* is the last thing. I'm bringing Opa in. You might hear her in your ear."

"Doesn't she specialize in children?"

"Yeah, but I like her, and I don't like many psychs. Fine with you?"

"Yeah, fine with me."

"Turn your head," Paz said. Izabel did, and Paz put an earbud in her ear. Then she pulled her hair toward the front of her face, tugging it a bit. "Do you tuck your hair behind your ears?"

"I won't."

"Good," Paz said.

## CHAPTER THIRTY-THREE

"Hi, Patrick," Izabel said.

"Hello, Izabel. Do you really prefer íz-abel? Or would *ee-sa-bél* be better?"

"Either is fine."

"I'll go with *ee-sa-bél* then," he said.

She shouldn't have let him pick. It reminded her of how her mother said her name. No one said it like that anymore. She said, "I heard you wanted to talk to me."

"It's not so much that. But they are so insistent on talking to *me*. And if I'm going to sit here listening to someone, I'd rather it be you." He smiled.

She smiled back. "How did you sleep?"

"Okay. They have decent cots back there. How about you?"

"I slept well," Izabel said, but she didn't know what to say next.

"What is it?" he said.

"Honestly? I can't believe we know each other. That I've known you for weeks."

"Just a little," he said.

"My college was like that. I'd keep running into people."

"Where'd you go to school?" he asked.

"Villanova. How about you?"

He didn't answer.

"It's okay, if you didn't go to college—"

"I went to college." He looked uncomfortable at having lost control of the conversation already.

"Oh. Didn't like it?"

"I didn't get to finish."

"Me neither."

"Not many people your age did," he said.

"Yeah, that's true. But that's not why I didn't finish. I had to leave to take care of my mother."

He shifted in his chair—he suddenly looked furious. "How did you know about that?"

"About what?"

"My father."

"I—I don't know about your father. I was talking about my mother."

"I had to leave to take care of my father. They told you that. You made up that lie about your mother to try and what, get close to me?"

"Fuck you. I'm not lying."

Andy put her arm on Izabel's arm.

"I'm sorry," Izabel said. "Look." She got out her tablet, searched for a picture of her mother, and then showed him. "This is what she looked like before she got sick." She found another picture. "This is what she looked like when she was sick."

"Why did you take a picture of her like that?"

"She asked me to. She said, 'Remember me both ways.' Which I thought sounded dumb. Like someone on TV would say."

"Do you remember her both ways?"

"Some days I remember mostly memories from when I was a kid. Some days, mostly memories of her sick."

"Sorry I said you were lying."

"It's fine," she said.

"You've lied before."

"When?"

"On television," he said.

"Yes, I lied then," she said slowly.

"Why did you lie?"

"It seemed like the right thing to do."

He didn't say anything.

She heard Paz in her ear. "Ask about college again." That was the first time she'd heard Paz's voice through the earbud, and Izabel hoped she hadn't jumped in her chair.

"So where did you go to college?" Izabel said.

"Pratt," he said. "Would've been part of the last class to go through."

"An artist?"

"Yeah," he said. "Sort of."

"What's that mean?"

"I specialize in packaging. Not everyone thinks of that as art."

"Seems like an art to me."

"What do you do?" he asked.

She hesitated for the first time. She didn't want him to know about Cami. She tried to play off the hesitation as embarrassment. "I told you—I didn't finish school."

"So nothing?"

"I never figured out what I was good at."

"What do you do with yourself?"

"I don't know."

"Come on. What's a typical day look like for Izabel?" He looked happier now.

"I clean. I shop for things I need. I watch old television and read old news."

"Old news?"

She nodded. She pulled up her app and showed him. He took her tablet and scrolled through.

"You can pick other years," she said. "Forty years ago. Fifty. Whatever time you want to read about." She didn't like him having her tablet in his hands, but before she needed to ask him for it, he handed it back. "What's your day look like?" she asked.

"Hanging out at home, working on my projects."

"You clean and shop?"

He laughed. "I have groceries delivered. I have someone come in to clean."

"I've thought about that. Who do you use?"

He didn't answer.

"That would be a great name to have," Paz said in her ear.

"Maybe I should go if you don't want to talk," Izabel said, leaning forward, going up on her toes.

"No," he said. "I want to talk."

She sat back down.

Patrick said, "What would you even do with yourself—if you didn't have to clean either?"

"That's a shitty thing to say," she said, and he hung his head a little. She asked, "What was your dad sick with?"

"Cancer."

"Is he okay? Is he in remission now?"

This time Patrick was the one who hesitated. "Yeah," he said.

"That's lucky," she said.

"Yeah."

Paz said, "Take a break. Ask him if he wants food."

"Do you want something to eat? I'm getting hungry."

"Yeah, okay," he said.

Izabel got up to leave and Andy followed her. Paz and Opa met them outside the room.

"That was good," Paz said. "I'm going to find out more about his father. And someone's already digging up records from Pratt. Just give us ten more minutes."

"His father is definitely a pressure point," Opa said.

"What do you want to eat?" Paz asked.

Izabel shrugged. She could barely think about food.

"Order something," Paz said. She walked off one way and Opa went another.

"What do you want?" Izabel asked Andy.

"Something that doesn't need utensils," Andy said.

"Are you that scared of him?"

"Aren't you? He freaks me out."

"Yeah," Izabel said, but actually she felt fine. "Maybe falafel?"

"Okay."

Izabel opened the door again. "You like falafel?"

"Yeah," Patrick said.

When she closed the door, Andy said, "Who cares what he likes?"

Izabel made an excuse: "I'm building rapport." But she wasn't sure why she had asked him.

PAZ THOUGHT PATRICK was lying about his father, but she didn't know about what exactly. Officer Evans found which doctor Patrick's father had been seeing and got her on the phone. She sent over the list of medicines he was taking, and the address they had on file for where to send them. It was Patrick's address. And oxygen tanks were on the list. The next one was scheduled to arrive in a few days.

Paz sent officers back to the house to look for any signs of the father.

"I think he's dead," Paz told Izabel.

"Why would he lie about that?"

"Opa?" Paz said.

"Denial? Which could range from not wanting to tell you about it, to not having accepted it himself."

"I think he died right before the murders began," Paz said. "And Patrick's been using his father's oxygen tanks to do the murders."

"So we can connect him to the murders then?" Izabel said.

"That'd be circumstantial," Andy said.

"But," Paz said, "if his father had been living with him, shouldn't there be a ton of medical stuff at Patrick's place? There was nothing."

"My mother had a lot of equipment at the house when she was sick," Izabel agreed.

"Right," Paz said. "So why get rid of it?"

Opa said, "Maybe it does connect him to the murders."

"He must have picked somewhere," Paz said. "One place, to move it all to. We need to know places this time, Izabel."

The food arrived and an officer unpacked the bag, laying everything out for them.

Izabel asked, "Is someone looking at everywhere he took cars to?"

"Christ, little detective. Yeah, they sent us the list, but it's only addresses right now. We're looking them all up. You ready to go back in?"

Izabel nodded, put the file under her arm, and picked up two small paper boats of food. Andy picked up another two. They went back in.

"Sorry that took a minute," Izabel said.

"No worries," Patrick said.

THEY DIDN'T TALK while they ate. But as they finished, as Patrick crumpled a napkin over his small boat, Izabel asked, "Did you really apply to leave when everyone did? Like you implied at the privacy pods?"

"No," he said. "And you—you said it was a *long story.*"

"Yes," she said.

"Denied?"

"No, approved."

"Then why are you still here?"

He knew the answer. If he was the killer, he knew. She didn't know how to tell him without scratching some itch in him. She said, "I ended up crossing paths with the killer, but then they thought I was the killer, and they held me as a suspect."

"You?"

She nodded.

"There's no way."

Opa was in her ear now, "Tell him that they made you see me."

"They even made me see a therapist."

"Tell him what you told me," Opa said, "about what you were angry about."

"How'd that go?" Patrick asked.

"I think she thought I could be the killer, too."

"No." He sounded shocked.

"Yeah, because I'm still angry about what happened."

"To your mom?"

"Yeah, and to the world. I'm angry about how we're living as if we're in some wild utopia now."

"But not *that* angry. Not angry enough."

"No, not to kill anyone."

"But they thought so?"

"They thought that was the kind of anger, maybe, that they were looking for."

"Yeah."

"But you didn't apply to leave? Why not?"

"You don't have to answer that," Patrick's lawyer said.

"Not everyone applied," Patrick said.

"I know. But why didn't you?"

"You don't have to answer," his lawyer said again.

Patrick turned his head toward his lawyer, like he was looking at the lawyer's knee. "I don't want you to talk," he said, and then he looked at Izabel again. "I wasn't scared."

"Because you had oxygen at your house?"

"No," he said. "I didn't."

"I would've felt better if I had oxygen in my house, but I was always worried it'd explode or something. I thought, 'How stupid would that be, if I blew myself up before I got killed?'"

"Stupid," he said.

"Do you have a girlfriend or a boyfriend?" Izabel asked.

"No."

"Why not?"

"I'm not in a rush. I'm still young."

"Yeah. So you're just playing the field?"

"Yeah."

"Where do you take someone on a date?"

"Why? You want to go on one?"

"Depends on where you take people," she said with a laugh. She hoped it didn't come off as fake to him.

"I'd take you to a restaurant."

"Which one?"

"I'd let you pick."

"Whichever one's your favorite," she said. "I love finding out other people's favorites."

"I like Haruki's Sushi."

"I like it there, too."

"Yeah? You've been there?"

"Yeah. Lots of times."

"Yeah," he said.

"Where's your dad now?" Izabel asked.

He looked down again. "Home, I guess."

"I mean, where does he live?"

Patrick didn't answer.

"Here, I have a map," she said, bringing out the blank map. "Can you point to where?"

He didn't even lean forward.

"What about on this map?" She brought out the map marked with the killings.

Now he looked up. "Where do you live?" he said.

"I live right here." She pointed, landing her finger next to the dot on her neighbors' house.

"These last few weeks, too?"

"I've been staying with friends."

"Why?"

"I was scared after I came across the killer."

"Why would he care about where you lived?"

"Maybe he was worried I could identify him."

"But you can't."

He didn't say it like a question, but she answered it like he had. "No," she said. "Does your father live near me?"

"No," he said.

"Did he apply to leave?"

"No," he said. "He wouldn't leave."

"Why?"

"It's crazy how many people left," he deflected.

"Yeah. There are definitely a few empty houses now. Do you have empty houses around you?"

"I don't know," he said.

Paz said, in her ear, "Press him."

"All your neighbors are still there?"

"I told you—I don't know."

"Yeah, but you must notice who's coming and going from their houses, kids going back and forth to school."

"No, I don't."

"I mean, how could you not notice, like, if the lights are never on anymore?"

"No!" He nearly shouted it.

## CHAPTER THIRTY-FOUR

Paz's team searched every abandoned dome that was anywhere near Patrick's house. In one, they found everything: the knife, oxygen tanks, even a hospital bed that Patrick must have wheeled over in the night. Everything but Patrick's father.

They canvassed the neighborhood well into the night, woke up every family, went into their homes, scared the shit out of them, to see if anyone saw Patrick moving things, to see if anyone ever saw someone in a suit, walking around.

No one had.

And then the lab techs came back with nothing. No fingerprints, no hairs, no blood.

The police had everything and nothing.

But there was no doubt now that he was the killer. No thought that they'd gotten it wrong somehow. No. He simply was the killer, and the pieces were falling into place.

"Do you need me anymore?" Izabel asked Paz. She was tired

and wanted to go home. She wanted to see Cami and Jana. For the first time in a long time, she wanted to feel like a mother.

"He'll only talk to you," Paz said. "And I need motive."

"I don't know what else I can get you," Izabel said. "I don't feel like I'm good at this."

"I think you are," Paz said.

Andy said, "He's almost nice. And he's definitely smart. If they take him to court with a circumstantial case, he could walk."

"You need a confession," Izabel said to Paz.

"You think you can get me one of those?" Paz laughed. "Look, don't think about that. Think about motive. And ask him more directly about the murders. We don't have to come at him sideways anymore."

"Does he know we found everything?"

"No," Paz said. "I don't want him to know yet. Reveal it as you want to. If you'll go in again."

Izabel nodded.

"Watch out," Paz added. "He's had some time to think this through."

As soon as Izabel and Andy came into the room, Patrick said, "Hi, Izabel," and he sounded more like her mother than ever, like he'd spent the hours practicing her name.

"I want to ask you about the murders now," she said.

"What about them?"

"If you weren't scared, then how did they make you feel?"

"I don't know."

"Did they annoy you? How they disrupted things?"

"No, that's a shitty thing to say," he said, mimicking her back to herself.

"So they upset you?"

"They upset everyone."

"Did you know anyone who was killed?"

"No."

"Would you have been upset if you had killed someone you knew?"

"What?"

"I'm going to have to protest to this line of questioning," his lawyer said.

Izabel ignored them both. "It seems like the houses were chosen at random, and you said you date pretty frequently, so you could have easily—"

"Wait a second," Patrick said.

"—accidentally picked the house of someone you knew and killed them."

"I didn't kill anyone."

"Ms. Kalloe, I'm going to insist—"

"I said I didn't want you to talk," Patrick said to him.

Izabel kept going. "Would that have made a difference to you?" She started taking the photographs out of the file and putting them all over the table.

He looked away.

"Now, if I were the killer, like they thought, I wouldn't mind looking at these, because I would have felt that I had saved them from living in this fake, perfect world. But I'm not the killer, so seeing these families, all dead, it makes me sick. Does it make you sick?"

"Yes," he said, not looking at the pictures.

"Yesterday you made it seem like you killed them for the same reason that they thought I could be the killer."

"No, I didn't. I didn't kill anyone."

"That's how it seemed to me, too. I thought we were the same like that, maybe."

He looked at her, over the pictures.

"But now I don't think that. Now I think you killed them thinking you were saving them from having their hearts broken when their parents died."

"What?"

"Yeah, I think your dad died and it broke your heart and you didn't want anyone else to grow up and have their hearts broken." Her stomach turned, provoking him this way.

"My dad's alive."

"We can't find him. Where is he?"

Patrick didn't say anything but his eyes were getting wet. They shone in the light of the room.

"It doesn't matter," Izabel said. "That's not my point. It's that the connection I felt yesterday—it's gone. You don't get it. How shit it is here."

"Yes, I do."

"I don't believe you." Everything she said came out sharply.

"They act like we don't miss the air."

"No."

"They act like we don't remember lying in the grass in the sun."

"No." She shook her head. "You don't *really* get it."

"They act like their displays in the mall are good enough for us."

She shouted at him, "You're not angry about it how I am!"

He stood up and yelled, "I killed them because it's not real!"

Did that mean she could leave? She wanted to run out of the room. But Paz said in her ear, "That might be enough, but press him to confirm who he killed."

His lawyer looked frozen. She wondered if he'd actually come in here thinking Patrick wasn't the killer.

"Killed who?" Izabel said.

Patrick sat back down.

"Killed the people in these photos?"

"I didn't kill anyone."

"But you cut their houses, and that killed them."

He half-nodded. They couldn't use that.

"Can I get a moment with my client?" the lawyer said.

"Do you need a break, Patrick?" Izabel asked. "That's fine. And I'm sure I don't have to tell you—if I leave at this point, I'm not coming back in."

"I don't need a break," he said.

"Patrick—" his lawyer said.

"I'm fine," Patrick snapped at him.

"The first time you did it, did you know that cutting the house would kill everyone inside? Or did you think they might survive?"

"You don't have to answer that."

"I know," Patrick said. He looked at the lawyer's knee again. "Stop talking."

"That would mean the second time was more real, right? That time you knew what the consequences of your actions would be."

Patrick didn't say anything.

"That would be this family, the Berensons." Izabel pointed at a picture. "You didn't have time to stick around and see them like this, dead in their house. You probably didn't see them at all, until it was on the news. And then they used pictures of the family *alive*. You probably haven't seen them dead in their pajamas like this."

He looked at the pictures.

"I'm sure you'd imagined what they'd look like when they were dead. Did you get it right? Did you imagine the layer of pollen that would be on them by the time the police took pictures? That's the strange thing about these pictures really. All these different families, but the photos are hard to tell apart with the pollen. Their bodies and the floors, their beds. Some of the children never left their beds, like this one." She pointed to a different photo.

He still didn't say anything.

"It's an efficient and smart way to kill, in terms of how hard it made it for them to catch you. But it's not what I'd expect from a killer."

"How were you there the other night?" he said.

"You came to *my* house," she said.

"Not that night. And not the first time. The other night."

"When?"

"Don't play dumb," he said.

"Just luck," she said. "Like the first time."

"No," he said. "Your feet were bare. You chased the girl. But how did she know?"

"Why does it matter?"

He could sense that he was gaining control again, going after information she didn't want to share. "Because it didn't make sense."

"Not everything makes sense."

"I wouldn't be here if you hadn't shown up that night."

"You might have been, and you'd have another dead family in front of you."

"I want to know."

"You don't get to know," Izabel said.

"Then I'm done talking."

"You already admitted to killing them, what else is left?"

"Something, or you wouldn't still be in here."

"I'm just here to see what else you'll let slip."

"Screw you," he said.

Paz said, "I don't think you can get him back to the details of the murders. Get out of there."

But Izabel didn't want to leave anymore. "Where's your father?" Izabel said. "He's dead, but where?"

"I threw him over the edge of the town. I'm sure the plants have destroyed his body by now. What does it matter? Nobody cared about him when he was alive."

"I'm sorry," she said.

He was agitated, but his body was calm. She heard it only in his voice when he said, "I don't think people can't handle their parents dying. I'm not an idiot."

"Then what are you?" Izabel asked.

"I don't know," he said.

He seemed upset again. It seemed like he was actually considering the question. Izabel almost regretted asking it. She didn't know what she was either. What kind of person could she be, having gotten herself entangled in the most abominable crimes of the last ten years, and enjoying it?

She felt a single strand of self-hatred move through her like a worm. And if Patrick was like her, which she knew he was, to some extent, then he felt it, too.

She opened her file to the list of murders. "Did you cut through the house at Fourteen Third Street on the night of April eighth resulting in the deaths of Karen, Peter, Tamy, and Tavi Coughlan?"

"Don't say anything," the lawyer said.

But Patrick said, "Yes."

She went down the list and he said yes to all of them.

## CHAPTER THIRTY-FIVE

When they got out of the room, Andy hugged her. "I never want to do anything like that ever again," Andy said.

Izabel nodded.

Opa and Paz came out from the adjacent room. Opa hugged her, too.

"Look at you," Paz said. "You got a confession."

"Is that it then?" Izabel asked.

"Well, court's not going to love the interview. Wasn't exactly a model of professionalism, was it? But we didn't violate his rights, so I think we'll be alright."

"And I don't have to see him again?"

"You'll see him at trial. Star witness, remember?"

"Yeah."

"You okay?" Paz said.

"I can't quite believe it. That it's done."

"You can talk to Opa about shit like that." Paz laughed. "Seriously though. You ever thought about working for us?"

"The police?"

"On the federal level. Profiler. Interrogator. That sort of thing."

"No," Izabel said.

"Would you think about it?"

Izabel didn't say anything for a second.

"What?" Paz said.

"I didn't even finish school."

"You know how the kids do it these days—I'd take you as my shadow. You've got good instincts, and you're absurdly brave, like so absurd you might want to talk to Opa about that, too." Paz laughed again.

Opa smiled, but she clearly didn't love Paz's jokes about her work.

"Think about it," Paz said. "You'd have to move to the capital, but they're going to move you down there for the trial anyway."

"Why will the trial be there?"

"The first thing that lawyer will do is petition to have it moved."

Andy nodded. "He'll argue that a jury of his peers from this town will be biased against him."

"And he's not wrong about that, is he?" Paz said.

"I have to talk to Kaito about it."

"Yeah, yeah. And it's no rush. Just wanted to make the offer."

"Thanks," Izabel said.

And Paz left them.

Andy said, "I need to go pick up Hestia. But you better come see us before you move anywhere."

"We will," Izabel said.

Now it was just Izabel and Opa standing there. Izabel said, "I guess you'll want to see me soon?"

"I don't care when you come in, but I want you to lean on me as much as you need to. A trial is a difficult thing."

"You coming to the capital, too?"

"No," Opa said. "But before that. And I know some good people there who I can refer you to."

"Can we sit?" Izabel said.

They walked over to some chairs. Behind them was another poster. There wasn't a monster on this one, but a shadowy portal, drawn in the same style. This one had a placard underneath it. It read: *Monsters of Our Past, Monsters of Our Present*. It had information about the installation, how the posters wouldn't be framed, how they would be scattered through the town. And it had information about the artist, an accountant, an officer's wife, who had been drawing since she was little. This was her passion project. Her side project. Maybe her exploration of humanity's dark side, too, as she felt it. And maybe she was actually processing her feelings, through her art, in a healthy way.

"You look pale, Izabel," Opa said.

Izabel looked away from the poster. "Am I like him?" she asked.

"Like Patrick? No. And I never thought you were. I never thought you could be the killer."

"Never?"

"Never," Opa said.

"You told me to be careful of the moment when you realize you don't have control."

"Is that how you feel now?"

"I don't know. I don't know if I feel like I have no control or more control than I'd ever dreamed of having. We had a plan and it worked."

"It did."

"I want to go work with Paz."

"But?"

"I don't know if it's my ego making that decision."

Opa smiled at her. "You're about ten minutes out from an exhilarating interview. Give yourself a break. Give yourself a minute."

"Do the elevator exercise?" Izabel joked.

"Never a bad idea," she said.

Izabel rubbed her eyes.

"You should go home," Opa said. "The adrenaline is going to wear off and you're going to crash."

Izabel nodded.

At home, Izabel told them that he confessed. Jana cried. Cami rubbed Jana's back and told her it was okay. Kaito scooped up Cami in his arms and squeezed her until she complained about it. Izabel held Jana and then Cami squeezed herself in between them until she had Izabel to herself.

"I have to lie down," Izabel said.

"I'll come with you, Mommy," Cami said.

So Izabel went to sleep in her own bed and Cami lay down beside her for a few seconds. Then she started to climb all over the bed. She settled near Izabel's feet and pulled on each of Izabel's toes. But Izabel was so tired, she didn't care, didn't react, and eventually Cami left the room.

Kaito woke Izabel and asked her if she wanted dinner or wanted to sleep more.

"I want to eat," she said.

He sat down on the bed.

"I didn't tell you everything," she said.

"You haven't told me anything yet."

"I don't mean about interrogating him. Afterwards, Paz offered me a job. She said I could be her shadow."

"Wow," Kaito said. "Do you like working with her?"

"I do."

"Then I think that's amazing," Kaito said.

That surprised her. She said, "I thought you wouldn't like it. I thought you'd think it was too dangerous."

"I think you've been looking for something you like for a long time," he said. "I'm glad you found it."

That was true. Her life had been interrupted over and over by things she couldn't control. Sometimes she felt like she only *fell* into her life with Kaito, fell backward into it. And she'd wondered what her life would have looked like, if she'd always been moving forward, toward one desire or another, never stopping and never stopped.

"We'd have to move to the capital," she said.

"I can do that," he said.

"She said we'd have to move anyway for the trial."

"Then that works," he said. He smiled.

"I think I'm really happy about this," she said.

THE FOUR OF them sat around their dining table. The late sun was coming in bright, casting a rectangle of light on the floor.

"I've been offered a position as a shadow," Izabel said.

"With who?" Jana asked.

"Inspector Paz."

"I like her," Cami said.

"If I take it, it means we have to move to the capital."

"No!" Cami said. "We just got home!"

"I know," Izabel said.

"You want to take it?" Jana asked.

"Yes."

"And I want to go, too," Kaito said.

"Why?" Cami said, upset.

Izabel pulled her onto her lap. "It would make us happy. It's important for people to be happy."

"I'm happy *here*."

"I know."

"*You're* happy here," Cami told her.

"I am, but I would be more happy there."

"You didn't say people needed to be more happy."

"It's important for people to be the most happy they can be. And for them to keep on asking themselves what would make them the most happy."

"But you're happy here," Cami said.

"But once you realize you'll be happier somewhere else, sometimes you stop being as happy where you are."

"But you have me."

"You will always make me the happiest."

"Then we don't have to go."

"Don't you think I will be able to make you happier if I'm happier?"

Cami didn't say anything.

Kaito said, "If there were ever something we could do to make *you* happier, we would do it."

"I'm happier here."

"But you don't know yet what things might make you happy in a new place," he said. "I hear there's a crayon factory in the capital."

"Crayons?"

"With all sorts of exhibits for kids."

"Like what?"

"Stations where you can make your own crayon labels and stations for drawing."

"On paper?" Cami asked.

"Yeah. My parents took me once," Jana said.

"Did it make you happy?" Cami asked.

Jana nodded. "Super happy."

"I will *try* it," Cami said.

Izabel and Kaito both kissed her.

"Is it okay with you?" Izabel asked Jana.

"Yes," Jana said. "I would like to leave, too." Then Jana looked at Cami, and then back at Izabel and Kaito. "What about Elm?" she said.

Kaito and Izabel hadn't talked about Elm yet, but Izabel knew what had to happen, and she was sure Kaito knew, too. She said, "We have to say goodbye to tree friend if we're moving."

"That's true," Kaito said. "We'll be too far away to see tree friend anymore."

"But I'll be able to hear my tree friend," Cami said.

"No, honey," Izabel said.

"I can still hear tree friend when I can't see them," she said.

"No, I understand that," Izabel said, "but we have to say goodbye."

"No."

"People don't have tree friends."

"They used to."

"Maybe they did, but they couldn't hear their tree friends in their heads."

"You don't like trees."

"What?" Izabel said.

"You don't like them!" Cami screamed.

If Cami were older she would have run into her room, away from Izabel. But at this age, she buried her head into Izabel's chest and cried and wiped her nose on her shirt. It was Izabel who hurt her, but it was Izabel's comforting that she wanted. And Izabel did comfort her. She held her and kissed her and told her everything would be okay.

## CHAPTER THIRTY-SIX

Lucy had Izabel's family squeeze into a circle in her office. Once they were settled, Lucy found Elm quickly.

*"I'm glad you're okay,"* Cami said to Izabel, as Elm.

"Thank you," Izabel said.

*"He did not kill you."*

"No."

*"Does that mean he is not a bad man?"*

"No, he is. He would have kept killing families."

*"Then he is not like the trees."*

"He was never like the trees. He didn't save anything with his actions."

*"Not even himself?"*

"No."

*"How do you know?"*

"It's not like the trees. Nothing flourishes, if he's saved."

*"So you understand why we did what we did?"*

Izabel felt sick. "Logically."

*"You are no longer upset with us, then."*

"I didn't say that."

*"Do you forgive us?"*

"No."

*"Okay,"* Elm said.

"Do you care if I forgive you?"

*"Yes."*

"Why?"

*"Your family is the first I have had contact with. You are* representative *in a way."*

"I can't ease your guilt."

*"Will you turn Cami against me?"*

"No," Izabel said. "I'd never do that."

*"I have seen humans do that to children before, about many things."*

"I promise."

*"But you do want me to leave her?"*

"We do," Kaito said.

*"Even if she does not want that."*

"She could be in danger if you don't leave her."

*"No, I would not hurt her."*

"Not from you," he said.

"From other humans," Izabel said, "who would want to understand the connection you two have."

*"I see,"* Elm said. *"Then I will go."*

"Thank you." Izabel and Kaito said it together.

*"I will say goodbye to her tonight and will be gone by morning. She will need you all."*

"We'll be there," Jana said.

Cami turned to look at Jana. *"Good."*

They waited for Cami to look away from her, but she didn't.

*"Do you forgive the trees?"* Elm asked.

"Yes," Jana said.

*"You're not mad?"*

"Not about that," Jana said.

*"About your parents?"*

"Yes."

*"I'm sorry I could not help save them."*

"I heard that you tried," Jana said. "Thank you."

Cami nodded and finally turned her head away from Jana. *"Is there anything else?"* Elm asked.

Izabel and Kaito looked at each other.

"No," Izabel said.

"Thank you again," Kaito said.

"Yes," Izabel said.

Elm didn't respond. Cami came back and said, "They're not gone! I can still hear my tree friend!"

"Your tree friend will say goodbye tonight when you can say goodbye back," Kaito explained.

"No," Cami said. "I thought they would convince you that they could stay."

"Your friend agreed with us," Izabel said.

"No, they wouldn't."

"They did," Jana said. "So maybe it's the right thing to do, right?"

"Maybe," Cami said.

"Thank you, Lucy," Izabel said.

"Thank you!" she said. "I've never been part of anything quite like this."

Izabel smiled.

The family shuffled out of the office, past the rooms of the spiritual center, where, from one, they heard someone shriek. Izabel watched as Cami took hold of Jana's hand.

IZABEL COULDN'T SLEEP. She was worried that Cami would be different when Elm was no longer inside her. What if the tree left and took part of Cami with them? What if she didn't remember Jana? What if she didn't remember any of them? What if Cami didn't wake up at all?

Or what if she was fine, but she resented Izabel forever for making the tree leave her? That seemed entirely possible when Izabel considered how long she had resented the trees for taking her mother. When she considered how long she would continue to grieve her mother. The more she thought about it, the more she was sure Cami would wake up and never smile at her again. She'd smile at Jana, and Kaito, after a day or two. Izabel would see those smiles, but that's it. Izabel would leave to work with Paz in the mornings and Cami would squirm out of her hugs.

In the same way the job had filled her with excitement, this filled her with worry. Suddenly she was sure she'd made every wrong decision she could make. Probably since falling in love with Kaito and being happy when the world was dying.

To fall asleep, Izabel thought about opening her app, but something about it didn't appeal to her anymore. Instead Izabel tried to imagine her childhood home, to build it in her mind. A good memory of her mother's living room. A framed photograph. Her mother's coasters. But she kept seeing the room covered in pollen, shattered glass on the floor, the vines having broken through the windows. She saw giant lazy pumpkins on the couch where she used to sit in her mother's arms.

IN THE MORNING, Cami ran into Kaito and Izabel's bed. She pushed her arm under Izabel's neck and hugged her.

"Good morning," Izabel said.

"Morning, Mommy," Cami said. "Did you get a good sleep?"

"Yes. How about you?"

"I said goodbye to tree friend."

"You remember?"

"Yeah."

"Are you sad?"

"Yeah."

"I'm sorry, mi amorcito. Is there anything I can do?"

"Play LEGOs?"

"Would that help?"

"Yeah!" Cami said.

"Okay, why don't you go get them out and start building and I'll meet you in there after I brush my teeth? Did you brush your teeth?"

"No. I can't do it myself!"

"Oh, then come brush your teeth with me."

Cami was already jumping out of the bed and heading for the bathroom.

"She seems okay," Kaito said, rolling over.

"I think she is," Izabel said. She leaned over and kissed him.

Walking to the bathroom, a feeling was there, that she was perfectly in control of her life. She decided to trust it.

## ACKNOWLEDGMENTS

CREATING THE WORLD of *Clean Air* required the help of so many generous people.

Thank you to Nicole Cash, who I interviewed about her work as a Licensed Clinical Social Worker. Her insights into working with children were invaluable as I wrote Opa's scenes with Cami.

Thank you to Damon Rich, urban planner, designer, and artist, who talked with me about cities and the history of cities when I was designing this strange microcosm of a town.

Thank you to tarot reader Jenna Matlin, who let me record a session where I took on the persona of Izabel. I had no idea what would happen in that session and it guided Izabel's path in so many ways.

Thank you to PennFuture, the Pennsylvania Department of Environmental Protection, the Bay Area Air Quality Management District, and *Willamette Week*. I wanted to capture how our communal recent past works in this singular near future, and I couldn't have done it without your words.

Thank you to Green Engine and all of their wonderful staff. I wrote this book there, often looking at the beautiful wall of plants that could never exist in *Clean Air*!

Many, many friends read this book and supported me through

writing and revising it. Thank you Eleanor Stanford, Lynne Beckenstein, Linda Gallant, Rachel Mennies, Maximiliano Schell, Carla Bruce-Eddings, Sarah Lyn Rogers, Rosser Lomax, Natalie Shapero, Sarah Einstein, Nicky Arscott, Dawn Lonsinger, Mariel Capanna, Nadine Darling, Tracey Levine, Tyler Goldman, Rebecca Fortes, Julie Langsdorf, Sara Curran, Vikram Paralkar, Amy Jo Burns, Kristen McGuiness, Hetal Kapadia, Hunter McLendon, and Catie Rosemurgy.

Thank you always to my agent, Sarah Yake.

Thank you to my editor, Abby Muller, and to everyone at Algonquin Books.

Thank you to my family. To my son, Aaron, first and forever. To Cris, Nick, Vic, Bian, Kiet, Noah, Sandy, Bob, Maya, Michael, Adam, Ian. And to my mother, Barbara, who died in 2019, but who read and loved this book just as it was, and I'm so glad that I keep finding more people who love it as she did.